HANGING ROCK

HANGING ROCK

Robert W. Callis

iUniverse, Inc.
Bloomington

Hanging Rock

iUniverse books may be ordered through booksellers or by contacting:

iUniverse
1663 Liberty Drive
Bloomington, IN 47403
www.iuniverse.com
1-800-Authors (1-800-288-4677)

Because of the dynamic nature of the Internet, any web addresses or links contained in this book may have changed since publication and may no longer be valid. The views expressed in this work are solely those of the author and do not necessarily reflect the views of the publisher, and the publisher hereby disclaims any responsibility for them.

Any people depicted in stock imagery provided by Thinkstock are models, and such images are being used for illustrative purposes only.
Certain stock imagery © Thinkstock.

ISBN: 978-1-4620-4096-4 (sc)
ISBN: 978-1-4620-4097-1 (ebk)

Printed in the United States of America

iUniverse rev. date: 07/28/2011

This book is dedicated to Gary M. Carlson, my best friend when I was growing up into manhood and the inspiration for one of the characters in this novel. Were Gary alive today, he would be pushing me to join him in an adventure searching for buried Confederate gold.

It is also dedicated to the memory of my great-grandfather William Main, who served as a private in Company I, 102nd Illinois Infantry Regiment from 1862 through 1865. He entered the Civil War as an 18 year old boy and came home a 21 year old man after surviving many incidents during Sherman's March to the Sea. One of those incidents included a brush with civilian guards trying to protect wagons near Hanging Rock, South Carolina, in February of 1865.

March 6, 1866

The rider peered into the gathering dusk as his horse slowly made its way down the dusty rutted pike. The road was surrounded on both sides by a thick pine forest. The rider was dressed in shabby, old clothing and the soles on his shoes were almost worn completely through. Everything he wore, from his worn shoes to his battered black slouch hat was covered with a fine gray dust. He was a small man, about twenty-three years old with a pale, almost unhealthy complexion. His dark hair was long and shaggy and covered the collar of his threadbare coat. He had the look of someone who was lost or at least puzzled to find himself in unfamiliar surroundings.

He reined in his horse and slowly dismounted. He tied his undernourished mount to a nearby log and pulled his canteen off the saddle horn. The horse appeared relieved at a chance for a rest from his burden. The man took a long drink from the canteen and then poured some water on a dirty neckerchief and used it to try to clean his grimy, unshaven face. Temporarily refreshed, he sat down on the dead log he had used for a hitching post and again stared intently around him. Still apparently unsure of where he was, the man pulled a dog eared map from inside his coat and seemed to be trying to match the map up with his current surroundings. Shaking his head in disgust, he replaced the map in his coat and pulled a small piece of jerky from his coat pocket. He silently chewed on the dried meat, pausing only to drink another swig of water from the canteen.

His horse lifted her head from an attempt to crop what sparse grass existed near the old log, her ears twitching. Suddenly four horsemen burst around a corner of the road and headed straight for the man and his horse. All four of the riders were dressed in what appeared to be white sheets with eye-holes cut in them. Initially frozen with shock, the man jumped up and grabbed for his horse's reins. The horse was spooked by the oncoming ghostly riders and pulled at the reins, her hoofs dancing in the dust as she attempted to free herself and thus making it impossible for the man to successfully remount. He finally got the horse to stand still long enough to pull himself into the saddle. He jabbed his boot heels into the horse's flanks to enable both of them to escape an uncertain fate.

Before he had ridden twenty yards, one of the white robed horsemen pulled even with him, and he felt a sudden excruciating pain as the man's sword cut into his right shoulder. His right arm and hand went numb, and he felt himself slip out of the saddle and fall to the ground. The pain in his shoulder and the hard fall to the road knocked him unconscious.

When he awoke, he was tied to a tree, his shoulder bleeding badly. He was surrounded by the four robed horsemen, who were now on foot. The shortest of the four saw him open his eyes and announced, "He's awake."

The tallest rider stepped forward and took the man's hair in his hand, jerking his head up. "Who are you, Yankee, and why are you looking for the Phelps barn?"

"You're mistaken. I'm not lookin' for any barn. I'm just passin' through these parts."

The tall rider's response was to smash his pistol butt against the wounded man's badly damaged shoulder, causing him to scream out in pain. "Don't lie to me, you goddamn Yankee. We found this map in your coat pocket. We know you asked directions to the barn back in Hanging Rock. What's this here map for? Where'd you git it?"

"I don't know, I . . ." The tall rider interrupted him with another hard blow to his damaged shoulder. The wounded man screamed in pain.

"Who sent you? Who ya'all workin' for?" The silence from the Yankee was met with two more hard blows against his damaged shoulder. The pain from the blows caused him to pass out again.

When he awoke, he was tied up and gagged and slung over his horse like a sack of grain. The four mounted men were leading his horse to what appeared to be the edge of a farm. The man knew by the growing darkness that about an hour had passed since he had been attacked. He wondered where they were taking him. He was regretting the day he had decided to come back to South Carolina from his modest home in Illinois.

Without any warning, the horsemen halted. Before the Illinois man could figure out where he was, two of the men had dismounted and pulled him down from his saddle. The two of them carried the trussed up man over to the edge of a sturdy wooden fence, which seemed to surround some sort of pen. At the count of three, they heaved him over the fence, and he fell heavily into the muddy ground in the pen. As he began to catch his breath, the over-powering smell of shit invaded his nostrils along with the smell of his own blood. He thought he must have lost control of his bowels from the pain. The two men leaned over the fence to check he was still securely tied, and then all four of them mounted up on their horses and rode off.

The man tried to keep from panicking. He knew he was badly wounded and bleeding profusely. He knew he might not last the night without medical help. He thanked God he was still alive. He told himself he had been through bad times during the war and had managed to survive all of them. In an effort to figure out where he was, he struggled to turn over and finally managed to roll onto his side. As his eyes adjusted to the gloom, he could see the outline of movement in the shadows at the far end of the pen. Then his heart almost stopped as he realized what his fate would be. The shadowy figures began to slowly move toward him, grunting as they advanced. The hogs had initially been frightened by the activity at the end of their pen, but now their curiosity and the smell of blood in the pen had overcome their initial fear. The gag kept the man from crying out as his fear overwhelmed him and he soiled his trousers.

CHAPTER ONE

THE PRESENT

The tall young man dressed in faded denims and a sweat-stained cowboy hat took a deep breath of the cool clean air. His skin was dark, tanned by the ever-present Wyoming sun, and his black hair seemed to slip down the side of his face like it was spilling out of his hat. He never grew tired of the taste of mountain air, and today was no different than the first day he drew a breath in Wyoming.

Carson "Kit" Andrews could feel fall in the air, even on a sunny early September day. He pulled out the letter he had just received and read it for the second time. He was standing on top of the butte that rose above his father's ranch house. From there, he could see for miles in all directions. The flat rock he often used for a bench was on the edge of the small, spring-fed pond that provided the ranch house with a secondary water supply. Kit often came up to the rock at the end of the day to watch the wildlife come to drink from the pond and watch the sun set in the west. The air was growing cooler as the sun went down as it did every night in Wyoming, regardless of the season. He was always amazed at how much the sun influenced the temperature in his adopted state.

His friend, personal trainer, and instructor Chris Connor was gone. Connor had set out the previous month to try and find Kit's father, who had disappeared two years before. Kit had used every argument he could think of to try to make Chris let him go along. Connor had insisted that he go alone. He had made it clear that as skilled as Kit had become, he was still not in Connor's league and would only make the search harder if Connor had to look out for Kit as well. He had promised to notify Kit if he learned anything, and if he did need Kit's help, he would contact him.

"If I get in trouble, you will be much more help to me in Wyoming than being with me." he had told Kit. Kit wasn't buying that. He knew if Connor needed help, his first call would be to Woody, who was both Kit's father's close friend and his attorney.

Kit had heard nothing from Connor, and he had been gone for almost two months. Connor had told Kit he would contact him by e-mail around the middle of each month, and in another week it would be time for Connor's first e-mail.

Kit re-read the letter he had received that day from his cousin Johnny Andrews in Altona, Illinois. Johnny was a farmer, and he farmed what had been the original homestead farm of the Andrews family in Knox County, Illinois. Kit's great-great grandfather William Andrews had purchased the farm in 1873. Kit knew the history of his great-great grandfather and the farm. William had emigrated to the United States with his father and uncle from Scotland in 1855 at the age of twelve. When he was eighteen, William enlisted in Company I of the 102nd Illinois Infantry Regiment of the Union Army. He served in the Civil War with General Sherman and fought the Confederates from Chattanooga, Tennessee, to Atlanta, Georgia. From there he was part of the famous march to the sea and the capture of Savannah, Georgia. When the war ended, William was in North Carolina. After the war he returned home and began to work on farms in Knox County, Illinois. By 1873 he had saved enough money to add to his mustering out army bonus and buy the farm.

Johnny had written to Kit to let him know they were going to tear down the original farmhouse, as it was beyond repair. The old frame farmhouse was a small story and a half building with a dirt floor. Kit knew it had been used as a tool shed when the current farmhouse was built in 1903. Johnny and Kit's cousin Beverly Andrews-Krans had decided to make a family event out of the occasion. They planned to take pictures of the family in front of the old house before they tore it down and then frame the pictures with salvaged red painted wood siding from the old building.

Kit had not been very close to his family on his father's side as his mother had always told him his father was dead and had never taken him to any Andrews' family gatherings. He smiled as he remembered how his cousin Beverly had tracked him down in Chicago a few months ago after reading about him in the Chicago newspapers.

They had written about Kit when he had testified as the only eyewitness in a murder trial. She had phoned him and re-introduced herself. Before he could mount any kind of a protest, she had driven up to Chicago to meet him and have dinner. Before he knew it, she had his e-mail address, mailing address, phone number and announced that he was back on the family Christmas card list. His cousin struck him as a woman who was seldom denied what she wanted. Beverly was one of those rare individuals who drew people like a campfire and they gathered near her for her warmth and light. When she walked into a room, people stopped to look. When she spoke, people listened.

Kit had called Johnny and agreed to attend the house-razing back in Illinois. He planned to fly to Chicago first and arrange to see Tang Kelly, the closest thing to a girlfriend in his life. They met in Kemmerer, Wyoming, her hometown, and she was now an assistant curator at the old Chicago Fields Museum of Science and Industry. The idea of a trip back to Illinois to see Tang and the family farm appealed to him. He could even stop and see his mother, although that was one meeting he was not looking forward to. Still the trip would allow him a chance to meet some of his father's family and get to know them better.

As Kit looked up from the letter, the sun had almost slipped behind the mountains to the west. He rose from the flat rock and made his way down the butte on the narrow trail. By the time he reached the ranch house, he was actually smiling.

Once in the ranch house, Kit turned on the inside lights as he made his way to the kitchen. A quick search of the refrigerator narrowed his supper options to about three items. He settled for some of Mrs. Carlson's frozen home-made chili and set the bag out to thaw. Kit made his way to his bedroom. As he passed his father's locked bedroom, he stopped and looked at the door. Although he had passed by this door many times, he had never been in the room and he knew that Connor had never been in the room either. Connor had told him that the room was off limits, but the room was a direct link to a father he had never known.

Taken by a sudden wave of curiosity, he tried the door. It was locked. He carefully looked at the lock. It was not a complicated system. His father had built the ranch house with security in mind, but he had apparently not worried much about the door to his own bedroom. Kit withdrew an old credit card from his wallet and inserted it between the lock and the door jamb. With a slight push, the door sprung open. Kit paused in front of the newly opened door. This was his father's house and his father's bedroom. Kit had last seen his father when he was two years old. He felt a strong inner desire to know more about his father than he had learned in Kemmerer from his father's friends, including Connor.

He stepped inside the room, found the light switch and flicked it on. He was in the center of a bedroom slightly larger than his own. It was sparsely furnished with a large bed, a side table with a lamp, a dresser, and a television set and stand. He moved slowly across the room and came to the door of a closet. He opened the door and flipped on the light. It was a large walk-in closet. At the far end was a good-sized safe. The walls were lined with clothes on racks and shelves. There were expensive suits, military uniforms, work clothes, hunting clothes and even a tuxedo. Against one wall were racks containing shoes and boots.

As Kit walked toward the back of the closet he could see something large and framed hanging above the safe. It was a huge picture frame and in the frame were over twenty photos, each mounted separately. Kit stepped closer to examine the photos. They were all of Kit at various ages of his life including a picture of him at his high school graduation and one at his college graduation. There was even one of Kit playing soccer in a high school game.

The father that Kit had never known had managed to secretly keep tabs on him as he grew up and had taken the photos as memories of his son. Kit stared at the photos for a long time and was embarrassed when he realized tears were running down his cheeks. He turned to leave, but before he walked out, he stopped and pulled an old worn leather jacket off the rack and held it close to his face. He could smell the slightest trace of what he was sure was Old Spice aftershave. Kit replaced the jacket, turned out the lights, and silently left his father's bedroom, making sure the door was locked, and headed back to the kitchen and his waiting supper.

Before he drove to Salt Lake and the airport, Kit stopped by Elmer's Paint and Body Shop in Kemmerer. As he walked up to the open garage door of the old building, he glanced at the faded hand-painted sign over the door. "Elmer's Paint & Body Shop. If we can't fix it, it ain't broke." Kit was still smiling when he tapped an elderly gray haired old man on the shoulder of his greasy coveralls. "Elmer, how the heck are you doing?"

"Hey there, Kit. I thought you might be by. Care for a cup of coffee?"

Kit politely declined, knowing full well that the locals were not sure which was heavier, used crankcase oil or Elmer's five day old coffee.

"Suit yerself," said Elmer as he refilled a battered tin cup from an ancient Mr. Coffee that might have originally been white, but was now the color of rancid grease.

"I suppose you wanna see yer truck."

"If you can spare the time, I'd appreciate it."

Elmer let Kit through a maze of old auto parts and barrels partially full of stuff that even Elmer was not sure of. He led the way through a doorway covered with an old blanket, also the color of grease, or something like it.

On the other side of the blanket was an empty one car stall, painted in a brilliant white. When Elmer hit the light switch, the room reflected the light off the spotless walls and floor. The stall was empty except for Kit's old 1949 GMC pickup. The pickup had been rebuilt and was minus the hood, radiator, and front fenders. The rest of the truck was spotless and done in primer paint.

"Another month and I should be done," said Elmer.

"What do I owe you up to now?" Kit asked as he was taking out his wallet.

"You don't owe me nothin' till I finish the dang job. I woulda been done sooner, but I couldn't find a good used driver-side door anywheres. I hadda fill in all them bullet holes and that took some time. Somebody sure musta been pissed at you or the truck. I filled in more than thirty holes. That ain't countin' all them dents of the bullets that just bounced off. Musta been some of them fool greenhorn Californian deer hunters huntin' outa season."

"O.K. Elmer, I'll settle with you when you're done." Kit took one last look at his beloved old truck and followed Elmer through the blanket door back to the chaos that lay beyond.

Kit had bought the old truck when the Chevy he drove from Illinois was damaged as he slid off the road in a spring snowstorm. The heavy doors of the old GMC had saved his life when hired killers had tried to ambush him and his close friend Swifty Olson. The killers had used pistols and their bullets couldn't penetrate the heavier metal doors of the old pickup truck. Kit had Andy Bain tow the truck into Elmer's and instructed Elmer to do the best he could in fixing it up. It had become a personal crusade to Elmer who had walked around the damaged truck muttering, "They don't make 'em like this anymore."

Kit knew the finished product would be worth waiting for. He walked back out to the street and climbed into his new Ford F-150 pickup. It was a nice truck, but it did not have the same appeal to Kit as did the old GMC. He started the engine and headed for the airport in Salt Lake City.

CHAPTER

TWO

Kit stepped from the taxi and walked up the steps to the entrance of the Field Museum. He stopped near the main entrance to check his appearance in the reflection of a large window. Satisfied with what he saw, he made his way past throngs of young children being held in check by their adult supervisors and finally arrived at the service desk. The polite young black man at the desk checked his admissions list and then asked for Kit's driver's license. Satisfied that this tall, young cowboy in front of him was the same person on the picture ID, he gave him a plastic pass that clipped to the front of Kit's shirt and gave him directions and a map. Kit had been here before and knew how to get to Tang's office, but he also knew the drill and patiently waited until the young man had finished his detailed instructions. Kit nodded his thanks and headed for the office section of the museum.

Occasionally, people would almost stop and stare at him. Their attention made Kit smile. He was pretty sure they did not get too many visitors wearing cowboy boots, jeans, a bright blue cowboy shirt, and a cream colored Stetson. Less than two years ago, he had visited the museum when he was living in Chicago. That day he was pretty sure he was dressed in shorts, t-shirt, and tennis shoes. He remembered he had gone at the insistence of his best friend, Willie Nelson, who had insisted they get some "culture."

The thought of his friend, who had been murdered several months ago, caused a wave of sadness to flood over him. He stopped in front of an exhibit, staring at it, but not seeing it as his mind was somewhere else. It seemed impossible that Willie was dead. Just a few months ago they had been in this very museum, laughing and having a great time. After a couple of minutes the feeling passed, and Kit resumed his trip to Tang's office.

Tang's real name was Mustang Kelly. She was born and raised in Kemmerer, Wyoming. Her father had been hoping for a boy, and when she was born, he had insisted on the name Mustang in the hope she would at least be a tomboy. Tang had been very much a tomboy, working in her father's garage and becoming a very good mechanic. She loved cars and trucks and working on them. She had gone to college at the University of Wyoming and had majored in anthropology. She was lucky enough to get a job at the Field Museum and had risen to the post of assistant curator.

When her father died, she had quit her job to go back to Wyoming, to take over his business and help take care of her mother. She found the business was in serious debt and she worked tirelessly to build up the business and pay off the debts. Realizing she might work for years before she could pay off all the debts, she had turned to hiring Mexican illegal immigrants to help her do some Indian grave robbing to obtain pottery and other artifacts and sell them to people she knew would buy and ask no questions. Kit had stumbled onto the grave robbing and had used a ruse to scare the superstitious Mexicans away. He then offered to loan Tang the money to pay off the debts and allow her to pay him back, "when she could."

Tang then was able to get her job back in Chicago and Kit had been back to see her two times since she left Kemmerer. Even now Kit could see her in his mind's eye. She was of medium height with a trim figure, red hair, light skin, and piercing green eyes that reminded him of emeralds. She had a great smile and a happy laugh that she had used often around Kit.

The first time Kit had shown up at the museum, he was able to surprise Tang. This time she was waiting outside her office with her hands on her hips, trying to look very official and professional. She wore a green suit, white silk blouse, and high heels. She knew Kit was fond of her in green. Her attempt to look very professional was betrayed by her huge smile. She was literally grinning from ear to ear.

Kit took her in his arms and lifted her off her feet and crushed her body against his. He looked her in the eyes and said, "You are one fine looking woman, Miss Kelly."

Tang squealed with laughter as he kissed her full on the lips. The kiss was long, as he enjoyed the feel of her soft lips and the taste of her lovely mouth. Kit finally released her, and she looked up at him.

"Wow, you sure know how to sweep a lady off her feet!"

"Thank you, ma'am. I'm mighty pleased to see you."

Tang laughed and told him to wait while she got her purse and coat. Soon they were walking out the entrance where Tang hailed a cab. "Usually I take the bus, but today I think we can afford a cab."

"Where are we headed, if you don't mind me asking?

"Well, I thought about going to the art museum or the aquarium, or the zoo, but then I thought, what the heck, let's go to my apartment and see what we can find to do there."

Kit smiled to himself and held her in his arms in the back seat of the cab. She looked great, she smelled great, and she felt great nestled against him. Suddenly he was really glad to be back in Chicago.

The next morning Kit left Tang's apartment about ten minutes after she left for work. He took a cab to Midway Airport and waited for his short flight to the airport in Moline, Illinois. Moline was about 45 minutes from Galva and his cousin Beverly was meeting him at the airport. In his three years in Chicago, he had only used O'Hare Airport on those few occasions when he had flown anywhere. He had never been to Midway and was surprised to see that it had been completely re-designed and renovated. Kit found a seat facing the center of the concourse at his designated gate and waited for his flight.

According to his ticket, the flight would take less than an hour. Kit and his travel bag had breezed through airport security and the overall pedestrian traffic was manageable. When he had lived in Chicago, everything seemed normal. Now he found himself amazed by the traffic on the roads, the crowds of people in the airport, and the general sense of congestion. He found himself watching the people hurrying past his waiting area and getting a kick out of how outlandishly dressed some of them seemed to him. "Sure don't see that in Kemmerer," he thought. Normally he might have felt a little out of place dressed in cowboy boots and a Stetson and would have been the object of a number of stares by passers-by. Instead, he sort of melted in to the background as scores of people passed by dressed in outrageous get-ups that he was pretty sure their mothers would not approve of.

About an hour and a half later, he was walking down the stairs that were built into the door of the small turbo-prop commuter aircraft on the tarmac of the Moline Airport. Kit and the line of people in front of him headed for the terminal building that was located a short distance away. The terminal looked small compared to Salt Lake City and Midway, but it proved to be adequate for the traffic that passed through its doors. Kit and his fellow passengers advanced into the terminal and through a security area that separated his group from waiting passengers with the use of portable ropes. Several security people stood in the area, apparently there to make sure no unauthorized people slipped through the ropes.

Once clear of the security area, he had no trouble finding his cousin Beverly, and she knew at a glance that the tall good-looking cowboy was her cousin. Beverly was a tall woman with reddish hair that was more bronze than red. She had a dark complexion and dark brown eyes. She was wearing a stylish pantsuit and sporting several sizeable diamonds. Beverly looked like the classy woman she was.

She led him outside the terminal to a nearby parking lot and a waiting large, black Cadillac. Kit knew that

Beverly was married to a very successful small town lawyer in Galva. His name was Schuyler Krans, but everybody knew him as "Sky," a nickname he had received in the second grade. The drive to Galva took about an hour as they passed through the flat and slightly rolling terrain of Western Illinois. Unlike Wyoming, where there were lots of open space and lots of nothing, Illinois was green. They passed fields of corn and soybeans and other things Kit wasn't sure he could identify. This was definitely farm country. During the drive, Beverly tried to bring him up to date on all of his relatives while peppering him with questions seemingly all at the same time. Kit enjoyed himself immensely. Beverly was one woman who made it easy for him to talk, and he could tell that she was also a good listener who did not miss a thing he said.

Before long, the seemingly endless waves of green cornfields thinned out as they reached the outskirts of Beverly's home town. Galva was a small Midwestern farm town that had been founded in 1854 to serve the farms in the area and also as a terminal for the Chicago, Burlington, and Quincy Railroad, now known as the Burlington Northern. The town of about 2,800 people was built around a square, and running north and south in the middle of the square were the railroad tracks.

As they drove around the square, Kit took note of the usual small town array of stores including a small grocery store, a drug store, a funeral home, a café, a couple of gas stations and a diminutive motel. In addition was a large old building that housed Swanson's Hardware Store, clearly the largest business in town. They passed by a bank and Beverly noted that Sky owned the building the bank was housed in and had offices next to it and above it. He also owned the old firehouse next to the bank building and used it to store the vast amounts of antiques that he and Beverly had no room for in their home.

They drove to the north side of town, along the east edge of Wiley Park. The park was large and well cared for with huge old towering trees, a bandstand, playground, and basketball court. Beverly's home was a large and spacious two-story house that had been built in 1902. It had a huge front porch that faced the park. A driveway on the west side of the house ran from Fourth Street in the front and exited on Fifth Street behind it. The yard was a block deep. Kit noted that many of the homes along the park were of similar size and architecture. He was pretty sure this had been the "uptown" neighborhood from the day it was laid out by the town's founders.

Beverly showed Kit to his room, a large bedroom with an attached bathroom on the second floor. She left him to unpack with instructions to join her in the kitchen when he was finished. After unpacking, Kit washed his face and hands in the bathroom and made his way down the beautiful wood staircase to the first floor. He noted that a rich Persian carpet had been made into a runner for the stairs with brass hardware holding it in place. The bright colors of the carpet meshed nicely with the rich walnut finish of the wooden stairs.

The house had been beautifully restored and looked like it must have in 1902, yet the kitchen was bright, modern, and large with its own dining area. As he stepped into the kitchen, Kit was immediately besieged by two cocker spaniels. Beverly was a pet person. She appeared out of nowhere and shooed the dogs away and had Kit sit at the table while she poured two cups of coffee. As Kit was looking around the room, he saw a huge black and white tomcat lying on the base of what appeared to be a liquor cabinet. The cat eyed Kit suspiciously, gingerly got to its feet, stretched and then slowly made his way down to the floor from the cabinet and casually strutted across the floor to the living room. Clearly the cat was the master of the house.

"Who's the giant cat?"

"That's Sylvester," replied Beverly. "He was Sky's cat when we got married, and he just assumes it's his house and the rest of us are temporary guests that he has to tolerate."

"What about the dogs? How do they get along with the cat?"

"The dogs have learned to leave Sylvester alone. When he gets tired of the dogs, he just bats them on the side of the head and sends them flying. That's why they leave him alone."

Beverly was refilling their coffee cups when the back door to the kitchen flew open and in strode Schuyler Krans, who was immediately surrounded by the two yelping dogs.

"Hello Mr. Barney. Hello Little Dog. How've you boys been today?"

Schuyler looked up from the attentive dogs. "Well, you must be Mr. Carson Andrews. It is certainly a pleasure to meet you," he said and he stepped forward and shook Kit's hand. "Can I get you a drink?"

Kit told Sky that he would love a drink and before he was comfortably back in his chair, Sky had poured two martinis and placed them on the kitchen table.

Schuyler was a large man who carried himself with a regal bearing. He was balding with a pear shaped body and a large head. He looked every inch like a judge out of the 1880's. He wore a navy pin striped suit with a fashionable silk tie and a light blue dress shirt. The suit was accented by the colorful large red suspenders that Sky wore under his suit coat. He had a loud booming voice that he used in public and in business. Kit was to later discover that once Sky got to know you, he conversed in private at a more normal octave level. Kit was to find Sky educated, very well read, and blessed with a large and slightly off-color sense of humor.

That night, as Kit slipped under the covers of the canopy bed in his room, he marveled at how he could have such interesting relatives and have known nothing about them until he wound up in Wyoming by accident. He was very glad he had decided to come for the family reunion at the farm.

After breakfast the next morning, Schuyler headed off to work at his law office, and Beverly and Kit headed for the farm in Altona with Beverly driving the Cadillac. The farm was about three miles out of Altona, a small farming town of maybe five hundred souls. They drove the last two miles on a gravel road. As they approached the farm, Kit was surprised to see that it looked like it probably did in the early 1900's. The big white farmhouse was set back from the road. A sidewalk ran from the large covered front porch out to the road and was flanked by huge pine trees that had to be well over one hundred years old. An old grove of walnut trees along the back side of the house served as a windbreak and the barrier between the yard around the house and the beginning of plowed fields.

Just past the house was a small, detached two car garage with a dirt floor. Beverly explained that her grandfather used to sit in his old Ford in the shaded garage and listed to the Chicago Cubs baseball games. Either the garage was a cool, private place to listen or he was just escaping the watchful eye of his wife, Beverly's grandmother. Surrounding the house and farmyard in a sort of L-shaped formation were several sizeable barns and machine sheds. Between the barns and the garage was a small story and a half building that was painted a faded red like the rest of the barns and sheds. Beverly explained that the building was the original farmhouse that they were planning to tear down today. Although the small building still looked to be in good shape, she explained it was no longer structurally sound. There were several other vehicles parked in the farmyard and Beverly pulled into an empty space and parked the car.

Kit had come dressed for work wearing jeans, a denim long sleeved shirt, and work boots. He was quickly introduced to his cousin Johnny, who handed him a pair of leather work gloves and a small wrecking bar. Beverly introduced him to everyone including her uncle William, Johnny's father. William was about ninety years old, but still in pretty good shape. He had the appearance of a handsome ageing movie star. His handshake was hearty and firm. He caught Kit staring at his right hand where the tip of the index finger was missing. He smiled and said to Kit, "Don't look so surprised. When you work long enough with machinery, sooner or later you make a mistake."

Kit blushed and started to apologize, but William just laughed it off. "Well, I think we oughta get started," he said.

Everyone gathered around the front of the old farmhouse for a group picture. Beverly was an amateur photographer and had won several awards for her black and white photos in competitions. She had an expensive looking camera placed on a tripod and after getting a satisfactory group placement, she moved to the front of the house with everyone else and operated the camera by remote control. After three pictures she decided she had enough, and the family divided up into work crews to demolish the 150 year old building. Beverly's plan was to give everyone in the family a picture framed with the wood from the old red farmhouse.

The men placed ladders against the building and began to take off the roof. Johnny had arranged for a large metal dumpster to be placed within a few yards of the old farmhouse and soon copious amounts of wood shingles were finding their way into the dumpster. Within two hours, the roof was off. The workers were careful as they labored to dismantle the rest of the house, as the aged barn wood would be sold to collectors and people who valued it in remodeling projects. Enough of the wood would be kept to make the frames for the family pictures.

At noon they broke for lunch. Beverly and the rest of the women had set up several tables and chairs under the shade of the walnut trees and served up an old fashioned farm lunch of fried chicken, mashed potatoes and gravy, green beans, corn on the cob, and pickles. There were pitchers of coffee, water, iced tea, and milk. In the middle of the tables were baskets of fresh baked bread and cups of butter.

Kit found out he had worked up a good appetite and ended up taking seconds, which got approving nods from the women who had prepared the meal. During lunch he chatted with his cousin Judy and her husband who lived in Georgia and his cousin Tom, who turned out to be literally a rocket scientist working for a large defense contractor in California.

Their lunch break complete, the men then returned to the task of working to dismantle the building. Kit had been taking down the boards of the inside walls when he made an unusual discovery. As he used his small wrecking bar to pull an old board away from the outside wall, something fell out of the cavity behind the board. He finished pulling the board off and after placing it on a pile of boards on the dirt floor of the old farmhouse, he knelt down and picked up the object he had disturbed. It was a small, leather bound notebook about eight inches long and about four inches wide. It was held together by a couple of rawhide thongs. Kit took the notebook out of the farmhouse and showed it to Johnny. They decided to put it aside and deal with it when they had finished demolishing the farmhouse.

It was almost four o'clock in the afternoon when the last remnants of the old farmhouse were finally removed and only bare ground and piles of old barn wood planks remained. In honor of the occasion and the history of the building, the men washed up in hot water and bar soap in old metal bowls, just as their ancestors had done at this same spot a century and a half before. They returned to the shaded area with tables and chairs under the walnut trees. This time the ladies served up ice-cold beer and snacks. Kit retrieved the old notebook he had found and sat down next to William and Johnny.

"Have you ever seen this notebook before, Mr. Andrews?" asked Kit.

William took the notebook and turned it over in his gnarled hands. "No, I've never seen this before."

"I wonder how it wound up inside the wall of the old farm house?" Johnny remarked.

"Well, my guess is this might have been my father's or his father's and they put it behind the wall for safekeeping and then forgot about it. Does it have dates or names inside?" asked William.

Kit carefully untied the old rawhide thongs. They were fairly rotten and came apart in his hands. The leather cover was in pretty good shape and although hard and rough to the touch, it had survived the years hidden in the wall intact.

Kit opened the notebook. At the top of the first page was a barely legible date and after a few moments of studying the page, Kit was able to determine that the year was 1862. The book's pages contained faded writing, made with what appeared to be the lead of a pencil. The pages were almost impossible to read although now and then Kit could make out a date or a word. The last entry was on April 12, 1865.

When Kit told William that date, the old man's eyes lit up. "That notebook must have belonged to my grandfather William. He enlisted in the Union Army in 1862 when he turned 18 years of age."

Pretty soon all of the family had gathered around to see the mysterious notebook. After a good deal of back and forth discussion, it was decided to let Beverly and Kit take possession of the notebook and see about getting it restored so their ancestor's writings could be read and understood. Kit promised to use his contacts at the Field Museum in Chicago to have the notebook pages restored to a readable level and then have the entire notebook copied and printed so each family member could have a copy. The general feeling among the family members was the notebook should then be turned over to the Knox County Historical Center in Galesburg.

By six o'clock, the tired but happy workers had gathered up their belongings and left the farm until only Johnny, his wife Patsy, William, Beverly, and Kit remained. Kit was tired and his clothes were a little wet and grimy from the dirt of the old building and the sweat from his body. He had forgotten about the high level of humidity and how it seemed to sap the energy right out of your body. He felt good about being part of the family working on a historic project. Kit had noticed that right after being introduced, he was treated as if he was part of the Andrews family and had always been around his relatives. It was a good feeling, and he savored it. He and

Beverly said their good-byes and headed back to Galva in the black Cadillac, now covered with dust from the gravel roads. Beverly obviously made no distinction between gravel and paved roads as she drove just as fast on either one. The big car fishtailed as it left the gravel road and made a hard left turn onto the asphalt highway. Kit just grinned to himself.

That night Schuyler took Beverly and Kit out to the Midland Country Club for dinner. The clubhouse and the golf course were located about halfway between Galva and Kewanee. It had been the only private club in the area for over fifty years. Galva now had a golf course at Lake Calhoun, but it was not as spiffy or prestigious as Midland. Everyone at the club from the bartender, wait staff, and patrons all seemed to know Schuyler and greeted him with his nickname Sky.

The meal was excellent and Schuyler entertained them with a steady patter of local history and who was who and who did what to whom. Kit found the information fascinating rather than boring. Schuyler was reportedly the richest man in Henry County, although he was far from ostentatious. His membership in the Midland Country Club was based on two things. One, his father had been a member and Sky had taken over his father's law practice and his place in the community. Two, Galva was not full of great eating places and the food at Midland was excellent. Sky was a man who appreciated good food and good drink. After a day's hard labor and two excellent meals, Kit was fast asleep shortly after his head hit the pillow.

CHAPTER
THREE

Kit was on the phone to Tang at 8:15 A.M. the next morning. He explained to her about the discovery of the notebook and what they thought it was. She promised to find out who could do the restoration job and then call him back. After breakfast, Beverly hauled out a huge old bound book that was entitled *The History of Knox County*. The book had been published in the early 1930's and included biographies of the more noted local citizenry. William Andrews had an entire page dedicated to his life.

When he finished reading the biography, Kit was impressed. A young farm hand had gone off to war for over three years and come out unscathed. In addition, he had saved his mustering out bonus and added to his savings for eight years of hard work as a farm hand. In 1873, he had saved enough to buy the farm in Altona. This was no small feat for a young man who inherited nothing from his parents but a good set of values and a penchant for hard work.

He had come far for a young man who left Scotland at age twelve and sailed across the Atlantic, landed in New York City, and then traveled by train to Chicago. That was the end of his formal education. He immediately began the work of a man as a farm hand. Then he joined the Union Army at age eighteen and traveled through Tennessee, Georgia, South Carolina, and then North Carolina. He marched in the grand review at the end of the war in Washington, D.C. He then took a train back to Chicago where he was mustered out of the army. He took a train south to Galesburg and then walked fifteen miles to his home. All this was during a time in U.S. history when people often never traveled more than thirty miles from where they were born.

Kit estimated that William had purchased the farm at the ripe old age of twenty-nine. Kit was sure the notebook was about his three year stint in the Union Army and since William had served under General Sherman during his legendary march to the sea, Kit was sure it would be very interesting reading.

Shortly before noon, Tang called back. She told Kit while there were several good places in Chicago that could do a good job of restoring the notebook, there was a man near Galva she would highly recommend. Tang felt this particular gentleman could do a good job, and he would probably be able to do it more quickly and cheaply than anyone in Chicago. Kit wrote down the name, address, and phone number and thanked Tang profusely. She made him promise to share a copy of the notebook with her as payment for her spadework.

Kit replaced the receiver on the phone and looked at what he had written down.

Dr. Henry Haselmayer, Professor of History, Knox College, 1328 Lombard Street, Galesburg, Illinois. Phone number at work is 309-932-3669.

Kit quickly dialed the number and found himself talking to a receptionist at the college. He was transferred to Dr. Haselmayer's assistant who informed Kit that Dr. Haselmayer was currently teaching a class and was unavailable. Kit then made an appointment for nine o'clock the next morning.

At 8:45 A.M. Kit was sitting on a bench outside Dr. Haselmayer's office at Knox College in Galesburg. The college was an old liberal arts school with a rich tradition. The campus was over a hundred years old with well kept grounds and impressive historic buildings. Kit had noticed the school's mascot was a Siwash. "What the hell was a Siwash?" Kit wondered.

A rich bass voice sort of rumbled out of the hallway at Kit. "Well hello, Mr. Andrews. I have been looking forward to meeting you."

"You have? I was not aware you knew who I was," responded a surprised Kit.

The man in front of Kit was short and very round. He appeared as if his head was set on top of a pumpkin. His legs must have been short as it seemed his gleaming black wingtip shoes stuck out at the bottom of the pumpkin. He had hair the color of salt and pepper, cropped very close on his head. He wore thick black rimmed glasses and was dressed in a three piece pin-striped suit with a white shirt and a yellow bow tie.

"Well, I had the luxury of talking to Ms. Kelly at the Field Museum and she informed me that she had referred you to me. I have a great deal of respect for Ms. Kelly and her fine institution. Please come into my office and have a seat.

Kit entered a small office that was surprisingly neat and orderly. The walls were lined with bookshelves filled with volumes of books of all sizes. The floor was an ancient hardwood and largely covered with a tasteful old rug. Dr. Haselmayer seated himself on a large green leather chair behind a huge walnut desk with a glass top. Nothing was on the desk except a telephone and a desk lamp. Kit seated himself on one of two green leather upholstered chairs in front of the desk.

"Now, Mr. Andrews, how may I be of service to you?" said Dr. Haselmayer.

Kit gave Dr. Haselmayer a rambling outline of the history of his great-great grandfather and ended with the discovery of the notebook.

"Ahh, a rare opportunity for a glimpse into the history of your ancestors. Excellent find! Did you bring the notebook with you?"

Kit nodded and produced the notebook wrapped in a couple of old, but soft cotton dishtowels from Beverly's kitchen.

Dr. Haselmayer took the notebook from Kit and laid it down on his desk. He then carefully unwrapped the dishtowels and set the notebook under his desk lamp. He paused to bring out a large old-fashioned magnifying glass and began to carefully study the outside of the notebook. Then he reached into a drawer in his desk and took out a pair of thin white cotton gloves and a thin silver bar that was about eight inches long and thinner than a dime. He used the gloved hands to open the notebook and the silver bar to gently turn pages in the notebook. After about five minutes of examining the notebook, he closed it and returned the bar, gloves, and magnifying glass to his desk drawer.

"Do you think you can restore the notebook?" asked Kit.

"Yes, Mr. Andrews, I believe I can. The book is in excellent condition. The writing appears to have been done with pencil and the lead on the pages has faded over time. The pages are in excellent shape considering their age. Your great-great-grandfather's notebook was of very high quality for the times and the quality of the paper has helped in the preservation of the writing."

"Can you give me some idea of how long this will take, Dr. Haselmayer?"

"I believe I can have it fully restored within a week. I do have classes and other research work, but this is something I do on the side. I thoroughly enjoy restoration and am anxious to see what thoughts and events your great-great grandfather has preserved for us."

"A week would be great. I'm staying at my cousin's in Galva and you can reach me at this number." Kit wrote down Beverly's phone number and address as well as his cell phone number on a card and handed it to Dr. Haselmayer.

"Mr. Andrews, you have not inquired as to the cost of this restoration?"

"I am happy to pay whatever you consider is fair. It's not everyday that a piece of family history falls in your lap. I want to restore the notebook and share it with all the members of the Andrews family."

"I assure you, Mr. Andrews, the work will be satisfactory and my fee will be fair."

"Thank you, Dr. Haselmayer. I look forward to your call."

Kit spent most of the next four days getting a grand tour of Galva and the surrounding area. He and Beverly visited several area cemeteries where she pointed out the graves of many of their ancestors. Kit was pleased to see that even in the small town cemetery of Altona, the cemetery was well kept, the grass mowed and the tombstones in good shape. He noted that the grave of his great-great grandfather William was part of a family plot that was set off by small granite cornerstones with the letter "A". Within the plot were several graves including his great-great grandfather and his wife and his great grandfather and his wife. All four of them lived to at least the age of eighty-three with William having lived until he was eighty-four.

He learned the history of Altona, Galva, and the neighboring village of Bishop Hill. Most of Bishop Hill, an early communal society, was now an Illinois State Park. He and Beverly visited Lake Calhoun, a man-made lake about six miles from Galva. Beverly explained that their great grandfather had been one of the founders of the association that created the lake. The lake had been established as a recreational area and had a large clubhouse with a swimming area, clay tennis courts, and a picnic area.

The lake was surrounded on three sides by a dense forest of old pine trees. Over the years the lake had filled in with silt and the clubhouse had fallen into disrepair. A few years ago, a local couple had purchased the lake and the land around it from the association. They were dredging the silt from the lake and had rebuilt the clubhouse. Kit was amazed to see the second floor of the clubhouse had a huge ball room with large fireplaces at each end. There was a bar area with the original dumbwaiter to bring food up from the kitchen on the first floor. There were also several decks attached to the second floor that made it seem even larger. The first floor housed the locker and shower rooms, offices, and a fully equipped kitchen, as well as a snack bar.

Beverly explained that they were still working on dredging the lake. Currently the clubhouse was available for wedding receptions, meetings, parties, and reunions. On the weekend, Sky took Kit to see some of the dozen or more farms that he owned and leased out to area farmers. It was soon apparent to Kit that Sky had not gotten wealthy by accident. He had a keen eye for a bargain and made a point to tell Kit that he bought farms that were marginal rather than the best farm land as the difference in profit on crops to a land owner was not very much and made the lower land price an even better bargain.

Probably the most unusual place for Kit was the Jacobsen Swedish Bakery. It was a simple storefront building in downtown Galva. Years ago there had been an active bakery behind the front of the building where the display cases were located. Today all the baking was done in the Kewanee bakery location and the goods transported to Galva. There were all kinds of breads, rolls, and coffee cakes on open shelves. What was missing from the store were any employees. There were none. Instead there was a box with a slit in the top to place your money. On the wall behind the showcase was a large menu of the bakery items with their prices. There was a notebook on top of one of the showcases to make a special order or to let them know that you did not have the correct change and needed some change back. Special ordered baked goods were in a separate showcase with the names of the folks who made the order in front of them.

"You mean this entire store operates on the honor system?" said an incredulous Kit.

"That's right. Sky thinks that most people actually overpay and never ask for repayment. The store has operated this way for at least ten years," replied Beverly.

The specialty of the store was something called rusks, which to Kit seemed like cold toast. Rusks came in several flavors including Beverly's favorite, cinnamon.

Beverly went on to explain that rusks were a Swedish specialty and Galva was a predominately Swedish town. Swedes are big coffee drinkers and rusks are used to dunk in their coffee.

Kit and Beverly had returned from the bakery, as well as the small grocery store that served Galva, and were putting away their purchases when the front doorbell rang. Beverly returned from the front door carrying a package in the traditional colors of Federal Express.

"Guess what this is?" she said to Kit in a teasing voice.

Kit took the package from her and noted it was from Dr. Haselmayer and quickly tore it open. He extracted the original notebook, wrapped in tissue paper and then took out a bound paper manuscript. He placed the wrapped notebook on the kitchen table and sat down in one of the wooden chairs and opened the cover of the manuscript. He was amazed to see that in the front of him was a manuscript that was a copy of the notebook, but in clear and legible print. "This is wonderful," he said to Beverly. "Dr. Haselmayer did a great job. This will be easy to have copies made for all of the family."

"Don't forget your favorite cousin when you get those copies," Beverly replied.

"Don't worry. I won't forget."

Kit then began to read the words of his long dead great-great grandfather, written almost a century and a half before.

September 12, 1862

Today I went to Knoxville and enlisted in the Union Army. I am part of the One Hundred and Second Illinois Infantry Regiment. My father gave me this notebook and I will try to write down what I see and do in the army.

September 19, 1862

We have been training in Peoria since we got here by train. This is the second year of the war for the suppression of the rebellion. Most of the men who train us are veterans who have fought against the Rebels. I am proud of my uniform, but it is made of wool and is god awful hot and itchy in the heat of Peoria. We work hard, but we eat regular.

October 2, 1862

We are finally leaving Cairo. We boarded cattle cars on the Peoria, Burlington, and Logansport Railroad and were soon gliding along the broad prairies east of the Illinois River.

October 18, 1862

We reached Jeffersonville, opposite Louisville, Kentucky, and are finally issued guns. They are French muskets, not the rifles we were hoping for. I am in I company, under Captain King.

October 26, 1862

We have been marching for 12 days. We camp every night and march all day. It is very warm. Our knapsacks are heavy with three days rations and forty rounds of ammunition as well as spare clothing. That and a heavy musket make for quite a load.

October 30, 1862

We awoke to three inches of snow! We then marched 20 miles to Salt River. It is very cold. I already miss the heat of a few days ago.

November 11, 1862

We have camped on the shores of Lost River for 7 days to rest and refit. The camp is pleasant with good weather and lots of hickory nuts, walnuts and persimmons.

November 26, 1862

We passed into Tennessee last night. Weather is cold with considerable snow. We are glad for our tents.

December 10, 1872

We set up winter camp at Fort Thomas, near Gallatin, Tennessee. Many have underground chimnies or fire-places in their tents. We have a home-made chimney. We received long delayed supplies, which includes cans of preserves, piles of cakes, green apples, dried apples, cheese, and choice butter. Also welcome were warm mittens and stockings and writing paper, pens, pencils, and postage stamps.

April 28, 1863

We are breaking our winter camp. The weather has been awful. Many men sick and some have died. Roll call of the company is down to 700 men from our original number of 921. The losses are due to sickness, death, and desertion. We embarked on a train and after a couple of hours, the train halted suddenly as we were attacked by rebels! They had removed a rail and planned to rob the train. They were surprised by our presence. We killed two and captured four. Five of our boys were wounded and two died.

June 1, 1863

Found field of large blackberries! We had stewed blackberries, blackberry pies, dumplings, and blackberries with milk. What a treat!

August 2, 1863

Set up camp in Lavergne. Built log huts and did not use tents. Company area has about 50 houses with 3 streets.

October 8, 1863

Colonel Smith had 4 companies including I Company converted to mounted infantry. He also managed to get 225 Spencer Repeating Rifles and Colt revolvers. I marvel at the magic of such a weapon and vow to use it effectively.

February 26, 1863

We are leaving winter camp at Lavergne. Have spent months patrolling area and hunting rebels without much luck.

March 22, 1863

While camped in Wauhatchie Valley, had a foot of snow fall on us. Men had great snowball fight.

April 14, 1863

Had grand review for General Thomas. Our reward was to give up our horses. Were ordered to exchange our Spencer Rifles for Springfield rifled muskets. Orders to begin march to Lookout Mountain came before exchange of weapons. Thank goodness.

May 13, 1863

Moved to right of Resaca where Rebels were. Moved through groves of young pine trees. Pushed back Rebel skirmishers. No one hurt.

June 12, 1863

Was part of a patrol that ambushed a group of Rebels. We counted bodies and found we had killed twelve and captured twenty. They were dressed in ragged clothes that were in worse shape than ours. They were tough, but pretty hungry. None of them had shoes.

"How about a cup of coffee?" said Beverly.

Kit was startled by the intrusion into his concentrated reading. "That would be great. I'm sorry I'm ignoring you, but this is so darn interesting."

"No problem. Just what exactly does the notebook have to say?"

"Well, William seems to try to write down what he thinks is important and while he does not write in it on a regular basis, he writes in it often enough to get a picture of what is going on with him."

"So it is like a diary?"

"No, it is not a diary. He writes in it when he thinks he has something worthwhile to write about. Sometimes he writes about the war, but mostly he writes about things that happen to him, both good and bad."

"That sounds great. I can't wait until I can get a copy to read. How much did the guy from Knox College charge you for this?"

"I didn't see a bill. The only thing in the package was the manuscript. I'll check in the back of it for a bill."

Kit opened the manuscript to the last page and the back cover. There he found a small handwritten note.

Mr. Andrews:

I hope you have found my work timely and satisfactory. I enjoyed reading William's account of his time in the Civil War. I think you will find a very interesting story of his in the spring of 1865. Good luck to you in South Carolina. My fee for this work is $800. Please remit to me at the address on the envelope.

Respectfully

Dr. H. Haselmayer

Kit was puzzled by the note and handed it to Beverly.

"Why are you going to South Carolina?" she asked after reading the note.

"I have no idea what he's talking about. I've never been there, and I don't know anyone in South Carolina."

"Well, maybe you should skim the rest of the manuscript to find out what happened in the spring of 1865 and that will tell us what he meant."

"I think you're right."

Kit picked up the manuscript and began to skim the pages looking for a date that would tell him he had found entries in the spring of 1865. Finally he found what he was looking for. Under the date of February 26, 1865, was a much longer story than any of the other entries. This one went on for several pages.

February 26, 1865

We just left camp at a place called Hanging Rock. There was a small stream that had cut its way though some large rocks and one big rock hung out over the others about twenty feet up in the air. Locals say this was where the British lost two battles in the Revolutionary War. After the battle in 1776, the British hung six American soldiers from the rock and hence the name. I and my tent mate Nathan Bates are up for foraging duty tomorrow and hopefully we will be successful. Foraging has been much harder since we entered this heavily wooded part of the state. Farms seem to be few and far between.

February 27, 1865

    Today was the strangest day of my life. I am trying to write it down carefully as I want to remember everything that happened. Bates and I along with most of Company I, were on foraging duty and walking down a narrow dirt road surrounded by tall pine trees. Suddenly we heard shooting and we rushed forward to the sound of gunfire. We came upon two of our company, Jesse McQuade and Charlie Hartsell. Both had been wounded and had taken cover behind some downed trees. They told us they had come upon two mule drawn wagons hidden in the woods just off the road. The wagons had been guarded by civilians with shotguns and they had opened fire on the two soldiers. Both fled, but were wounded. Soon we were joined by the rest of Company I and we forged ahead under the leadership of Captain Murphy. At the sight of our well armed force most of the civilian guards surrendered and some fled into the surrounding woods. We did not give chase. We investigated the wagons and discovered they contained two large safes from the Bank of South Carolina. There was also a large amount of clothing. Captain Murphy obtained the combinations of the safes from one of the civilians, and they were opened under his supervision. The contents of the safes included over one million dollars of confederate bonds and twelve gold bars, each weighing about 25 pounds. There was also $5,000 in newly minted federal gold coins, assorted silver and gold jewelry, and about $200 worth of new Confederate postage stamps

    Captain Murphy had just finished making a written inventory of the safes and wagons when a mounted detail from the provost marshal rode up. A Captain Daniels was in charge and after talking with Captain Murphy, and verifying the contents of the wagons, he gave Murphy a receipt and took charge of the wagons, mules, and safes, leaving only a few mules that some of the civilian guards had been riding.

After the provost marshal's detail was out of sight, I told Bates that something didn't feel right and it was awful coincidental that a mounted detail showed up right where we found them hidden wagons. Bates thought I was out of my head, but I convinced him that we should check on them. I had a feeling they were there to meet the civilians and were not expecting to see the 102nd Illinois.

I talked Sergeant Nystrom into letting Bates and I take two of the captured mules and do some foraging. Soon Bates and I were on the dirt road tracking those two wagons. They wasn't hard to track as the wagons were heavy and made deep ruts in the dirt road. I had a feeling that them nine cavalrymen were Rebs dressed like ours. After about twenty minutes, we could hear them up ahead of us. The road twisted back and forth in the heavy woods, and it was easy to stay out of sight. After an hour, we passed an old church on our left. There was a small graveyard next to it. It wasn't much of a church, but it did have a small cross on the top of the roof. It needed paint real bad. The graveyard looked like it was pretty overgrown with weeds. About fifteen minutes later we crossed a sizeable creek over a stone bridge. In front of us we could see the forest getting thinner, and it looked like the beginning of a meadow. To keep from being seen we pulled off into the trees that bordered the meadow and dismounted. We tied off our horses and began moving to the edge of the tree line on foot.

In front of us, the road entered a large meadow of about 80 acres. We had to wait until they moved all the way through the meadow before we could get back on the road or risk being seen. They stopped about halfway through the meadow and turned off the road to their right. We could see a sizeable barn on the edge of the meadow. It was built on a small hillside and was two stories high. The lower portion of the barn was stone and the upper portion was made of rough hewn planks that looked more like hardwood than the pines that surrounded the meadow. The barn rose to a peak with a loft above the main door. At the nave of the roof was a cross about two feet high and eighteen inches wide that had been cut all the way through the wooden wall. Like the old church we had passed, the barn was unpainted.

The wagons were pulled up to the front of the barn and the large barn door was opened. It was getting to be almost dark and several lanterns were lit inside the barn. With a fair amount of moonlight and the light from the lanterns, it was easy to see the inside of the barn from my vantage point in the trees. The lanterns inside the barn also seemed to light up the cross in the nave of the roof. The men used planks and ropes to unload the two safes into the barn. Then they took shovels from the wagon and began to dig up the dirt floor of the barn. They dug for almost an hour until they had a pretty sizeable hole. Then they used planks, ropes, and two of the mules to slide the safes down to the edge of the newly dug hole. They then carefully lowered the safes into the hole with planks and ropes. They proceeded to cover the safes with timbers from inside the barn. After they were done they began to shovel dirt over the timbers.

I noticed the one posing as an officer did none of the labor, but merely gave orders. Soon five of the men were doing the digging while the officer and three others seemed to slowly drift back away from the hole. At a hand signal from the officer, he and the three men drew their side arms and quickly shot the other five men without any kind of warning. They then threw the five bodies into the hole and picked up the shovels and began covering them with dirt. In about fifteen minutes they had filled the hole and raked the surface level and covered it with loose straw to hide their activity. The four paused to drink from a bottle the officer had produced, and then they blew out the lanterns and closed up the barn door. They mounted their horses and led the mule teams, wagons, and the five spare horses away into the darkness of the night, heading for the other side of the meadow. I noted that they continued on the road still heading to the east.

Bates stood up as if to leave, and I pulled him back down to the ground with me. I wanted to make sure they were actually gone. I took a piece of paper I had in my pocket and by the remaining light of the moon, I did my best to make a map of the barn and how we had arrived there. When I was finished, I motioned silently to Bates and we slowly and carefully made our way back to our mules. We rode back to our camp on the same road. We knew that the men who had posed as Union cavalrymen were in reality Rebels. We also knew that five Confederate soldiers had been killed by four men who were killers and thieves, not soldiers.

Bates and I decided not to report what we had seen. No one would believe us if we did and the war was almost over. The two of us made a pact to come back five years after the war and see if the treasure was still there. We agreed that we would come back together or not at all. It was likely that the four killers would be back to claim their loot, and all we would find was an empty hole. Still it would be worth a try and, if nothing else, we would see that those five Confederate soldiers got a proper military burial.

I tore the map in half and gave half to Bates and secreted the other half in the side of my notebook. I hope I have done the right thing.

The next entry was dated some time later.

April 12, 1865
Lee has surrendered with his whole army!

That was the last entry in the notebook.

Kit felt something brushing against his leg, and he looked down to see Sylvester rubbing against his leg and purring loudly.

"Well, you must have done something to impress old Sylvester. He never warms up to strangers and to him, everyone is a stranger."

Kit looked up at his cousin and joined in her laughter. "Maybe Sylvester knows about the treasure," he said.

"What treasure?"

Kit then related the story of what happened to their great-great grandfather on that fateful day, February 27, 1865.

CHAPTER FOUR

By dinnertime, Kit had been on the phone with Swifty and filled him in on the story of the Confederate buried treasure. Swifty had immediately agreed to join Kit on a treasure hunting trip to South Carolina. Kit had e-mailed his friend with a list of things he wanted him to pick up at Kit's house and bring with him.

They agreed to have Swifty drive his truck from Wyoming to Illinois. Kit knew some of the equipment Swifty would bring would be things that he could never take on an airplane. The truck would give them a good base of operations and provide them with all the gear they might need for this type of expedition.

Kit made a list of things he might need that he could get locally and borrowed Beverly's Cadillac to drive to Galesburg, where he filled his shopping list. Kit knew it would take Swifty about a day and a half to drive to Galva. He spent the interim time on Beverly's computer downloading maps and information on South Carolina and details about the area around Hanging Rock. Kit also researched the Bank of South Carolina and the history of Company I of the 102nd Illinois Infantry Regiment in the Civil War. By the time Swifty finally pulled his truck up in front of Beverly's home in Galva, Kit had amassed a great deal of information.

Swifty's arrival called for introductions all around, and Kit was relieved as Swifty was on his best behavior and made a very good impression with Beverly and Sky. Swifty was soon regaling Beverly and Sky with stories of his various adventures with Kit in Wyoming. Swifty looked every inch the cowboy he was, from his worn cowboy boots to the hand tooled belt holding up his jeans to the slightly sweat stained Stetson cowboy hat on his head. Swifty's smile was infectious and so was his laugh. It was hard to believe this animated and very funny man was also a skilled commando and a trained killer.

After lunch, Sky went back to work and Kit and Swifty went out to the truck to conduct an inventory of their gear. After half an hour, Kit was satisfied that Swifty had brought everything he had requested and more. He was also sure Swifty had managed to include some items he was not revealing to Kit. Swifty had a history of making sure he was prepared for the worst even if he didn't let Kit know just what that might include.

When they were finished with the inventory, Swifty asked Kit to show him the manuscript with William's account of the Confederate treasure. After he had finished reading, Swifty looked up and said, "When do we leave for South Carolina?"

"In a day or so," replied Kit. I ordered a few things, and they should be here by Federal Express tomorrow."

"That suits me. I'll grab my knapsack and you can show me where I bunk."

Kit took Swifty to the second floor of the huge old house and opened the door to the bedroom next to his.

"Wow," said Swifty. "This looks like a room at the Plaza Hotel in about 1915!"

Kit smiled. Swifty was correct. The house had been restored to its turn of the twentieth century glory and the bedrooms were quite large for such an old house.

After supper that night, Kit and Swifty worked at the kitchen table with the information Kit had downloaded from the computer.

"Here is what I think we should do," said Kit. "We drive down to Columbia, South Carolina. Columbia is the capital of the state and is where most of the museums and historical centers are located. You drop me off at the airport and then you go to the State Archives Building and get as much research on the Hanging Rock area as you can.

We have to try to find any evidence of the landmarks on the map. We'll need current maps, and if possible, some aerial maps."

"Where are you flying off to?" asked Swifty.

"I'll fly down to Charleston and rent a car. I plan on making a visit to the main office of the Bank of South Carolina, which is located in Charleston. I need to find out if they have a record of the safes and their contents. I want to know if they ever turned up and if the bank got its money back. If they did, then this will be a scenic trip to find the old sites for history's sake and not a treasure hunt."

"What a pity that would be."

"Hey, odds are that the four killers came back after the end of the war and dug up the treasure. With our luck their descendants are probably running a bunch of Taco Bell restaurants that they bought with the proceeds from the treasure."

"Taco Bells? What a lack of imagination."

"To each his own. I just think there isn't much chance that someone hasn't found and recovered the treasure by now."

"You never know. Criminals are usually stupid. Maybe they didn't survive the war."

"Even if the gold is long gone, there are five families who deserve to know what really happened to their sons, husbands, and fathers. Those boys were soldiers, and they deserve a proper military burial."

"I can't argue with that."

"I wouldn't expect you to."

"Well, only one way to find out. Where's the airport on this map?"

They left Galva right after having breakfast with Beverly and Sky. Kit and Swifty had thanked their hosts profusely for their hospitality. As they were driving out of town, Kit had Swifty stop at the local florist shop to have some flowers delivered to Beverly as a token of their thanks.

They drove east to Interstate 74 and then headed south towards Knoxville, Tennessee. From there they would drive southeast to Columbia. Kit figured it would be about a two day drive. The big Ford F-250 pickup truck did not ride as smoothly as Beverly's Cadillac, but it was still quite comfortable. They developed a pattern of driving for about two and a half hours and then stopping for gas and changing drivers. After ten hours of driving, they stopped for the night in Cairo, at the very bottom of the state of Illinois.

"Man, this is a long state! I can't believe we have been driving for ten hours and we are still in Illinois. Are you sure we can get to Columbia in two days?" said Swifty.

Kit laughed. "Most people are like you, Swifty. They have no idea of distance in a place like Illinois. Here in Cairo we are south of places like Louisville, Kentucky, and Richmond, Virginia. We should get to Columbia by tomorrow night unless we run into bad weather."

"I sure as hell hope so. Other than a few humps and hills, this state is awfully flat and kind of boring."

"People say that same thing about driving through southern Wyoming on Interstate 80. When we cross the river tomorrow morning you'll see a change in scenery."

They stopped for lunch about halfway between Nashville and Knoxville. The weather had been good and other than a light rain shower mid-morning, the trip had been uneventful. True to Kit's prediction, they entered the city limits of Columbia, South Carolina, about six o'clock in the evening. They found a motel on the outskirts of Columbia and after a quick supper they were in their rooms fast asleep by 8:30P.M.

Both men were up early and had breakfast at a nearby pancake restaurant. Kit had made a list of places for Swifty to visit and a checklist for him to use at each location. He was pretty sure that Swifty would have the best luck at the state historical society and the state archives building. Nevertheless, he was leaving nothing to chance. Swifty's job was to find out all he could about the area around Hanging Rock and specifically to see if he could locate where the old barn had been.

Kit had a strong hunch that a barn like his great-great grandfather had described was possibly still standing due to how it had been built. He knew that after all these years, it was more likely that it was gone. Swifty would also look for the church with the graveyard and the creek with the stone bridge. Again, it was likely that none of those landmarks still existed except for the creek.

Swifty dropped Kit off at the Columbia airport. Kit was traveling with his backpack as his only luggage. That allowed him to take the backpack as carry-on luggage and keep it with him on the airplane. The airport was nothing special. Kit closed his eyes and opened them again. As he looked around, he could have been in any of a hundred medium sized airports in the United States. Passengers here in Columbia looked just like the ones he had seen at Midway Airport in Chicago and the airport in Moline, Illinois. After getting a reservation and a ticket for Charleston, he engaged in a couple of hours of people watching and decided that Midway had a greater number of weird looking folks wandering around in the terminal.

By eleven in the morning, he was on a small jet headed for Charleston. The flight was quick and soon they were touching down at the Charleston airport. There was a light rain falling as Kit and the other passengers deplaned down an open portable stairway to the tarmac. After a short walk in the rain they were in the terminal, which was modern, bright, and clean. Kit made his way to the rental car counters and rented a mid-sized Ford equipped with a GPS from Hertz. The rental cars were in a lot adjacent to the terminal. By the time he had finished with the paperwork and headed out to the lot to secure his car, the rain had stopped.

Kit exited the airport and pulled onto Interstate 26, which took him into downtown Charleston. He had read a lot about the city and was eager to see it. As one of the original walled cities of North America, Charleston had been an English colony and one of the first successful seaports in America. Many of the buildings pre-dated the American Revolution. Here were so many churches that Charleston was known as the "holy city". Each church had adjacent cemeteries that featured famous Americans including several signers of the Declaration of Independence. Kit thought it amazing that Charleston was also known as where the American Civil War had started with the siege and fall of Fort Sumter. He knew the city was a peninsula bordered on both sides by rivers that ran into the Atlantic Ocean. At the end of the peninsula was the entrance to the harbor from the Atlantic. In the middle of the harbor entrance was the small island that housed Fort Sumter, now a national historic site.

He turned down King Street and slowly moved south on the one-way street with the traffic. King Street was full of all kinds of stores with nationally known names. The old buildings were spectacular and many looked exactly as they did three hundred years ago and were in excellent condition. Before long, he had wended his way on the narrow street to the south end of the city. Here was a large park known as the Battery. The Battery Park was bordered on the north by huge old mansions that predated the Civil War. On the east and west were the channels of the Cooper and Ashley Rivers and to the south was the Atlantic Ocean. The park was marked with huge live oak trees with a border of palmetto trees to the south. Sprinkled throughout the park were statues and various types of Confederate artillery pieces permanently mounted on concrete bases. From this location, the Confederates had shelled Fort Sumter until its surrender.

Kit parked his car and walked across the park to the seawall at the south end. The seawall was constructed of large rocks interspersed with large palmetto trees and ringed the edge of the park on two sides. Kit stood there and gazed out to sea where he could just make out the hazy outline of Fort Sumter. While he watched, various types of boats and larger ships passed by his location. Kit felt a sense of peace and serenity. He then knew that Charleston was his kind of place. He also noted that a combination of heat and humidity was causing him to sweat like he had been building fence or roping calves. He stepped back into the shade of a towering live oak tree in the park and felt a cooling sense of relief.

Kit found a seat on a park bench in the shade of several palmetto trees right next to a statue saluting the brave defenders of Charleston. He began studying a map he had obtained of Charleston. Just as he had thought, the city was like a peninsula with the Cooper and Ashley Rivers on each side. The actual working harbor side of the peninsula was on the east side with the Cooper River. For many years this had been an important naval base as well as an important shipping port. The naval base was now closed and the land was being redeveloped for private use.

The activity of the port was somewhat diminished from its heydays, but there had been a recent upsurge due to cruse ships. With new terrorist threats, many security issues had surfaced in the aftermath of the 9-11 incident, and many ports were ill equipped to handle the security problems dealing with thousands of containers being shipped in and out of the ports. The ensuing slowdown of handling cargo had caused untold problems in the shipping industry. Cruise lines found themselves as poor cousins to cargo lines and sought ports where they could be handled more quickly, with their customers undergoing less hassle.

The beautiful old city of Charleston was an easy answer. Tourism was already the major industry in the city and the hotels and restaurants were ideally suited to handle the crowds of tourists waiting to board their cruise ships. In the two hours that Kit had been sitting in Battery Park, he had seen several large cargo ships and two cruise liners entering the harbor. He also saw fishing boats, pleasure craft, and even Coast Guard vessels.

Kit returned to his map. The older and more interesting part of the city was on the east side of the peninsula and the main thoroughfare appeared to be East Bay Street. He remembered he had not told Swifty where he would be staying. On Beverly's advice he had made reservations to stay at the Market Pavillion Hotel. He knew it was in downtown Charleston, close to the harbor and on the end of the area known as Market Street.

Market Street contained a series of long, open-air roofed bricked buildings, much like barracks, that ran east and west with North Market Street running along the north side and South Market Street running along the south side. The property and the buildings had been given to the city by a local family before the Civil War. The buildings were to be used by people to buy and sell goods, but the deed specifically prohibited the selling of slaves. It reminded Kit of a kind of organized flea market that sold everything from t-shirts to delicately created baskets hand-made out of the native sweet grass.

Kit had a two o'clock appointment at the Bank of South Carolina with the Vice President in charge of operations. He had learned through his telephone call that she was also in charge of the history of the bank and he felt she might be the best person to help him in his search. He found the location of the bank on his map and noted it was on Meeting Street. His cell phone rang, and he fished the tiny phone out of his shirt pocket. The caller was Swifty.

"Hey, how's Charleston? Are the women there as good looking as they say?"

"Swifty we're looking for information, not women."

"Maybe you're limiting your search to historic stuff, but I was born to multi-task."

"So what have you learned in Columbia, Mr. Multi-task?"

"Well, I got a lot of information on Hanging Rock and some of it is pretty surprising. It seems that a good deal of the land near Hanging Rock is now part of the Andrew Jackson State Park. Most of the park is located in the north end of the state and this part is separate, like an island. Hanging Rock was a British post garrisoned by the Prince of Wales' American Regiment, part of the British legion and a large force of Loyalists, all under the command of a Major John Carden. On August 6, 1780, General Thomas Sumter made an attack on this position with a band of Patriot Militia and won a great victory, even though they were short of ammunition and outnumbered two to one. One of the impressive rock formations in the vicinity of the battlefield is the huge boulder known as the "Hanging Rock."

"You mean this was Americans fighting Americans, just like in the Civil War?"

"Apparently so. Later in the war, a British colonel named Banastre Tarleton captured six American soldiers and hanged them from the rock."

"Is that how it got the name, Hanging Rock?"

"That's not real clear. Apparently the rock hangs out over a gulch about twenty feet below it. Also the colonel was known in the war as "Bloody Tarleton." I was amazed to find out how many battles were fought in South Carolina in the Revolutionary War. According to my sources and they might be a little biased, but there were more Revolutionary War battles fought in South Carolina than in any other of the original thirteen colonies."

"Really, I don't think I ever heard that."

"Their big heroes are Daniel Morgan, General Sumter, Francis Marion, who as better known as the Swamp Fox, and Lighthorse Harry Lee. There are guys we never hear much about."

"That's all very interesting, but what did you learn about the area round Hanging Rock? Did you find any old churches or rock bridges over creeks, or old two story barns in large meadows?"

'I didn't find anything that looks or sounds like our landmarks, but a lot can change in 140 years. The biggest positive is that this area is still pretty much rural and hasn't been developed or changed a great deal. I spent two hours looking at aerial photos of the area and have a few clues, but we need to see them on the ground."

"Great! What else did you find?"

"Not much yet, but I have an appointment with the Director of the State Historic Museum tomorrow. I think he can get me into almost any place we want to look. Do you have any bright ideas?"

"I do have an idea. We know the date that the five Confederates were killed, and that they were part of a unit of nine men. See if it is possible to check through the Confederate Army records and find out if any group of five men were reported missing, killed, or captured on that date by any units in the area. That might give us an idea of who they were. They might even have relatives still living in the area."

"Good idea. I'll check that out tomorrow. What did you find out at the bank?"

"I have an appointment there in an hour. Hopefully I can find out what may have happened to the safes and the treasure. I'll call you tonight and give you an update."

Swifty hung up and Kit headed for his car. He didn't want to be late for his appointment at the bank, and he could always wait in the air-conditioned comfort of the bank lobby.

Kit was surprised to find the magazines in the bank waiting area had actually been published in the current year. After his arrival at the main lobby of the bank, he had been directed to an office on the third floor of the old bank building. The building had been constructed before the Civil War and had undergone several renovations. It still retained a basic Greek look with its marble columns and spacious marble floors. Kit had been ushered to a small waiting room next to the very old and very creaky elevator he had just arrived in.

He could see that this waiting room was part of a small lobby that was surrounded by a semi-circle of office doors. There were four of them. All of them were about eight feet high and made of solid walnut with curious smoky glass as a window in the upper half of the door. The offices were guarded by a matronly, gray-haired secretary, who appeared to have stepped out of the cover of Life Magazine in 1950. At one point, Kit coughed and that was enough to buy him a disapproving glance from the guardian secretary.

Finally, at exactly 2:00P.M, the guardian stood up and announced that the Vice-President would see him now. She led the way to the door on the far right and after knocking, she opened the door for Kit to enter. He stepped into a beautiful old office paneled in what he thought might be pecan wood with many built-in shelves. The shelves were full of books and artifacts. The walls contained framed historic maps and documents. The ceiling was at least ten feet high and made of tin hammered into patterns. The furniture consisted of an antique desk that was fairly small and a low round table with four upholstered chairs around it. It was too low for a conference table and too large for a coffee table.

"Good afternoon, Mr. Andrews. My name is Ellie Lynn Main. I'm in charge of the operations of the bank. How may I be of service to you?"

Kit was struck by how normal she sounded. There was none of that southern drawl he had heard so much about. He was also struck by how attractive she was. She was dressed conservatively in a navy suit with a white silk blouse. She had beautiful eyes and a trim figure. Her hair was jet black and featured a short, conservative cut that framed her face. It was when she smiled that Kit almost lost focus. She had the greatest smile he had ever seen. It attracted his eyes despite his efforts not to stare at her.

"Are you all right, Mr. Andrews? You look a little pale."

"Yes, yes, I'm fine. I was just surprised by your lack of a southern accent."

She laughed and it was a lovely, tinkling sort of laugh. One that was both attractive and genuine.

"Oh, that. You have to get used to Charleston. It's an English colony and has been since it was founded. You'll hear very little of the southern drawl in the city. If you go outside Charleston, then you will hear what you apparently expected to hear. I've never liked the stereotype of southern women with magnolia mouths."

"Magnolia mouths?"

"Yes, that's what we call them. I have always suspected a good deal of what you hear is more of an act than an accent. Now, what brings a Yankee from Wyoming to an old bank in Charleston, South Carolina?"

Kit liked the fact that she had a sense of humor and yet did not stray far from the business at hand.

"Well, I am here to try to unravel a mystery from the past."

"What sort of mystery?"

"I'm researching the loss of two bank safes and their contents from the Bank of South Carolina in February of 1865."

"That would be just before the end of the Civil War."

"That's correct. It was right before the end of the war."

"This happened here in Charleston?"

"No, it happened in the northern part of the state near a place called Hanging Rock."

Kit noticed that Ms. Main had produced a legal pad and had begun taking notes.

"I've heard of Hanging Rock, but I'm not familiar with it. How did the bank's safes end up in a place like that?"

Kit then took Ms. Main through the history of what happened on that day in February of 1865. He ended his story with the capture of the wagons and safes and omitted the events that occurred later.

"Let me get this straight. Two safes belonging to the Bank of South Carolina were captured by the Union Army near a place called Hanging Rock around February of 1865?"

"That is correct."

"So what does this have to do with me and the Bank of South Carolina?"

"I have reason to believe that the safes wound up in Confederate hands before the end of the war, and I would like to determine if they were returned to the bank along with their contents."

"Now, that is something I can probably help you with. It will take a little time as our records during the war are now stored on microfiche. Having the approximate date is also helpful. How can I get in touch with you?"

Kit gave her his cell phone number and told here where he was staying.

"Oh, the Market Pavilion. That's a very nice hotel."

"So you've stayed there?"

"No, I've never stayed there, but I have friends who have and they loved it. I have been to their bar on the rooftop. It's really nice."

"There is a bar on the rooftop?"

"Yes. They have a swimming pool and a bar on the roof. You can sit on stools all around the rooftop and look out over the city. It's really a great view at night with all the lights and the ships in the harbor."

"I'll have to check that out."

"You do that and let me know what you think. With a little luck I should have an answer to your question by tomorrow."

Kit rose and shook Ms. Main's extended hand. Her hand was small, but her handshake was firm.

"Thank you for seeing me and agreeing to look into my question."

"You're welcome. I'm happy to help. After all, this could turn out to be helpful to the bank."

As Kit descended to the ground floor in the old rickety elevator, he could still see those beautiful eyes and that dazzling smile.

Kit checked into the hotel and was ushered into a very comfortable room on the fourth floor. The bellhop explained to him that the computer card which served as his room key also was to be used in the elevator. The roof of the hotel was open to the public as it featured a swimming pool for the hotel guests, and a rooftop bar for the general public and the hotel guests. The elevator would only stop at the fourth floor and open for a hotel guest who used their room key card for that floor. Kit appreciated the explanation and the extra security that the system provided him. He checked his cell phone for any calls from Swifty and finding none, he stretched out on the large king-sized bed and was soon fast asleep.

He was awakened by the sound of his cell phone ringing. He rolled over and found the phone on the night stand. It was Swifty.

"Hey cowboy, what's shakin'?"

"Hey, yourself. What time is it?"

"Oh, did I interrupt your beauty rest or were you having more fun than I am?"

"Not likely. I just crashed for a couple of hours. This humidity sucks the life out of you."

"You must be getting soft. I love hot weather. This is nothing. You should spend some time in Panama. Now, that's hot and wet."

"I'll stick with the air conditioned hotel room. Here in Charleston they mix the temperature and the humidity level and create what they call a comfort zone."

"My idea of a comfort zone is faster horses, older whiskey, and younger women."

"I think I've heard this song before. So, tell me, what have you uncovered about our mystery?"

"Glad you asked. I had a good talk with the director of the state historical society, and he gave me some good names and source areas to search. I think I hit pay dirt with one of the names."

"How so?"

"I ran down a guy named Stonewall Jones. He's a real Civil War buff, and he hangs out at the museum all the time. I'm pretty sure Stonewall is a nickname. His real first name is probably something dorky like Dewayne. He must be at least seventy-five years old. He wears a gray getup that looks something like a Confederate uniform. He's pretty chipper for a guy his age."

"What are you doing hanging out with old weird guys?"

"This weird old guy is a walking encyclopedia on the Confederate Army. He's spent years in the records of the museum and the records of the Sons of the Confederacy. He says he can find the names we're looking for if we give him a couple of days."

"How much does he want?"

"He wants fifty bucks a name, and I think that's a bargain."

"You bet it is. See if he can get us the names of the bad guys as well as he names of the five who got killed. That might help us trace down what happened after February of 1865."

"Hey, that's a good idea. The beauty rest must have helped your brain. It sure couldn't help your looks."

"Very funny."

"I'll check with old Stonewall in the morning and call you with an update tomorrow night."

"Try to call when normal people are awake."

"Partner, there's nothing normal about either one of us."

Kit was in the shower when the room phone rang. He grabbed a towel and ran for the bedside table and the phone.

"So how are you managing to cope with our humidity?"

"Well you might not believe this, but I am dripping all over the floor in my room as we speak."

Ellie Lynn laughed. It was again that tinkling laugh that also sounded so genuine.

"You're right, that sounds a little hard to believe even in Charleston."

"Actually you caught me in the shower and I'm still trying to dry off with one hand and hold the phone with the other."

"I'd say I'm sorry, but that wouldn't be the truth."

"Somehow this does not sound like Southern hospitality."

"Actually, that is why I called. I have some news for you and would like to buy you a drink. That is if you still have any dry clothes left."

"You're very funny. Today everyone's a comedian."

"Oh, what else happened to you?"

"Never mind. I can manage to look foolish without any help from anyone else."

"I'll be you can," she said. Then she laughed again.

"When and where?"

"How about we meet at your hotel bar on the roof in about an hour?"

"I'll be there. You'll be able to identify me without a problem. I'll be the guy in the wet clothes."

She laughed and hung up the phone.

CHAPTER FIVE

One hour later Kit was sitting on a metal stool at a small round high table near the edge of the roof of the hotel. Instead of sitting with a view of the city as the other occupants of similar tables were doing, he was seated with his back to the skyline so he could get a clear shot of the elevator doors. The elevator was the only way in or out of the rooftop bar unless you counted the stairwell or the rusty fire escape. Kit had arrived about twenty minutes early and was nervously stirring a swizzle stick in his drink. It was slightly dusk and the lights that illuminated the rooftop were on and becoming more apparent.

Kit was wearing well-worn jeans, cowboy boots and a white polo. In a nod to the sunshine and heat of Charleston, he was also wearing a pair of high quality Serengetti sunglasses. He heard the sound of sirens and turned and peered over the low wall that surrounded the rooftop to see what was happening. So far in his visit to Charleston he had not heard a single siren or even seen a police car or ambulance, let alone a fire truck. The sound of the siren seemed to echo from the buildings below and then he caught sight of the flashing red and blue lights. A police car had sped by on East Bay Street and was quickly gone, taking the noise of the siren with it.

The touch on his shoulder almost caused Kit to jerk backwards.

"Whoa there, cowboy! I assure you this native is friendly!"

She had slipped up next to him while he was distracted by the siren. He felt foolish and was sure that his face was red with embarrassment.

Ellie Lynn flashed that disarming smile and the nervous tension and apprehension seemed to evaporate under its warmth.

"You surprised me. I can't believe I didn't hear you approach. You were as silent as an Indian."

"Well, I am blessed with good genes, but they are English, not Indian. My father was born in a town called Buffalo, Wyoming."

"You're kidding me, right?"

"No, he was born on a ranch outside of Buffalo, graduated from the University of Wyoming and spent his life working for the Federal Government. He was posted here in Charleston when I graduated from high school. When he got transferred again, I stayed here and graduated from the College of Charleston. I went to work for the bank right out of college and that brings us up to now. That gives you my story in thirty words or less. Now I'd like to hear your story. You seem a little too polished to me for a cowboy from Wyoming. You asked me for some information and I managed to find it. Before I divulge what I found, I'd like to know who I am giving it to and why. I think there is more to the story you told me at the bank."

"I am truly floored. There aren't many people in Wyoming and those that do live there seem to know each other. Are your grandparents alive?"

"Yes, but they now live in Arizona in a retirement community. They got older and tired of the winters in Wyoming, and they sold the ranch. Grandpa did hold onto a twenty acre parcel in the foothills of the Big Horn Mountains that has a small cabin on it. They spend at least six weeks there every summer."

"Buffalo is a truly pretty part of Wyoming and so are the Big Horn Mountains."

"I'm waiting."

"Excuse me?"

"I'm waiting to hear your story. You show up today with this strange story about lost bank vaults and treasure in South Carolina and turn out to be a cowboy from Wyoming. Things like this don't happen every day to a girl like me."

Kit put up his hand in a show of surrender. "O.K. I get it. What would you like to know?"

"Everything."

"Everything?"

"Yes, everything."

Kit looked across the table into those lovely eyes and the disarming smile. Ellie Lynn was an attractive woman. Not knock-down gorgeous, but one of those women who got better looking the more you looked at her. She also had this air of honesty and sincerity that seemed to surround her. He decided that telling her the truth was a good idea. He also had the feeling that she had the ability to tell if he was lying to her or holding out on part of the story.

"If you want the whole story, it is going to take a little time."

"I'm sitting here waiting. I have plenty of time."

"Are you free for dinner? Can I buy you dinner while I tell you my story?"

"Dinner is fine, providing I pick the restaurant."

"You have a deal. Where are we going?"

"Give me a minute and I'll let you know," she said as she pulled out a cell phone and placed a call and made a reservation for two.

She closed her cell phone and looked up at Kit. "Anson's has room for two in about fifteen minutes. It's about a block from here, and it's an easy walk."

She stood up and headed for the elevator with Kit in her wake.

Ellie Lynn pointed out landmarks on their walk to the restaurant. The narrow streets were full of vehicles and the even narrower sidewalks teemed with tourists.

"I would guess that tourism is a big deal in Charleston."

"Tourism is the big deal, period."

They had crossed the street and headed up a side street. To their left was a huge parking lot that took up about a city block. On their right were old historic buildings. Parked along the curb of the large parking lot were several horse drawn carriages.

"More tourism?" asked Kit.

"Yes and no. They give guided tours of the neighborhoods of Charleston. Most of the guides are very good and the tours are very informative. They're also a lot of fun."

"I see the horses seem to be wearing large diapers?"

"Of course the horses wear diapers. Otherwise you would have to be very careful where you step." Ellie Lynn flashed him that dazzling smile and said, "We're here."

Anson's turned out to be a small, cozy restaurant that looked like it probably did in the early 1800's. They were escorted to a table in the rear of the restaurant and provided menus.

Kit ordered an iceberg wedge salad with blue cheese and crab cakes. Ellie Lynn also ordered the wedge salad and a grilled sea bass. They each had a glass of wine and before they knew it, their meals had arrived. Kit found the salad delicious and under the lettuce was a base of sliced beefsteak tomatoes that were better than any he had ever eaten. Then the waiter placed a small cup of soup in front of him.

"What's this? I didn't order soup?"

"I ordered it for you," said Ellie Lynn. "This is a specialty of Anson's and South Carolina. It's called She Crab Soup."

"She Crab Soup? That sounds weird to me."

"Just try it. If you don't like it, I'll finish it and pay for it myself."

Kit hesitated for a second before trying a spoonful of the soup. He was not a picky eater, but he had always been a little hesitant on trying out new foods. His reaction was immediate.

"Wow, this is delicious. It looks like some kind of cream chowder, but not like any I ever tasted. This is great."

Ellie Lynn laughed, her eyes seemed to sparkle with her laughter.

"I thought you'd be unable to resist the charms of She Crab Soup."

"You got that right. This is delicious. I can't believe I never even heard of it before."

"It's pretty much a South Carolina dish, and I don't think I have ever seen it on a menu any place else in my travels."

By then the small cup of soup had disappeared, and the waiter brought them their entrees. Kit found the crab cakes to be as good as any he had ever tasted. Judging from the way Ellie Lynn was attacking her sea bass, the feeling was mutual. He made a mental note to remember the name of the restaurant. They both turned down the lovely display of desserts and settled for cups of coffee. Kit looked at his steaming coffee cup and smiled.

"What are you smiling about?' asked Ellie Lynn.

Kit then told her the story about how he first tried to make coffee in a sheep camp and what a disaster that turned out to be. He finished the story by telling her the proper way to make cowboy coffee by bringing the pot of water and the coffee grounds to a boil and then adding some cold water to make the grounds sink to the bottom of the pot.

Ellie Lynn made a face and said, "I'll take Starbucks, thank you."

"Actually, it's pretty good and especially on a cold morning in the high country of Wyoming."

Ellie Lynn just smiled and stared at him.

"Did I spill something on myself?'

"No."

"Then why are you staring at me like that."

"I'm waiting for you to come through with your promise and tell me about yourself. A deal is a deal and we're done with dinner."

Kit told her about growing up in Illinois without a father and working in Chicago after graduating from college. Then he told her the story about he and his two friends witnessing a murder and how he fled to Wyoming to hide after his two friends were killed for what they had seen. He left out some parts of the story, but was careful to include learning that his father had not died when he was little and finding out that he was the beneficiary of a trust established by his father. He told her about Swifty and the shootout with the killers who had been hired to eliminate him as a witness. When he was done, he realized that he had deliberately left out any reference to Tang Kelly.

When he looked across the table, he realized that Ellie Lynn was staring at him intently. Her eyes had gone from laughter to something much more intense and focused.

She broke off her stare and smiled. "Good grief that is quite a story. It sounds like something you would see in a movie. You're lucky to be alive."

"I'm alive because I am blessed with some very good friends. They took very good care of me when I needed help."

"It sounds to me like you had some hand in how that all turned out. You've made quite a change from city boy to cowboy. I'm sure your parents are very proud of you."

"Kit then explained the not so tender relationship he had with his mother, the queen of guilt, and that he had not seen his father since he was two.

"Still, it sounds like your father kept a close watch on you when you were growing up, and surely your mother is not all that difficult."

Kit could not keep from laughing out loud. "My mother loves me and I love her, but you have to do it on her schedule and be careful to fit it into her moods."

"Now that I've enlightened you with my not so glorious past, what did you find in the bank records about what happened to the two safes we talked about?"

Ellie Lynn reached down into her purse and pulled out a small slip of paper. "The safes belonged to a branch of the Bank of South Carolina located in Camden. Apparently the bank hired a teamster to move the vaults out of Camden and away from the approaching Union Army. The records of the Union Army revealed that they took possession of the vaults and their contents and turned them over to the provost marshal's office on the same day they found the safes. After that, the trail ends. The safes were never returned, and they never were entered on the books of the Union Army provost marshal for that area. They just simply disappeared."

Ellie Lynn looked up from the paper she held in her hand. "There is one other thing. The inventory of the safes mentioned in the Union Army report matches the bank records except for one item."

"What item is that?"

"The bank records list the contents of the safe and the list does not include any postage stamps, but the Union Army report does. It's possible that the stamps were normally sold by the bank in those days and they just tossed them in with the rest of the valuables before the safes were moved, but we have no record of the bank's ever owning them."

"What about the jewelry and diamonds in the report?"

"They were being held for safekeeping by the bank for several customers in Camden. They did not belong to the bank. Everything else in the vaults did belong to the bank, except the postage stamps."

Ellie Lynn sat back in her chair and folder her arms in front of her. "Now I have a question."

"Yes?"

"You told me in the bank this afternoon that you believed the vaults wound up in Confederate hands. How could you possibly know that?"

Kit looked down at the floor to avoid her direct look. He liked this woman and decided he could trust her with the truth and was probably going to need more of her help.

"I'm going to tell you a story about what happened to those safes back in February of 1865." He went on to tell her about his great-great grandfather and what happened to him back on that fateful day in the spring of 1865 near Hanging Rock, South Carolina.

"So your great-great grandfather never went back to try to find the safes?"

"No, he never did. The plan was for him and a man named Nathan Bates, his tent mate, to wait five years and let things die down. Then they would go back to see if the Confederate killers had returned to retrieve the treasure or not. If the treasure was gone, they would still use the trip to see that the five Confederates killed were given a proper military funeral and their families would know what happened to them. After five years passed, my great-great grandfather tried to get in touch with Nathan who lived in nearby Henry County. Nathan had left the area four years before and had never returned and never been heard from. William decided that it was too big a risk to go back down South alone. He stuck the map in his notebook and hid it in the wall of the house."

"Well even if the treasure is long gone, your great-great grandfather was right. Those poor boys that were killed deserve better and their families have a right to know what happened to them."

"I don't disagree. My plan is to find out who they were and let their families know."

"How are you going to do that?"

"I have my partner, Swifty Olson working on the historical records in Columbia as we speak. He's found some old codger named Stonewall Jones. Apparently Jones is a Civil War buff and one who knows his way around those old records better than anyone who actually works there."

'You mean he's not a government employee?"

"No. Swifty says Stonewall is just a strange old coot who hangs out at the historical center and does private research for a fee, payable in cash, of course."

"I see."

"What do you mean, you see?"

"Well, I've never heard of this Stonewall Jones person and I've been pretty active in local research for the DAR."

"The DAR?"

"You know, the Daughters of the American Revolution. Perhaps you've heard of us?"

"You're in the DAR?"

"Yes. Were you expecting a three cornered hat and a powdered wig?"

"No, no. I meant no disrespect. I'm just a little confused."

"Confused about what?"

"I thought we were talking about research on the Civil War."

"Historical research is historical research. You may not be aware, but there were more Revolutionary War battles fought in South Carolina than in any other state in the thirteen colonies. The history of the state includes the Revolutionary War, the War of 1812, and the Civil War.

"Okay, I stand corrected," said a pleading Kit as he held up the palms of his hands as a sign of surrender.

"Look, Kit. As a member o the DAR, I've worked on several research projects that tapped many sources of history in the state. One of the projects I worked on included the two battles fought at Hanging Rock. Does that ring a bell?"

The light finally went on in Kit's head.

"So you know good sources of information that might also be useful in our search for the bank vaults and the treasure?"

"Yes, I do. I think it's a little premature to call the contents of the vaults a treasure. The contents remain the property of the Bank of South Carolina and their customers, assuming the jewelry mentioned had been placed there for safekeeping."

Kit finally smiled. "Did you think we were going to steal the treasure?"

"No, I didn't think that. Who is this Swifty character?"

"Swifty Olson is my partner. I thought I told you about him."

"As a matter of fact you did mention him, but you gave no details. Just who is this Swifty guy and why does he have a name like that?"

"Swifty is my partner and best friend. We got to know each other in Wyoming. He saved my life. He's a former Army Ranger. He left the Army and returned home to Wyoming where he grew up. I hired him as my bodyguard when my life was threatened, and he came to my rescue more than once."

"He sounds like quite a guy."

"He's the best. I trust him completely."

"How is he at research on Civil War history?"

"Ouch! I think I get your point. You think maybe he could be doing better than placing his bet on a guy named Stonewall Jones?"

"Hey, this Stonewall guy may be fine. Lots of times I've found that volunteers knew more about where to find things in archives than the so called professionals did. I just think it's a good idea to pursue more than one avenue."

"Is that an offer to help?"

"Boy, are you ever slow. Of course it is. If we can find those safes, it certainly isn't going to hurt my career at the bank. Plus the historical aspect of it is very intriguing. Last, but not least, the families of those five Confederate soldiers deserve to know what happened to them. The five also deserve to be buried in a proper cemetery with full military honors. The South is very big on honoring Confederate dead. So am I."

During the slightly heated exchange Kit had observed a transformation take place. Ellie Lynn's features changed from light-hearted to steely determination. Even her eyes took on an assertive look. By the end of the exchange, he could see her features soften, as she could see she finally had his undivided attention.

"Welcome to our little team, Ellie Lynn."

"I hope I don't regret this, Mr. Andrews."

"You won't have any regrets. I really appreciate your offer of help."

"You're welcome. I'll start working on the research tomorrow."

"Does the DAR have regular meetings and stuff like that?"

The smile returned to Ellie Lynn's lips and her eyes.

"Yes, the Charleston chapter meets monthly. I serve on the research committee and we often do individual research for families trying to trace their ancestors back through the Revolutionary War period. Why do you look so surprised?"

'I guess I thought an outfit like the DAR was stocked full of old ladies having tea or something. I never expected to meet a member as young and attractive as you."

Ellie Lynn blushed, her skin turning red at her throat and moving up to her hairline.

"Thank you for the compliment, Mr. Andrews. I think you would be further surprised to find out that we have a lot of young women in the DAR chapter. Charleston has been around since before the Revolutionary War and many of those families are still represented today, and their daughters are proud to claim membership in the DAR. It's another way of honoring their families and their family history. As a mater of fact, we're having a fund raising auction on Friday night. If you will still be in town then, I'd love to take you as a guest."

"I'll make it a point to be here. I'm not passing up an invitation like that. I look forward to meeting more members of the DAR if they're all as charming as you," said Kit with a tinkle in his eye.

Ellie Lynn burst out laughing and Kit soon joined in.

Several minutes later they were standing outside the restaurant in the warm, humid dark night. Kit wrinkled up his nose as the distinctive odor of horse manure invaded his senses.

"Wow. Where is that smell coming from?"

"That is not exactly the remark a southern lady expects from a southern gentleman, Mr. Andrews," said a grinning Ellie Lynn.

"We both know I'm no southern gentleman. I'm sorry, but it seems so strange to encounter that smell in the middle of a city."

"Look around you," said Ellie Lynn. "This area is surrounded with the stables of the various companies who operate horse drawn carriage rides in the city. They are strictly regulated and licensed. Only so many carriages can be out at any one time, and they may only travel in the residential areas to the south side of the city in the morning. Trips in the afternoon and evening are restricted to the business district?"

"How many stables are there?"

"I'm not quite sure, but I think there are about six or seven."

"That seems like a lot."

"Carriage rides are big business as they cater to tourists. The rides are conducted by very knowledgeable drivers who provide oral history lessons on all the landmarks they pass in the carriage. It's a slow and interesting way to see the details of the city and its history."

By now, Kit had been observing the carriage traffic near the restaurant. He noted that each carriage was capable of holding about six passengers and were drawn by one large draft horse. There were larger wagons that held about a dozen people on benches that were pulled by two large draft horses. Each horse was wearing a large white diaper.

Ellie Lynn noticed his attention to the carriages and she smiled. "Unfortunately they have not yet developed Pampers for horses so we are left with the old fashioned cloth kind. Fortunately for all of us, they work well."

Kit walked Ellie Lynn back to her car, which was parked near the hotel. They stood close together and Ellie Lynn looked up at him, her beautiful eyes shining.

"Thank you for dinner and a lovely evening, Mr. Andrews," she said. As he bent his head down toward her, she turned her head slightly away from him. She reached out and took his hand and shook it. "Good night," she said as she slipped into her car and drove away.

A slightly surprised Kit stood as though frozen in place, shocked by what had just happened. He felt like a fool and could tell that he was flushed and slightly embarrassed. After a moment, the feeling passed. Once again he had proven to himself that he had almost no skill in reading what women really wanted or expected. He had thought he felt a connection, but must have been mistaken. He glanced at his watch and realized he needed to call Swifty and give him an update. He quickly moved through he hotel doors and up to his room.

Swifty answered on the second ring.

"Where the heck have you been? I've been expecting your call for over an hour now. Don't tell me you actually got lucky?"

"I've been busy working on getting more help in digging up information on Hanging Rock and the nine Confederates."

"Nine Confederates? I thought I was supposed to be looking for the five who never came back?"

"I got to thinking about that. If we find the five who got killed, then chances are we will be able to find the four who did the killing. They were a unit, remember. They might even have descendents still living around here. If we find the barn and the treasure is gone, we might be able to trace it back to them."

"Sounds like a plan. How are you gonna get more help?"

"I met with the Vice President of Operations at the bank today. She was able to find out that the bank never did recover the safes. That means that if the killers didn't come back for the gold, its still there."

"Fat chance the gold is still there. My bet is they came back after the war was over and dug it up and had a good old time with it. Wait a minute. You said "she" helped you? You mean "she" as in a female? Surely she was old and ugly."

"Nope. She's young and attractive and very helpful."

"How helpful is that?"

"She offered to help us research the names of the nine Confederate soldiers who were at Hanging Rock in February of 1865."

"She offered this out of the goodness of her heart?"

"No. She got me to tell her the story and she is interested."

"So you did get lucky!"

"Not hardly. She was very nice, but she had zero personal interest in me."

"Well, I can understand that. After all, you are kind of a dork. I wonder how she feels about the real manly type. Maybe she needs to meet me."

"Somehow I think you would probably strike out as well. I think she might be a little too sophisticated for you and me."

"Sophisticated? Not my kind of woman. I prefer them with more hormones than brains, as you know."

"That's certainly a surprise to every woman you have ever met, I'm sure."

"Hey, that's not nice. I'll have you know I'm going to see a waitress I met for a drink when she gets off work tonight. She seems very impressed with me."

"I'll bet. Have you heard anything from this Stonewall Jones?"

"Nope, not a word. He said it would take him two or three days and he'll call me here at the motel."

"Good enough. I'll check in with you tomorrow night and we can compare notes."

"How long are you staying in Charleston?"

"I'm not sure. I think I'll pay a visit to the State Historical office here and try to get some help. Maybe Ellie Lynn will come up with something in her search."

"Ah, Ellie Lynn. So now we have a name."

"That gives you about 110% of what I've got, partner. Talk to you tomorrow."

"I'll try not to stay out too late tonight and keep the fun level down to a mild roar."

Kit smiled to himself and hung up the phone.

CHAPTER
SIX

Swifty had chosen to stay at the rather modest Holiday Inn Express. His reason for the choice had nothing to do with price, quality of accommodations, or the age of the facility. The motel was about a block and a half from a pretty lively country and western bar. After he hung up the phone with Kit, he pulled on his boots, checked his hair in the bathroom mirror, and headed out the door.

Swifty had assumed that a state capital like Columbia would have a large number of single women who were working at government jobs. He was correct. The bar was like most Swifty had frequented. It was dark and noisy. He took a seat at the bar and ordered a beer. Beer in hand he swiveled on his bar stool and looked over the room. It was packed with what he assumed were good ole boys dressed up in their cowboy best. There was no shortage of women dressed in tight fitting jeans and tops. Some of them would have been better off wearing something more loose fitting as tight clothes were less than flattering to them.

The bar also sported two pool tables, both of which were in use and a large jukebox complete with flashing laser lights that shot up into the ceiling when a song was played, which seemed to be continuously. There was a fairly small dance floor in the middle of the bar, but the number of dancers seemed to overwhelm the small space and there were dancers all over the bar, including between the tables. The walls were adorned with animal heads and cowboy junk including old harness, lanterns, and tools. Swifty noted that the major item above the mirrors behind the bar was a large Confederate flag. A quick look around confirmed that all the faces in the bar were white.

Swifty finished his beer and ordered a second. He had just paid for it when he felt a tap on his shoulder. A young woman with hair dyed platinum blonde was standing beside him. She was a little pudgy, but she was pretty and had an ample bosom.

"Hi there, cowboy. I don't remember seeing you in here before."

"Howdy, ma'am. I'm new to these parts. This is my first time in this place."

"Oh, you're a Yankee! Where are you'all from?"

"Born and raised in the great state of Wyoming, ma'am."

"Wow! Are you a real cowboy?"

"Yes ma'am. I've been one most of my life."

"I just love cowboys. Most of the guys in this place are just make-believe cowboys. I don't think I ever met a real one before."

"Don't be too hard on them, ma'am. There's nothing wrong with wanting to be a cowboy, even if it is the drug store kind. Any one who likes country and western music is all right with me."

"Well that sure includes me. I love country music. I once went to a concert and saw Willie Nelson. It was a blast."

"I'm sure it was. Course old Willie is a Texas boy and Wyoming cowboys don't have much truck with Texans."

"Oh, I didn't know that. Would you like to dance?"

Immediately Swifty was off the stool and took her in his arms. "What did you say your name was darlin'?"

"I'm Tina. What's your name?"

"My friends call me Swifty."

"What do your enemies call you?"

"I don't have any enemies. None that are alive, anyway."

"Oh, you sound like a real bad man!" Tina said with a smile.

"Bad enough for you, darlin'." He pulled her closer and felt her body press into his chest as they danced. They kept dancing and only stopped occasionally to have another round of beers. This was Swifty's kind of evening.

The loud ringing of the motel telephone woke Swifty with a start. He immediately rolled off the bed and landed on the floor with his knees bent in a fighting crouch. Then he realized where he was and what the noise was. He relaxed. He walked over to the bedside table and picked up the phone.

It was an automated wake-up call. Swifty looked at his watch and saw that it was seven in the morning. He could not recall asking for a wake-up call and decided it was the result of a clerical mistake in a cheap motel. He looked around the room but saw nothing out of place. His wallet was on the night stand and when he picked it up, a slip of paper fell out and onto the floor. He picked up the paper and opened it.

"Tina. 453-6207."

Just below the message was the lipstick imprint of her lips.

"Very creative" thought Swifty. Then he proceeded to wad up the paper and toss it in the wastebasket.

Twenty minutes later he had showered, shaved and was dressed and out the door to get some breakfast. As he scanned the menu of the small diner he'd found, he realized that he was supposed to meet the waitress from supper last night at the country and western bar. He didn't remember seeing her there and decided she must have shown up after he and Tina had left the bar. "Too many women and not enough Swifty," he thought with a smile.

By nine o'clock he was at the state historical center looking for Stonewall. The little old guy in the funny grey uniform was nowhere to be seen.

"Rats," thought Swifty. He got a cup of coffee at the cafeteria for the center and waited on a bench by the entrance. Still no Stonewall. Swifty cursed himself for not getting a phone number from the old guy.

He bought a newspaper from a vending machine and got a refill for his coffee. By ten o'clock he had almost finished the paper and there was still no sign of Stonewall. An article in the last section of the paper caught his eye. According to the article the Daughters of the Confederacy had an information center in Columbia and provided both on-line and staff access to their information base. Swifty tore out the article and found the location on the city map he had gotten from the motel. The center was not far away and after spending almost an hour and a half waiting fruitlessly for Stonewall to show up, he decided to see what he could find out for himself at the center.

The lady behind the receptionist desk at the Daughters of the Confederacy was middle aged, homely and weighed more than the chair she was setting on was designed for. "Still," thought Swifty, "a woman is a woman."

Swifty flashed the woman his famous smile and turned on the charm.

"Howdy, ma'am. My name is Swifty Olson from Kemmerer, Wyoming, a little place I'm sure you've never heard of."

The lady smiled and flashed a set of false teeth. "How can I help you, Mr. Swifty?"

"Actually, ma'am, my first name is Swifty, and you can call me Swifty if you like."

The lady actually blushed.

"So, how can I help you, Swifty?"

Swifty glanced at the name plate on her desk. "Well, Ms. Leon, I'm doing a search for some long lost relatives."

"I see. So what were the names of these relatives?"

"Well, that's the problem, ma'am. I know they were in the Confederate army and they were reporting missing on February 27, 1865 near a place called Hanging Rock, South Carolina. However, I don't know what their names were."

"They didn't have the same last name of Olson, like you?'

"No, they didn't. I think they might have been using assumed names, not their real names."

"Oh. Well, there were more than a few men who fought for the CSA who did not use their real names. Some were criminals and some were actually Yankees."

"Really! I didn't know that" said Swifty with a look of admiration on his face.

Ms. Leon blushed again. Apparently no one had wasted much attention or flattery on her recently.

"Well, it is a little known fact."

"I'm sure it is."

"I would advise you to use the date of February 27, 1865. You can do a chronological search and find out what outfits were located near Hanging Rock on that date and then look at the unit rosters. You can also check the reports for the following day to see if there were reports of men missing. I must warn you that the date you have mentioned was a chaotic time. The Confederate Army was falling apart and the record keeping was probably pretty spotty. Still, it is worth a look, don't you think?

"I certainly do," said Swifty.

"Let me take you to a computer and show you how to use it for your search."

Ms. Leon showed Swifty to a cubicle with a computer and showed him how the menu worked and what he needed to click on to do his search.

"Just come and see me at the desk if you need any help," she said with a crooked grin.

"I most certainly will," said Swifty. "And thank you for your kind assistance." He sat down at the computer and pulled out a notebook and pen from his jacket pocket. It took a few minutes before he had figured out the program and was able to maneuver his way through the menu to the chronological listing of events and reports that he was looking for. He was dismayed to see that there were over twenty Confederate units located in the Hanging Rock area on February 27, 1865. The good news was that most of them had been depleted in numbers through death and desertion and the roster lists of the units were not very lengthy.

When Swifty finally looked up from the glare of his computer screen, his back hurt him and he could swear his eyeballs were sore from the eyestrain of staring at the detail on the small computer monitor screen. He went to the receptionist desk and had Ms. Leon explain to him how to print out what he had found. She explained that the charge would be fifty cents a page. Swifty thanked her and returned to the cubicle. He knew that the Confederates had been mounted and so he decided to make a list of all the units, but only printed out the cavalry units along with their rosters and casualty reports for February 27 through March 5, 1865. He hit the print button for each page he wanted and then returned to the receptionist desk. He had printed out 38 pages and paid Mrs. Leon the $19.00 along with a $20 donation to the Daughters of the Confederacy. Ms. Leon practically gushed when she gave him his receipt.

Swifty asked her if she might have a large envelope that he could put the copy pages in and she provided one complete with the logo of the Daughters of the Confederacy. She refused payment for the envelope.

"You'all come back and see us again, Mr. Swifty."

"I most certainly will do that ma'am," he replied.

Swifty felt suddenly hungry. He looked at his watch. It was almost two o'clock in the afternoon. He headed for the nearest restaurant with a smile on his face.

CHAPTER SEVEN

Kit had a text message from Swifty telling him that he would call on Friday afternoon with a report. Kit then pulled out his portable notebook and plugged it into the phone jack in his room. The hotel advertised high speed broadband internet connections and he was quickly on line. Sure enough, there was a message from Connor. Kit eagerly downloaded the message.

Kit: am in Rome. Not to see the Pope to get forgiven. Leave that to you. Found clues that led me to look here. He had old friend from CIA who retired here. Found him and after convincing him who I was and what I wanted he told me he helped your father by supplying him with information on some Mafia big shot in Sicily. I will send you copies of the info via Fed Ex. Am headed for Sicily. Will keep u posted.

Connor

Kit took a deep breath. He had almost forgotten about Connor. Now he was worried. He knew the Fed Ex package had gone to his home in Kemmerer. He used his cell phone to dial a familiar phone number in Wyoming.

"Howdy." The rich strong voice of Big Dave Carlson seemed to flow out of the cell phone with the force of a thunderstorm.

"Big Dave. This is Kit."

"Kit! Where the hell are you?"

"I'm in Charleston, South Carolina."

"What the hell are you doin' in a place like that?"

It was just like Big Dave to get to the point and not waste time with formalities.

"I'm looking for some lost Confederate gold."

"Well, hells bells, why didn't you say so. You need some help. I hear tell that gold stuff is pretty heavy for a little feller like you."

Big Dave was well named. Kit had often compared him to a real life version of John Wayne. Big Dave was six foot four and weighed about 260 pounds on a good day. He was also one of the toughest men Kit had ever known. He had taken Kit in when Kit was on the run and treated him like a son. He was also one of Kit's father's best friends.

"I got an e-mail from Connor. He's in Rome."

"Connor! Did he find your daddy?"

"No, but he sounds like he is hot on the trail. He said he was sending me some information by Federal Express. I imagine it's at my house. Could you go out and pick it up and send it on to me?"

"Can do. Where do I send it?"

Kit gave Dave the name and address of his hotel. He could hear Big Dave writing it down, the pen probably looking like a toothpick in his massive fingers.

"I got it. I'll go out today and pick it up and get it out tomorrow morning at the latest. Are you O.K.?"

"I'm fine. Thanks for the help."

"No problem. Let me know what's going on. Connie worries about you."

Connie was Dave's wife and she also had treated Kit like a son. She and Dave had lost one of their sons in the Gulf War. Kit had been the recipient of some of his clothes when he would up stranded on their doorstep in a spring Wyoming snow storm.

"Tell her hi for me and that I'm fine. Tell her I'll bring her back a gift from Charleston."

"I'll do that. You call if you need help."

"I'll be fine. I got Swifty with me."

"Yeah, but who's gonna keep him out of trouble?" laughed Big Dave.

Kit chuckled to himself as he broke off the connection.

A quick search confirmed that the rest of the mail was spam and Kit deleted it. He switched the notebook over to word processing and updated his findings on the search for the Confederate gold. He paused as he entered Ellie Lynn's name in the memory. He felt himself blush as he remembered how stupid he had felt the previous evening when he tried to kiss her and she avoided him. He let the thought pass and then finished up with all the data he had collected. He went back on line and sent an e-mail to his cousin Beverly to let her and Schuyler know he was in Charleston and added his room number at the hotel. He signed off and closed up the notebook and slipped it back into its small carrying case and placed it in his carry-on bag.

Kit sat down on one of the over-stuffed chairs in his room and looked through the tourist guidebook he had found on the coffee table. He marked a couple of sites with his pen and then located them on the attached map. Satisfied with his work, he called the main desk for the valet and asked for his car to be brought up front. If he was in Charleston, he decided he would see a few of the sites just like any other tourist.

Kit was soon in his rental car and driving on the huge new suspension bridge over the Cooper River. He followed the signs and found the site of Fort Moultrie in Mt. Pleasant. He enjoyed the museum and the tour of the restored old fort. It had served to protect Charleston against the British in the Revolutionary War and remained a fort until World War II. He then drove to Port Freedom and toured the decommissioned Navy warships anchored there.

Most impressive was the aircraft carrier Yorktown. Scattered on the flight deck of the old carrier were all types of aircraft from the last fifty years. Kit finished his tour with a ride on the tour boat out to Fort Sumter in the middle of the Charleston harbor. The fort looked surprisingly small and isolated. Kit tried to imagine what the Union troops there had felt when they were surrounded on all sides by Confederates. Here is where the Civil War began. The main bombardment of the fort had come from Battery Park. The park was the very place where he had sat in the shade of huge live oak trees over two days ago. Had he already been her for almost three days?

The parade ground in the center of the fort was dirt baked hard as concrete by the relentless sun. It was less warm in the battlements where the thick concrete walls offered shade and a sense of coolness. The trip back on the tour boat was highlighted by the breeze coming from off the ocean waves. Before Kit knew it, he was ashore. He left his rental car at the hotel with the valet and walked to a nearby crab shack restaurant. While it was obviously kind of tourist trap, he found the crabs tasty and washed them down with a couple of cold beers. Satisfied, he left a healthy tip, walked back to the hotel and was asleep by the time he hit the bed.

Friday morning Kit awoke to gray overcast skies and the threat of rain. He dressed in jeans and a polo and his boots. He had breakfast in the concierge's room on his floor. While he ate, he scanned his guidebook. Maybe it was a good time to look at Charleston from a horse drawn carriage. He found himself enjoying this unusual city and every block of it seemed to be lined with the pages of history.

He put on his cowboy hat and walked the short distance to the north side of Market Street where the stables for the various carriage companies were located. He found himself in front of the Old South Carriage Company and walked into the small plain office. A young woman behind the counter was dressed in a white blouse, grey slacks and sporting a red sash around her waist. On her head was a grey kepi or confederate Civil War cap. She appeared to be in her early twenties and had a fresh tomboy look to her. Her skin was well tanned and her blonde hair was pulled back in a pony tail. Her eyes were light blue and her face seemed to be devoid of any makeup. Kit could smell the unusual mix of lilac and horse sweat. He guessed the lilac smell was from her shampoo. She did not look like the type who put on perfume to work with horses.

"Hi there. How can I help you?" Her voice was high, like a young girl's.

"I'm interested in a carriage ride. Am I correct to understand that you can only go down into the residential district in the mornings?'

"Yes, sir. That's correct. You can take one of our scheduled rides in the larger carriages with about eleven other people or you can request a carriage just for yourself. Which would you prefer?"

"I hadn't thought about going alone. Wouldn't that be a little boring?"

"Oh no, sir. Our drivers are excellent guides and will provide you with an interesting oral history of all the homes you will see on your ride."

"In that case, how do I sign up?"

The blonde smiled and pulled a small radio from her sash. "Lew. I've got a customer for a single to the Battery."

She waited a few seconds and then her radio crackled and Kit heard a disembodied voice say "Ten minutes."

The blonde turned to Kit and explained the carriage would be out front in ten minutes. Kit paid her the fee in cash and pocketed the receipt. He left the confines of the small office and walked out on the sidewalk and stood under the shade of a tree. Even though the sky was overcast, the air was hot, humid, and sticky.

Almost exactly ten minutes later, the horse drawn carriage pulled up with a young man in the driver's seat. He was dressed exactly like the young blonde girl in the ticket office.

"Are you the gentleman who wanted a solo tour of the Battery, sir?"

"That would be me," said Kit.

Kit gave him his receipt and opened the small half door to the open carriage, using the small step suspended under the carriage frame he stepped up and into the rig. The carriage had seats on the front and back of the carriage, facing each other. Kit settled into the velvet upholstered back seat so he would be facing the driver and the horse at the front of the carriage.

The young driver looked to be in his early twenties, not too much younger than Kit. He turned in his driver's seat, located about as high as the top of the seats in the carriage, and faced Kit.

"My name is Earl, and I'll be your driver and guide. The tour will take us down to the Battery Park and will take about an hour. I'll try to explain everything we see, but please don't hesitate to ask questions at any time."

"That sounds good to me, Earl."

Earl clucked to the horse and gave the reins a light slap; the horse and carriage slowly moved forward. They soon joined a short line of carriages in front of a small booth.

"This won't take long, sir. Each carriage has to have a tour medallion when they go out and the city only allows so many for each area at any given time."

Kit could see there were actual medallions, each numbered, that were hung on the carriages. He also noted that their horse was a draft horse and was wearing the requisite diaper.

They started their tour by going past several very old churches and public buildings and Earl gave a pretty interesting history on each of them. Soon they were into the residential area that made up the south end of the city, ending with Battery Park. Kit noticed that because of the slower speed of the carriage, Earl was able to give a short oral history while they were still in front of or going by the building in question. Kit saw numerous mansions and very interesting large homes.

He learned from Earl that the homes had been rebuilt several times due to fires, hurricanes and storms, not to mention the bombardment of the city by the Union Army in the Civil War. He also learned that when rebuilding or renovating any building, a strict code was followed. Owners of such houses could not even change the color of the homes without permission from the city. As they were headed south, Earl pulled the carriage off to the side of the narrow street just before they were about to cross Broad Street. Earl turned in his seat to face Kit.

"This here is Broad Street. South of this street live the richest people in Charleston in some of the most expensive real estate in the South. When asked where they live, they will always say South of Broad. Those folks who are not quite rich enough live just slightly north of Broad." Earl then paused with a big grin on his face. "Do you get it?" he asked.

Kit had no idea what Earl was talking about and told him so.

"Well sir, those folks who live south of Broad are SOB's. Those people who live slightly north of Broad are SNOB's."

Kit grinned and he and Earl shared a good laugh.

As they made their way back from Battery Park on East Bay Street, Earl called Kit's attention to Rainbow Row, a series of stately homes, each painted a different pastel color. They also took a side trip on a street still made of cobblestones. The ride was very rough and the carriage bounced abruptly, even with their slow pace. Earl explained that ships coming into Charleston had used the stones for ballast and had unloaded them when they filled up with stores to be shipped out of Charleston. The English stones were then used to pave the streets of the city. The one hour trip was over too quickly for Kit. When Earl stopped to let Kit out by the parking lot on market Street, Kit decided to ask for a favor.

"Any chance I can see the stable you keep the horses in?"

Earl's face lit up in a smile. "Absolutely," he said. "I wondered if you were a real cowboy or just another tourist."

"Oh, I'm a tourist all right, but, yes, I'm a cowboy."

"Where're you from?"

"Wyoming."

"Oh, that explains your lack of an accent."

"Accent?"

"Yeah. We get a lot of loud cowboy types from Texas and Oklahoma and they have the twangy sort of accent."

Kit couldn't help but laugh out loud.

Earl clucked to the horse and they went about a block north of the office and then pulled through an alley into a large barn that was not visible from the street. The barn was about two stories high and had large doors at each end. There were stalls on both sides of the barn, a tack room, and a shop. Next to the far door was a small office. One of the stalls was larger and was full of hay bales and feed sacks. Next to it were bales of straw, piled up against the outside wall.

Earl drove the carriage about halfway through the barn and stopped. He stepped down from his driver's seat and Kit let himself down from the carriage. Earl explained how they operated the stable and rotated the horses. He introduced Kit to Barney, the stable manager. Barney was built like a blacksmith, which Kit suspected he was. He was bald, short, and stocky. He wore jeans and a t-shirt under a leather apron.

Neither Barney nor his clothes smelled like they had touched water recently.

"So you're a real cowboy from Wyoming."

"That's what they tell me."

"Well, what do you think of our little setup here?"

"This is very nice. I'm surprised to see a stable in the middle of a city like Charleston. How many horses do you handle in this stable?"

"Oh, we have abut ten today. Sometimes we have up to sixteen, but this isn't a high season and we have two horses ailing, so they ain't working right now."

"Where do you keep the other horses?"

"We have a deal with the outfit we buy our hay, feed, and straw from. They operate a large farm and hay brokerage business up by Hanging Rock and they keep our extra horses, including our sick ones, out on their pasture."

"I thought your feed supply looked a tad small for ten draft horses," said Kit as he pointed to the large stall he had noticed earlier.

"Space is real dear in Charleston. Hanging Rock Farm has a warehouse down by the harbor and they truck hay, straw, and feed into it. We call them with an order and they deliver with a small truck from the warehouse. It's real handy for us. They even pick up our horse shit and haul it back to the farm to use as fertilizer."

"All your horse shit? Where do you store it until they come by to pick it up?"

"See that steel tank by the back door?"

Kit turned around and then saw the stainless steel tank next to the door his carriage had just come through. It was like a small dumpster, only rounded on the top, like hatch on a submarine.

Barney laughed. "Looks like some kind of giant metal egg, don't it. They bring in a small garbage truck and it lifts the tank up and turns it upside down. The hatch locks open and the horse shit falls out into the opened container on the truck. Then they set the tank down and the truck's hatch is closed to seal the container. We open the top of the tank and dump in the horse shit from the horse diapers as well as the straw bedding from the stalls when we muck them out. The hatch keeps any odor from escaping so unless you were standing right next to it, you can't smell the shit."

"Pretty slick," said Kit.

"Works for us," replied Barney. "Hanging Rock Farm handles every stable in Charleston. Their prices are reasonable. If someone tries to compete with them, Hanging Rock Farm jut drops their prices until the new guys give up. Plus they give good service. All it takes is one telephone call, and they're here the next day. Sometimes they get here on the same day."

"I had no idea there was money in horse shit!"

"Well, it works for them and they do provide all the feed, hay, and straw we need. They don't cut their prices, but we needed a way to get rid of the horse shit and to keep the city happy and this system solves all our problems."

Kit thanked Barney for the tour and stopped to thank Earl who was putting a nosebag of oats on his horse. He gave Earl a twenty dollar tip and headed back to his hotel.

When Kit got to his room, he took out his cell phone and noticed he had a message. He was puzzled why the phone didn't ring, but he couldn't remember hearing it. He must have received the call when he was in a dead spot. He called up the number and heard a very short message from Swifty.

"You big goof ball! Why don't you answer your damn cell phone? Don't tell me you forgot to turn the damn thing on. When I see you again I'm going to have to retrain you. I had to get the name of your hotel by calling your cousin Beverly. I've faxed some information I found on the Confederates who may have been in the unit we are looking for. You should be able to pick them up at the front desk of the hotel. Call me when you get the stuff and look it over. You might want to check the battery on that two-bit cell phone of yours."

Kit smiled and took the elevator back to the first floor and the main desk of the hotel. Sure enough there were thirty-eight faxed pages waiting for him. He thanked the desk clerk and headed back up to his room. He spread the pages out on the hotel room desk and began to read and organize them. They covered roster reports and after action reports for February

27, 1865, through March 5, 1865. He was pleased that Swifty had covered a broader time period than just the one day.

The reports were hand written on pre-printed report pages and were difficult to read. Even though the author's handwriting was pretty good, some of it was faded and had to be read carefully.

Kit's first thought was to separate the roster reports by each unit and then try to match up the after action reports. The roster reports were apparently used for payroll purposes, but he doubted that many of the Confederate soldiers saw any pay at that time in the war. The roster reports were not much help. Some units mentioned on February 27 were not to be found in the March 2nd through March 5th reports. Kit assumed that they had moved out of the area or perhaps had ceased to exist. Entire regiments were down to company size. A large part of each daily report was made up of reported desertions. Kit could understand why. At that point in the war it looked like there was no hope and with spring coming, many men probably just headed for home to try to put in a crop to feed their families.

Frustrated with being unable to discover much with the roster reports, Kit turned to the after action reports. On the third page he read he found what he thought he was looking for.

After Action Report
February 28, 1865
Fifth South Carolina Cavalry

Patrol of nine men of Troop B were sent to met some civilian supply wagons northeast of Hanging Rock on evening of 2-27-1865. Captain Regret in command. Regret and three men returned early this am with five spare mounts. They ran into a Yankee ambush of a company of cavalry supported by infantry on Elmwood Road. Five troopers were killed or captured and Captain Regret and three troopers were able to escape. They eluded the Yankees in the woods and hid until dawn when they made their way back to camp. A second patrol was sent out immediately under Major Hargrove and they were unable to find any trace of the five men.

Reported as dead, captured or missing were the following:

1. *Pvt. Oliver J. Pratt*
2. *Pvt. D. Vonalt*
3. *Pvt. Wendell McKusker*
4. *Sgt. Andrew Conder*
5. *Pvt. Solomon Nix*

"Pay dirt" thought Kit. This had to be the right unit. The numbers jived with William's diary and five killed was the exact number he was looking for. Now he had to figure out the names of the three troopers who survived. He already had the name of Captain Regret. A careful check of the rosters under the Fifth South Carolina Cavalry showed Troop B with twenty one men including Captain Regret. For some reason, he had only taken eight men out with him instead of the entire troop. That was certainly lucky for the other twelve men who had remained behind. Kit decided that Regret was careful to not take too many men because he and his little band of three would have to overwhelm the others and they had been successful in killing five. More men might very well have been a problem for him.

A further check of the roster records revealed that Regret's first name was Ambrose. By carefully reading each report for February 27th and February 28th, Kit found that of the twelve men left behind, three were on sick call, two had deserted, and seven had been assigned to guard and tend to the unit's horse herd. After checking each name of the duty roster, he was left with three names.

The three accomplices were Pvt. Allison Clay, Pvt. Wilson Pickett, and Cpl. James Walsh.

Kit picked up the hotel phone and called Swifty on his cell phone.

"This is Swifty."

"I've got some good information from those lists you faxed me. I think I have the four guys we're looking for as well as the five who got killed."

"Great work. I knew you had it in you. With my training how could you possibly go wrong."

"What a load of bullshit. You're lucky to be able to turn a computer on and off."

"Hey watch your mouth. Did I or did I not find these reports?"

"I'll give you that, but I'm sure you had some help. Let me guess. Your help was female and you probably charmed the pants off her."

"Not exactly, but I was my usual charming self."

"I assume she was good looking?"

"Not exactly, but she did succumb to my charming personality and was very helpful."

"I'll bet."

"Hey, don't argue with the results. We got the names, didn't' we?"

"I'll give you that. I'll fax the names to you and have you check out the records in Columbia to see what happened to our boys."

"Fax them to me at the number at the top of your faxed pages. I'll get them here at the Holiday Inn Express in Columbia."

"Consider them on the way."

Kit went down to the small office provided by the hotel for business clients and typed up the names in his computer and printed them out. He then faxed them to Swifty at the motel.

Kit returned to his room and saw the message light lit on his phone. He dialed up the voice mail and was surprised to hear the voice of Ellie Lynn Main.

"Hey there, cowboy. This is just a call to remind you about the DAR charity auction tonight. The auction is at seven at the Charleston Place Hotel. I'll meet you in the front lobby. Bye."

Kit looked at his watch. It was already 2:00P.M. Then suddenly it hit him. What the hell was he going to wear? He had no idea what people in Charleston wore to charity auctions. He let the wave of panic wash over him and then felt it begin to subside.

"Be calm, be calm," he told himself. Then he picked up the phone and called the concierge's desk. He quickly explained his problem to the concierge and was pleased to discover that such events were not formal in the summer time, but casual wear meant very nice and usually very expensive casual wear. The concierge also sent him to a nearby men's store on King Street and called ahead to let them know what he needed. One hour later he was walking out of the store with a snazzy black shopping bag filled to the top with new clothes. He walked back to his hotel with a large smile on his face. He was starting to really enjoy life in Charleston.

At about a quarter till seven Kit arrived at the Charleston Place Hotel. He stopped at the entrance to the hotel and looked at his reflection in the glass of a large window. He was wearing a pair of black designer jeans with a long sleeve white cotton shirt. He wore a black leather belt trimmed with silver. His black cowboy boots were shined to a high gloss thanks to the hotel room service, and he wore his white Stetson cowboy hat. He was pleased with the reflection he saw and headed into the hotel lobby.

The hotel lobby reflected the look of the entire hotel. It looked old, sophisticated, and sleek. The architecture was a mixture of modern and classical. Everywhere Kit looked the view seemed to drip with the same theme, money.

Kit stopped by the edge of the main desk and surveyed the people in the lobby. The lobby was about a third full with people lining up at the elevators. An event sign by the front desk announced that the DAR Charity Auction would be in the Palmetto ballroom on the second floor of the hotel at 7:00P.M.

Kit was about to turn away from the sign when he felt a tug on his sleeve. There at his side was the much shorter Ellie Lynn Main. She was even more attractive than he remembered. She wrote a light blue summer sleeveless dress that seemed to fit her petite figure perfectly. She also wore shoes that matched the blue in her dress. Again he remembered that while she was not drop dead gorgeous, when she flashed that amazing smile her attractiveness rose to another dimension.

"Hello cowboy. Sorry I'm a few minutes late."

"No problem. I just got here myself."

"We might as well get in line for the elevator."

"After you, ma'am."

As they stood in line, Kit found himself looking over the attire of the other male guests trying to make sure he had dressed appropriately. He saw a lot of casual attire consisting of Dockers, loafers and polo shirts, plus a few light colored tropical suits mixed in with some seersucker suits. Kit relaxed knowing he would not stick out like a sore thumb and embarrass Ellie Lynn.

Ellie Lynn interrupted his thoughts. "I'm glad you could make it."

Kit smiled. "Me too."

They exited the elevator and were confronted by a series of desks manned by the staff of the DAR. Each table was dedicated to a section of the alphabet with a sign reflecting which letters were associated with which desk. Ellie Lynn took his hand and let him to the table for the letter M. Kit saw a series of name tags on the table and behind them sat a staff member next to a small cash box. Kit began to reach for his wallet when Ellie Lynn put her hand on his and said, "It's taken care of."

"You bought the tickets?"

"No. The bank buys several to support the DAR and I have two of them."

Ellie Lynn picked up her pre-printed name tag and had the clerk hand make one for Kit. She took off the adhesive backing and put it on his shirt above his left shirt pocket. Then she did the same with her own, placing it on the upper left portion of her dress. They were each given a bid card with a number on it and the card number was then registered next to their name by the clerk.

They entered the ballroom. There was a series of buffet tables loaded with food and three separate bars along one side of the ballroom. At the end, a podium was set up for the auctioneer and in front of the podium were rows and rows of chairs. On the other side of the ballroom was a series of long tables that Ellie Lynn explained contained the silent auction items. She told Kit that patrons could avail themselves of the food for free, but that drinks were cash bar only. The actual auction would start at 8:00. Between 7:00 and 8:00, the patrons made the rounds of the items on the silent auction tables and wrote down their bids and helped themselves to the food buffet tables and trays.

Kit and Ellie Lynn made their way along the silent auction tables, pausing now and then to examine an item that interested them. Kit noticed that many of the silent auction items were local works of art. There were watercolors, charcoal sketches, poetry, framed photographs and hand-made sweet grass baskets of all sizes and kinds. There was also a series of hand tied fly fishing lures, some hand carved wooden birds and ships, and silver and gold jewelry. Two items that caught his eye were a hand made knife and a small diorama of miniature civil war soldiers, Confederate of course.

Kit made bids on the knife, the diorama, and a small necklace made with amazingly thin strands of gold and silver. He noticed that Ellie Lynn had made a bid on a hand painted scarf, but nothing else. They made their way to the buffet tables and after filing their plates and finding two chairs toward the back of the ballroom, Kit offered to get them some drinks. Ellie Lynn told him she would like a glass of cranberry juice.

Kit went to the bar located at the back of the ballroom and found himself in line behind five other men. All of them were obviously on the same mission he was. The bar was manned by three bartenders, and all of them were busy. There was a similar line of thirsty patrons in front of all three servers. Kit watched patiently as two of the patrons in front of him were served and left the line with a drink in each hand. He was anxious to get back to Ellie Lynn and learn more about her. He found her very friendly and interesting. He also felt that she was maintaining her distance, and he wasn't sure why. His thoughts were interrupted by a commotion in front of the line next to him on his right. He turned to watch as a tall, well built man with a head of pre-maturely white hair cut very short was yelling at the bartender.

"What the hell are you trying to pull, you little jerk. I asked for Scotch, not this swill you just poured. When I say Scotch I mean single malt Scotch, not this blended crap."

"I'm sorry sir, but we don't carry single malt scotch. This is all we have to serve."

The tall white haired man reacted by reaching across the serving table and grabbing the startled bartender by the throat and actually lifting him off the ground. "Listen you little shit bird. You have exactly one minute to come up with some real scotch or you'll be sorry you were ever born."

The white haired man's face had become flushed and the veins on his neck stood out reflecting his apparent rage. Everyone at the bar, including the other bartenders seemed to be frozen in shock at the man's outburst.

Kit found himself stepping forward and placing himself between the angry white haired man and the distraught bartender to the surprise of everyone, including the angry tall man.

"Partner, I think you need to let go of this boy. Just step back and cool off."

"I ain't your partner and you're buttin' in where you got no business. Get out of my face or I'll crush you like a bug, cowboy hat and all."

Without even thinking about it, Kit executed a move Connor had taught him for just such a situation. Kit turned and brought his fist down on the man's extended right arm at the joint of the elbow, breaking the man's grip on the bartender's throat. In the same motion of turning, he stepped behind the man as he brought his hand down the man's left arm and then twisted it behind the man's back. Using the man's arm as leverage, he forced him forward and down until his face was on the serving table.

Then Kit leaned forward and whispered into the tall man's right ear.

"I'll let you go if you agree you'll apologize to the bartender. Otherwise I'll break your arm off and beat you to death with it. Which will it be?" Kit added more pressure on the arm to add emphasis to his words.

The tall man's eyes bulged out from his eye sockets from the pain that Kit was inflicting, and he quickly nodded his head up and down to indicate his agreement with Kit's offer.

Kit let him go and carefully stepped back.

The tall man slowly stood up, rubbing his sore left arm. He turned to the frightened bartender and said, "I'm sorry." Then he pulled a wad of cash out of his pocket, tossed a twenty dollar bill on the serving table, then turned and left the room as quickly as he could manage.

The entire incident happened so quickly that no one in the crowded ballroom had noticed it except the three bartenders and the approximately fifteen or sixteen men who had been waiting in line.

Kit resumed his place in line as the men standing there quickly made room for him. The bartenders resumed their jobs filling drink orders and the lines began to move forward as though nothing had happened. When Kit got to the front of the line, the bartender filled his order and refused to take his money.

"No way you're paying, man. Thank you for saving my friend's bacon from that angry dude."

"I didn't do much," said Kit.

"The hell you didn't. The last time I saw a move like that was in the movies. And I wasn't being choked at the time. I'd pay money just to see someone get the best of Harlo Clay.

"Save your money, son. It wasn't that big of a deal. Thanks for the drinks."

Kit tossed a five dollar tip on the bar and took the drinks back to where Ellie Lynn was seated.

They had just finished their plates of food and their drinks when a very attractive blonde who looked to be in her early thirties came up to them.

She was dressed in a very expensive green silk dress that showed off her well formed figure. She was a woman with the kind of curves that involuntarily drew a man's attention, and she obviously knew it. She had light blue eyes and pale white skin. She wore a beautiful and obviously expensive diamond necklace, diamond earrings, and a large diamond ring on her right hand. She wore no wedding ring. On closer examination, Kit decided hat she was probably closer to forty than thirty and she took great pains and probably a whole lot of money to look younger than she really was. Under the blonde hair, blue eyes and quite a bit of make-up, Kit detected a hardness which belied the sophisticated appearance she was trying so hard to project.

"My goodness, Ellie Lynn, how are you? I saw you come in and I just had to come over and meet your new escort. I don't believe I've had the pleasure of meeting him before."

Kit saw Ellie Lynn assume a forced smile and heard her say, "Kit, this is a friend and customer of mine, Ms. Wendy Regret. Wendy, this is my friend, Mr. Kit Andrews of Kemmerer, Wyoming.

"Wyoming! My word! You must be a real cowboy, Mr. Andrews."

"Well, ma'am, that's at least partially correct."

"Ellie Lynn, however did you manage to meet such a good looking man from as far away as Wyoming?"

Before Ellie Lynn could respond, Kit interrupted. "Actually Ellie Lynn's family on her father's side is from Wyoming. I know them well and told them I would look her up when I was in Charleston."

Wendy gave him a puzzled look. So did Ellie Lynn.

"Wyoming is a large state, but with very few people. When you live there you get to know pretty much everybody in the entire state. It's kind of like living in a small town. You know, the kind of place where everybody knows more than they should about everybody else."

Both the ladies joined Kit in laughter.

Ellie Lynn shot Kit a look of thanks.

"Well how long do you plan to stay in our fair city? Are you just visiting or are you planning to stay for a while?"

Ellie Lynn interjected at this point. "Wendy is one of the most successful Realtors in Charleston. She is also on the board of the DAR and a very good customer of the bank."

"Well, Ms. Regret, I'm just visiting, and I'll be going back to my home in Wyoming shortly. I truly am enjoying my visit to Charleston, and I must say I never had any idea that it was populated with such lovely ladies."

Both women seemed to blush slightly.

"My goodness Mr. Andrews, you are quite the gentleman for a Yankee."

"Actually Ms. Regret, during the Civil War, there was no Wyoming. It was just a territory and was settled largely after the Civil War by veterans of both armies.

"I must correct you, Mr. Andrews. In the South, we refer to it as the War of Northern Aggression."

"I stand corrected, Ms. Regret, and I will endeavor to remember that in the future."

"Well, it was a pleasure to meet you, Mr. Andrews, but I see some clients of mine that I simply must go and greet."

"The pleasure was all mine, Ms. Regret."

As soon as she was gone Ellie Lynn looked up at Kit and said, "You are such a big fat liar."

"Hey, I just thought a little fib on how we met was appropriate. Besides, she seemed to be a little too interested for my comfort level."

"I think she was just curious about you and then she wanted to find out if you were looking for a house she could sell you and make a commission."

"Well, I can't fault her for her taste or her ambition."

"She's a little too pushy for me. She's a good customer of the bank, so I'm nice to her. However, while she is very successful in selling real estate, she has a reputation for twisting the truth as it suits her."

"Her last name seemed somehow familiar to me."

"It's a very old name in South Carolina. Her family dates from Pre-Revolutionary War times. Her grandfather was a state senator and her father was a local judge. If I remember correctly, her great-great grandfather was a hero in the Civil War."

"He was a hero of the Civil War, not the War of Northern Aggression?"

"It must be my northern heritage, but to me it's the Civil War. Calling it the War of Northern Aggression is popular with many locals. Some even refer to it as the Late Unpleasantness."

"I'll stick with the Civil War. That's what all us Yankees remember it as."

"Wendy is right about one thing. You are good looking for a Yankee," she said with a grin.

"And you, Miss Main, are the loveliest rebel I have ever encountered," replied Kit.

This time Ellie Lynn truly did blush.

They were then interrupted by the announcement from the podium to take their seats as the auction was about to begin.

After the auction was over, Kit and Ellie Lynn went over to the silent auction counter and Kit discovered he had made the winning bid on the knife and the gold and silver necklace.

Kit paid the cashier and put the items in the pocket of his jeans. Then he looked around for Ellie Lynn. He found her talking with a tall blonde woman who appeared to be about the same age as Ellie Lynn. As Kit approached them, the blonde gave him a careful once-over. Kit noted that the look was one of careful appraisal, not just a cursory look. She was almost six feet tall and very thin. She was attractive in a fashion model sort of way, but Kit felt no chemistry when their eyes met. Kit walked up and before he could introduce himself, Ellie Lyn smiled at him and said, "Kit, I would like you to meet one of my friends from the bank, Samantha Butler. She also answers to Sam."

Kit smiled and took Sam's outstretched hand. Her grip was gentle, but firm and warm.

"How do you do, Mr. Andrews. Ellie Lynn has mentioned your name more than a few times to me."

"I do hope at least some of it was in a positive vein."

Sam laughed. She had a deep throaty laugh that some men would call sexy.

"I assure you I have yet to hear her say anything negative about you with the sole exception of you being a Yankee."

"So am I to gather the Civil War isn't over for you either?"

"No, Mr. Andrews, for we true southerners, the War of Northern Aggression is never over. We have managed to immortalize it and turn it into tourism. We never managed to beat you, but we will take your money."

Kit smiled. "You have me there, Ms. Butler. I love your city, but it is a tad more expensive than Kemmerer, Wyoming."

"I'm sure it is, and we would be very disappointed if it were not. Have you enjoyed your visit to Charleston?"

"I certainly have. Everyone I've met has been helpful and polite, especially Ms. Main."

"By now you have discovered Ellie Lynn is one of the nicest people on the planet, not just Charleston."

"I would agree with that assessment. Ellie Lynn mentioned that you work at the bank. What kind of word do you do there?"

"Ellie Lynn warned me that you were direct. I like that in a man. Actually I'm in charge of security for the bank. I'm kind of an in-house cop."

"You could have fooled me. You look nothing like any cop I've ever met."

"I'll take that as a compliment. Actually I was a cop before I took the job at the bank. I worked as a detective for the Atlanta PD."

"What caused you to make the change?"

"I got tired of all the politics and crap, and I found out that the longer you deal with criminals and low lifes the more you start to think like them. I saw no future in that, so I applied for the security job at the bank and here I am."

"I assume this was a good move?"

"It's turned out to be a very good move. Keeping up with white collar crime and high tech fraud is a full time job. The bank allows me to buy what I need and it keeps me on the cutting edge. I really enjoy it."

"I assume the hours and the pay and benefits are better as well."

"You are absolutely correct. The only thing similar to my old job is I still carry a gun."

"May I ask if you are carrying one now?"

"You can ask, but I prefer to keep that a professional secret."

"So the answer is yes."

"You are quick. Ellie Lynn said you'd be hard to fool."

"Well, I have to admit it isn't obvious."

"Have you figured out where I carry it?"

"Since you're not carrying a purse I would have to believe it is in the small of your back. My guess would be a small, single stack 9mm semi-automatic."

"Boy, you are good. You're right on both counts."

"If you two are done exchanging gun stories, I would like to remind you both that I am still standing here," said Ellie Lynn

"Sorry Ellie Lynn. I didn't mean to monopolize your cowboy, but he is really interesting. I have to get back to my date who will want to know why his cold beer is warm and his hot sandwich is cold."

Ellie Lynn and Sam both laughed while Kit just smiled politely.

Sam made her good-byes and disappeared into the crowd that remained at the food tables.

"Well, what did you think of Sam?"

"As a cop or as a woman?"

"As a woman, of course."

"She was very nice, and I can see why you like her."

"Did you find her attractive?"

"She looks like a model, but she's not my type."

"She's not? Why isn't she your type?"

"I can't really tell you. It's just that I don't feel any attraction to a woman like her. I liked her as a person and I think she's a really interesting woman, but she doesn't register on my Wow Meter?"

"You have a Wow Meter?"

"Absolutely. All guys have one."

"And just where do you keep this Wow Meter?"

"I could tell you, but then I'd have to kill you."

"You're very funny, cowboy."

"Well, are you ready to go home?"

"Lead the way, Mr. Andrews."

Kit and Ellie Lynn took the elevator to the lobby and made their way to the hotel exit.

"I have my car parked in the hotel lot. Would you like a ride back to your hotel?

"That would be great. Are you sure it isn't too much trouble?"

"It's not a problem. Charleston is pretty easy to get around in a car."

All too soon Ellie Lynn had pulled up in front of Kit's hotel. He turned in his seat to face her.

"Thank you so much for a great evening. I had a very nice time."

"Me, too. I'm glad you could come."

Kit paused for what seemed an eternity that was actually only a few seconds. Then he leaned forward toward Ellie Lynn. She put her right hand on his chest as if to ward him off. "I've had a lovely time. Please don't spoil it."

Kit heard himself apologize and found himself standing in front of the hotel watching the taillights of her car disappear into the darkness. He managed to recover his composure and headed back into the hotel and up to his room.

When Kit got to his room, the message light on his phone was lit. He called the main desk and was informed that they had a FedEx package for him. He went down to the main desk to retrieve it and was surprised to see it was the package Connor had sent from Italy, and forwarded to him by Big Dave Carlson.

He took the package back to his room and opened it. He removed a few typewritten pages and one handwritten page. He started to read the pages. Kit paused after a few minutes to get a Coke out of the mini-fridge and then resumed reading. When he was finished, he had a frown on his face. The typed pages were sort of an itinerary of Connor's trip with notes added. They ended with him headed from Rome to a small village in Sicily. Written in pencil at the end of the typewritten page were two words. "*Romano* and *dangerous.*"

The hand written page simply said "This is a trail of bread crumbs in case something happens to me. If you do not hear from me within thirty days, come running." The note was signed, "Connor."

Kit stuck the papers back into the envelope and put it in a pocket of the small notebook computer carrying case. He would just have to wait until he did or did not hear from Connor. He checked his calendar on his cell phone and entered a note reminder to come up in thirty days. He took the necklace and the knife out of his pocket and dropped them in the same pocket in the notebook computer carrying case where he had placed Connor's notes.

Kit undressed and slipped into bed. He was restless and could not fall asleep. He sat up and turned on the bedside lamp and looked at his watch. It was almost eleven. At first he thought he was restless because he was worried about Connor and the search for his father. He knew that wasn't true. Connor could take care of himself and if he needed Kit, he would let him know in no uncertain terms.

No, the problem was Ellie Lynn Main. He could not seem to get her out of his mind and he could not understand how he could enjoy someone so much and feel such a connection and still get blown off by her. This was two times in a row. Something was wrong, and he just could not figure it out. It wasn't like he asked her to have sex with him. He had just tried to kiss her good night after a pleasant evening together. Kit had a spotty track record in dealing with women, but this was more than just puzzling.

He got out of bed and pulled out the telephone directory from the drawer in the night stand and found her number. He picked up the hotel phone and dialed it. After three rings, he was about to hang up when she suddenly answered the phone. He felt his mouth get very dry and he was unsure of what to say.

"Hello. Hello."

"Uh, Ellie Lynn."

'Yes.'

"This is Kit Andrews."

"I thought maybe it was you. What are you up to at eleven o'clock at night?"

"Well, I felt I needed to call you and talk a little. Is this a bad time?"

"No, it's not a bad time. You probably rescued me from a bad talk show and even worse jokes. What is it you wanted to talk about?"

"I wanted to talk about you, and I specifically wanted to talk about you and me."

"I see."

Kit was teetering between panic and brutal honesty. He chose brutal honesty.

"Ellie Lynn, I'm having trouble understanding what I'm doing wrong with you that seems to prevent us from getting any closer. I think we're getting along great and suddenly I feel like someone threw ice water on me."

There was silence from Ellie Lynn's end of the phone.

Kit plunged ahead. "Look, Ellie Lynn. I find myself attracted to you and what I know about you has made me very fond of you. I thought you felt the same way, but when I went to kiss you tonight, you turned away. I guess I'm not the brightest bulb on the tree, but I'm having trouble figuring out why?"

After a brief pause, Ellie Lynn responded. "I'm sorry if I've hurt your feelings, Kit. That was not my intention. I hope I have not misled you."

"What do you mean by misled?"

"I really do like you, Kit, and I enjoy your company. But I want no part of any relationship. I'm single by choice. I try to make that very clear to any man I meet. I had a very long relationship with a man, and it ended very badly. I was betrayed and hurt by him. Without going into the gory details, I'll just say that this man cheated on me and stole from me. It wasn't just money he stole. He stole my trust and my faith in others. He hurt me physically and emotionally.

I've spent two years with a shrink trying to figure out what normal behavior was. Since then I just don't let anyone get close to me. I'm too afraid of being hurt and disappointed. I like you, Kit. You seem to be to be a very nice man. One of the nicest men I've been with in years. But I can't change who I am and how I feel. I've spent a long time building up my defenses against the disappointments in life, and I'm not sure I want that to change. I've worked hard to get where I am, and I'm happy with my life because I feel safe. If you are really interested in me then you are going to have to be willing to invest a whole lot of time getting to really know me and letting me get to really know you. At this point in my life, I don't allow myself to trust anyone. And to be perfectly honest, I just met you."

"I just met you and I like how I feel about that, Ellie Lynn."

"But you're a man. All the men I know are basically just looking for one thing from a woman and it's isn't love."

"It seems to me that you are trying to lump an awful lot of guys into one category."

"Maybe, but I've not seen anything in my experience to change my mind. When I talk to men, they're not looking at my mouth or my eyes, they're looking at my breasts. If you haven't noticed I don't have much in the chest department that would seem to invite so much attention. Yet they still stare at them. I want to say to them, hey, I'm up here, not down there. It's insulting. With most men no matter what you do, they seem to think it's some sort of come on."

"Do you think that about me?"

"No, Kit. You've done nothing to make me see you like I see most men, but I also don't know enough about you to feel safe. I should tell you that before I called you and met you for a drink, I did a background check on you."

"Really. What did you learn about me?"

"I learned that you are what you say you are. I used the bank resources and I checked you out on Google."

"How boring was that?"

"You may be a lot of thing, Mr. Andrews, but boring is not one of them. Your testimony in the murder trail in Chicago makes you out to be a pretty brave and honest man. I found absolutely nothing negative about you."

"Well I hope I got points for that."

"Actually, you did. That's why I met you for a drink."

"Can I ask how many points I got?"

"No, you may not, Mr. Andrews. A woman never divulges all her secrets."

"I know it's getting late and I'm sorry for keeping you up, but I would like to continue this discussion tomorrow. How about we meet for breakfast or lunch?"

"I'll settle for brunch at the King Street Bakery. How about we meet there at eleven tomorrow morning?"

"I'll find it and meet you there."

"See you then. Good night, Mr. Andrews."

"Good night, Miss Main."

Kit put down the phone and slipped into bed. This time he was asleep within minutes.

CHAPTER EIGHT

Kit was rudely awakened by a loud pounding on his door. He slipped groggily out of bed and pulled on a pair of jeans and searched for a t-shirt. The loud pounding continued.

"Hold your horses, I'm getting dressed," he yelled at the unknown person pounding on his door.

He finally located a t-shirt and pulled it on. He opened the door and there stood a grinning Swifty wearing his traditional garb of jeans, denim shirt, cowboy boots, and cowboy hat.

"Good morning, sunshine. Sleeping in, I see. Did we have a good time last night and are trying to recover or are we just getting our beauty rest?"

Kit didn't know whether to punch his friend or hug him.

"Very funny, you jerk. Why didn't you just call up to the room instead of pounding on the door?"

"Oh, I could have called up, but I thought this would be a lot more fun and who knows. I might've gotten lucky and found you in bed with some southern belle."

"In your dreams."

"Hey I want you to know that I've been known to have some very colorful and interesting X-rated dreams."

"Please. That's too much information for this early in the morning."

"Early! Have you checked out the current time my friend?"

Kit glanced at his watch and was astounded to see it was already nine in the morning.

"Shit."

"Now what's wrong?"

"I've got a brunch appointment with Miss Main at eleven."

"Well, get cracking and get cleaned up. I love brunch."

"You weren't invited, pal."

"I am now. Where you go, I go. We're partners, remember?"

"I don't think this is a good time, Swifty."

"Why? What did you tell her about me?"

"Enough."

"You can never tell a lady enough about old Swifty. You know women can never get enough of me."

"You live in total delusion, Swifty."

"Maybe, but it's a real happy place, Kit."

"O.K. You can come if you promise to behave."

"I always behave. It's just sometimes I behave badly," said a grinning Swifty. "Besides if you're meeting her at eleven, we can get there early and you can bring me up to date on what in the wide world of sports is going on down here."

By ten o'clock they were seated at a table at the King Street Bakery. The bakery was a small restaurant that specialized in breakfast and lunch. They ordered coffee from the middle-aged waitress, and Kit began bringing Swifty up to date including his evening out at the DAR charity auction.

Swifty listened carefully to every detail and when Kit was finished, he had several questions. "What did you say the bartender called the white haired dude you dumped on the bar?"

"Let's see. I think it was an odd first name. Oh, yeah, it was Harlo. I never heard of anyone named Harlo before."

"It's his last name I think we're in need of, partner."

"What was his last name? I think it was Kay or Cray or something like that."

"Was it Clay?"

"That was it! Harlo Clay. Why? What's the big deal about some drunk with a funny sounding first name."

"Well, if you read the stuff I faxed to you carefully, you would know that one of the four killers your great-great grandfather saw was named Clay. Maybe it's just a coincidence, but this bad tempered dude you tried to teach manners to might just be a descendent of the bad dude your great-great grandfather saw."

"His name was Clay?"

"The dude's name was Allison Clay, private in the Confederate Army. And in case you forgot, he was a killer."

"How do we know if they're related."

"We don't. We do a little research and try to find out if there's a connection."

"We can Google him."

"What the hell does that mean?"

Kit explained the powers of Google to a surprised Swifty.

"My boy has been getting educated. I'm truly shocked. I forgot you were a techno weenie."

"Systems analyst, not techno weenie, you hillbilly."

"Since you are just an ignorant flatlander from Illinois I can forgive you for your stupidity and lack of class. Nobody calls a cowboy a hillbilly and lives to remember it. But in your case I'll make an exception."

Swifty was expecting a smart ass remark from Kit, but Kit was sitting perfectly still and seemed to be staring into space.

"Earth to Kit. Earth to Kit. Come in Kit."

"Sorry. I just remembered something else from last night."

"Oh yeah, what's that?"

"I met this high powered lady realtor last night. She comes from an old line South Carolina family. Her name was Wendy Regret."

"Regret? As in Captain Ambrose Regret?"

"You got it."

"Now we're getting way too far over the line in coincidence land."

"Maybe, but I'm curious to see what the computer has to say when we Google her as well."

Their conversation was interrupted by the sudden appearance of Ellie Lynn Main. Unlike the other times Kit had seen her, she was dressed very casually. She wore white shorts, white sandals, and a light yellow polo. She wore no jewelry and very little make-up. She still took Kit's breath away.

"Am I interrupting something, Kit?"

"No, no, you aren't. Ellie Lynn this is my partner, Gary Olson. Most people know him as Swifty Olson. Swifty, this is Miss Ellie Lynn Main, Vice President of the Bank of South Carolina."

Both men had risen to their feet as Kit spoke.

"I'm very pleased to meet you, Miss Main. I've heard a great deal about you from Kit. You are every bit as lovely as he described you."

Ellie Lynn did not blush at Swifty's compliment. Instead she took it in stride and just smiled.

"And you, Mr. Olson are exactly the charming scamp I expected you to be."

Not missing a beat Swifty pulled out a chair and said, "Please join us for brunch, Miss Main."

Ellie Lynn laughed and her face lit up with her disarming smile and her flashing eyes as she seated herself at the table.

They waited as the waitress suddenly appeared and took their orders for brunch. As soon as she left, Ellie Lynn turned to Kit and said, "So why am I blessed with the company of two such charming Yankees?"

Kit smiled and explained Swifty's sudden appearance and his insistence on joining Kit for brunch with Ellie Lynn.

"So now that we have the formalities over with, can you bring me up to date on your search for the treasure?" asked Ellie Lynn.

"Treasure, what treasure?" said a stunned Swifty.

"She knows the whole story, Swifty. I told her after she offered to help us in our research. She has been very helpful."

"Oh! Well, if Kit trusts you, then so do I. Maybe you can help us out with a little coincidence that we seem to have come up with as a result of that little gala outing you two were at last night."

"What coincidence are you talking about?"

"It seems that Kit had a little confrontation with one of your less civilized patrons at the bar last night. Are you familiar with a dude named Harlo Clay?"

"Of course I am. He's from an old South Carolina family. The Clay family has been in the state since before the Civil War."

"What can you tell us about him?"

"He runs the Hanging Rock Farm just outside of Hanging Rock. They raise hay and grain. They're probably the largest hay and grain broker in the state. I think every farm and stable in South Carolina does some business with them. Harlo is the farm manager, and he's a cousin of the owners. He has a reputation as kind of a hothead, and he's had more than a few scrapes with the law. He always uses the family connections to get himself out of trouble. He doesn't usually attend many social events in Charleston. I think his cousins prefer to keep him on their farm, where he is out of the public eye and they can provide damage control over whatever kind of trouble he manages to get himself into. He also fancies himself to be quite the ladies' man. Frankly, he's the kind of man who gives me the creeps. Why do you ask about him?"

"He got into a little argument with a bartender at the charity auction last night and when Kit tried to intervene, he got nasty and Kit had to put him down."

"Put him down?"

"Well, figuratively speaking. Kit just slammed his head down on top of the bar and made him apologize to the bartender."

"Kit, you didn't say anything about that last night."

"I didn't think it was important, and I didn't want to upset you."

"Not important! I'd have paid money to see someone slam Harlo Clay face down on a bar in public."

All three of them broke out in laughter.

When Kit stopped laughing, he looked thoughtfully at Ellie Lynn and said, "You mentioned Clay works for cousins that own the farm. You wouldn't happen to know their names?"

"You met one of them last night."

"I did?"

"Yes. Surely you remember Ms. Wendy Regret. She was the blonde realtor who was almost drooling over you."

"She's Harlo Clay's cousin?"

"She certainly is. She and her brother, Lee Regret, own the farm and Harlo Clay manages it. Why are you interested in them?"

"Do you believe in coincidences, Miss Main?" asked Swifty.

"Actually, I almost never believe in coincidences, Mr. Olson. Bankers rarely do."

"It seems we have been able to come up with the names of the nine Confederate cavalrymen who swiped the bank safes from the Union Army and buried them back in February of 1865."

"You have?"

"Yep, we have. You might be surprised to know that two of the four, who killed their five comrades over the buried gold, had familiar names. They were private Allison Clay and Captain Ambrose Regret."

"Their names were Clay and Regret!"

"One and the same, we think."

"My God. Even I would have trouble thinking that was a coincidence."

"We plan to Google them to see if there is a connection."

"I can do better than that. As soon as I get home, I'll trace their lineage on the DAR data base. Both of their families are in the data base."

"That would be great," said Kit.

Ellie Lynn stood up and both men came to their feet.

"You boys are way too polite to be Yankees. Are you sure you're not from southern Wyoming?"

Kit and Swifty laughed.

"No, Miss Main. We're Yankee cowboys from Wyoming," said Swifty. "Although Kit here is actually adopted. We ain't real sure if he was born or hatched and we're pretty sure his parentage is questionable."

Now it was Ellie Lynn's turn to laugh.

"I'll call you on your cell phone when I finish the search," said Ellie Lynn, and with that she was out the door and gone from sight.

"My, my," said Swifty. "You know when she first came in, I thought she was a little plain. The longer I looked at her, the better looking she got. How does she do that?"

"I have no idea, but she does it to me every time I see her."

"Well, let's let her do her thing while we do our thing."

"And just what is our thing today?"

"Why you show me around this lovely city and hopefully some of its lovely females. What else could be more important?"

"You've got a deal," said Kit, and he left enough money on he table for the bill and a sizeable tip for the waitress.

CHAPTER NINE

Lee Regret was just finishing a leisurely breakfast on the shaded stone patio outside the family's historic home on Meeting Street in Charleston. Suzie the maid had just finished bringing him a pot of freshly brewed coffee and had finished clearing off his breakfast dishes. Having a good cup of coffee on this patio was one of Lee's favorite pastimes. Lee's slender frame was dressed in pressed tan Dockers with a white polo. He wore leather sandals on his feet, no socks. He took a sip of the fresh coffee and placed the cup back on the saucer as he stretched his long legs out under the wrought iron table.

Life was good, he thought. Life had been very good to Lee and his sister since he figured out a way to make their simple life as hay and grain farmers and brokers a much more rewarding enterprise. It had been almost five years ago when Lee had been approached by a well dressed Korean gentleman in a Charleston bar. The man had seemed out of place as it catered to the more blue-collar type of clientele and was not a place where a man of color would normally go willingly. Charleston was a very sophisticated and cultured city, but it was still a city in the South. Whites held the economic upper hand, and thus they also held the political upper hand in the city. It was very rare to see any non-whites south of Calhoun Street after dark unless they were working there. The exception to the rule was tourists. Charleston's main industry was tourism, and that brought people of all races into the city. That was fine as long as they did not stay and spent lots of money while they were there. Tourism was the reason that Lee had built up a good part of his business in Charleston.

Lee and his sister owned a larger farm in the northern part of the state near a small town called Hanging Rock. The farm had been part of a plantation owned by their great-great grandfather who had fought in the Civil War for the South. They had inherited the old rice plantation about ten years ago when both of their parents were killed in a car accident. Lee and Wendy were the only heirs. They inherited everything from their parents, including the ancestral farm. Lee had converted the land from rice to hay and grain. He then expanded the business to begin brokering hay and grain all over the state. He built up the business and had several warehouses on the farm to store the hay and grain he purchased from others and then resold.

Some of his best clients were the gentlemen farmers, who owned small farms and raised prize horses. In addition to the hay and grain, he also provided bedding straw, a by-product of his oat fields. As the agriculture in the state became more gentrified, so did the source of demand for his products and services. Lee had a fleet of trucks, both large and small, that picked up his purchases and delivered his sales. Then he became the primary supplier for the stables in Charleston that provided horse-drawn carriage rides for all of those tourists. It was big business in Charleston and was heavily regulated by the city. Lee provided a valuable service to the stable owners, as their stables were not large enough to store much hay and grain and the city would not allow them to store it outside. He provided just in time delivery of the hay and grain they needed along with the bedding straw. At the same time, he used sealed metal capsules to solve another problem the stable owners had with the city. He provided them with a sealed storage tank for their manure. His men picked up the units weekly and left behind a newly cleaned empty tank.

To support his Charleston operation, Lee had purchased a large warehouse at 313 Concord Street near the docks of the port of Charleston. It was only a block east of East Bay Street. The warehouse had both truck and train access, but Lee only used the truck access. Lee had bought the warehouse right after the Navy had closed down their base at Charleston and warehouses could be obtained cheaply. He could easily get double what he paid for the warehouse if he chose to sell in today's market. With the success of his operation, there was a fat chance of that happening.

The warehouse was the staging place for his operations in Charleston. He shipped hay, grain, and straw by truck into the warehouse. Usually this was about two semi-trailer truck loads a week. Then smaller trucks delivered the hay, grain, and straw during the week to the stables in Charleston as well to some of the larger plantations just outside of the city. The Charleston area had a great deal of wealthy people who owned horses.

Lee also stored the manure tanks in the warehouse and once a week they were emptied into a large semi-trailer after adjustable sides had been added. This was done by using a small industrial crane in the warehouse. The semi-trailers were then hooked to trucks and driven to the farm in Hanging Rock where the manure was spread over the farm's growing fields. The semi-trailers were then steam cleaned and loaded up with bales of hay and straw and sacks of grain for the return trip to Charleston. Lee had learned a long time ago that no truck should ever make a trip empty if it was possible to provide it with a cargo.

The deal had worked out well, but while it was a good living, it was still a lot of hard work. Lee had managed to "persuade" potential competitors that trying to compete with the Regrets was unhealthy. He had used any method necessary to eliminate any and all competition. He used everything from political pressure to bribery to strong-arm tactics. His methods were both legal and illegal. He didn't care what he had to do, but he would not tolerate interference in what he considered his god-given right to having an exclusive market for his business.

Until that night five years ago, Lee's only worry had been the potential repeal of some tax shelters his business enjoyed. Lee had spent a good deal of money supporting political candidates who advocated greater tax shelters for the poor farmer in South Carolina. Even with those shelters in place he still resented what he felt was a large chunk of cash he was forced to give to the government. What was particularly galling to him was how that money was spent on the blacks and the poor white trash in the state. Lee Regret was a chip off his great-great grandfather's old block. He was a racist to the core. He was also anti-government. On the surface he was a southern gentleman, a throwback to the plantation owner of the pre-Civil War days. Below the surface, he was a man who would stop a nothing to get what he wanted and to whom violence was second nature.

That night seemed longer ago than just five years ago. Lee had been sitting at the bar, complaining loudly to the bartender and those around him about the government wasting money on the niggers. He turned quickly on his bar stool when he felt a touch on his right shoulder. There stood the Oriental gentleman, dressed impeccably in an expensive Armani suit.

"Mr. Regret?"

"That's me. Who are you?"

"My name is Kim Song, Mr. Regret. I was advised by a Mr. Field that you and I might be able to do some business."

Lee was instantly on alert. Mr. Field was a local who owned several fishing boats and leased them out to shrimp fishermen. He and Lee had worked together in the past on several illegal enterprises. Field had connections with many of the ship captains whose vessels visited the part of Charleston on a regular basis. Field usually helped to smuggle contraband into the port and had used Lee's warehouse and his trucks to move the contraband out of Charleston and to a distribution point.

Lee had been paid well for each shipment, and he had never known the contents of the contraband nor did he want to. He was pretty sure the contraband shipments were drugs. After 9-11 security had tightened in Charleston as well as every port in America and the shipments had stopped. He had not heard from Field in over four years.

"Well, then. Perhaps we should talk in private," said Lee, gesturing toward a booth in the back of the bar.

"As you wish, Mr. Regret."

After they were seated, Lee asked, "How is my old friend, Mr. Field. Has he ever gotten around to cutting that long hair of his?"

Mr. Song was silent. He stared intently at Lee with black eyes that seemed devoid of any life. Then he spoke. "Mr. Field is bald. He has no long hair."

Lee relaxed. "That was just a test, Mr. Song. I like to know if I am dealing with someone who is telling me the truth."

"I assure you, Mr. Regret, I tell only the truth. This is about serious business and a business where lies are punishable by death."

"Before we begin, Mr. Song," said Lee, "put your right hand on the table. Now take your left hand and slowly unbutton the middle three buttons on your shirt."

Mr. Song did as instructed holding his tie to the side as he used his left hand to pull his unbuttoned shirt apart. "I do not wear a wire, Mr. Regret. I am not a policeman."

"One can never be too careful, Mr. Song. Now button your shirt back up and tell me about this serious business you mentioned."

"My country has need of a man with your resources and your abilities, Mr. Regret."

"What country would that be, Mr. Song. China?"

"No, Mr. Regret. I work for the government of North Korea."

"North Korea! What's a North Korean doing in Charleston?"

"We are in many smaller port cities of the United States, Mr. Regret. We wish to do business with Americans like yourself who wish to make money and not have to pay their government any taxes."

"How do we make money without paying taxes?"

'Your government does not collect taxes on income that they know nothing about. I assure you that they will not know about this income unless you choose to tell them which I think would be both foolish and unwise of you."

"I think I'm getting tired of you talking in riddles. Why don't you just try to get to the point and let me know what is it you want from me."

"You Americans are always in such a hurry. You always want to get to the point. As you wish, Mr. Regret. My point is that we wish to smuggle goods into the port of Charleston and we wish to use your warehouse to store them."

"Are you nuts! If we get caught, I lose my business, my warehouse and I go to prison. I'm not interested."

"Please, Mr. Regret. Hear me out completely. I do not wish you to just store the goods. I wish you to buy them from me and then use your trucks and your distribution system in the state to sell my product to others and make a great deal of money."

"Look pal. I don't deal in drugs. It's too dangerous. I've done a little smuggling in the past, but I never knew what I was smuggling and that was just fine. Those days are over and now I run a legit business."

"Your business has a good deal of debt, Mr. Regret. You are making a good deal of money, but most of it goes to pay back debt and pay taxes to your government. Is that not so?"

"How do you know that?"

"My government knows much about you and your family, Mr. Regret. We think you would make a fine customer for North Korea."

"If I were interested in your deal, which I am not, just what is this product you think I will buy and then resell for a profit?"

Mr. Song smiled. "Do you smoke, Mr. Regret?"

"Of course I do. So does almost everyone I know. I've been trying to quit for years. I'd think if your government knows so much about me you would know if I smoked or not. What about it?"

Mr. Song reached into his coat pocket and slowly withdrew it holding a package of Marlboro cigarettes. "This is your brand, is it not?"

"Yes, that's my brand. What has that got to do with this deal?"

"These cigarettes and this package were made in North Korea. We make them and smuggle them into your country. They are exact duplicates of your American cigarettes including the packaging. They only thing missing is the tax stamp. We sell them to you for twenty cents a pack. You smuggle them to your farm in Hanging Rock. Then you have your delivery trucks stop at all the small general stores, convenience stores, grocery stores, and taverns in the state and sell them the same packs for $2.75. They then place the packs in with their regular cigarettes and sell them for $5.00 a pack. You net $2.55 a pack and your customers net $2.25 a pack and none of this is reported and is income that is untaxed. My numbers are based on our experience in doing this same business with other parts of the United States."

"Your experience in this business? You've been doing this in other places already?"

"Last year we smuggled over two billion packs of cigarettes into your country."

"Two billion packs!"

"That is correct, Mr. Regret. This year we expect to double that number."

"But why do you use cigarettes?"

"My country is poor and harsh, Mr. Regret. We need hard cash to survive. We are a strong people and will do what we have to do to survive. This way we get the hard currency we need, and you get rich."

"I'll admit your story is hard to argue with, but how do you get paid? I'm not giving you any cash until I receive the merchandise."

"I completely understand, Mr. Regret. When you receive the goods in your warehouse, you will wire the required amount of cash to an account in the Cayman Islands. From there the money will be wired to several locations and become impossible to trace. Your cover story is that you are investing in a REIT headquartered in the Caymans."

"What the hell is an REIT?"

"It is an investment vehicle created in your country called a Real Estate Investment Trust. You invest money in the Trust which owns commercial real estate income producing properties. You share in the risk and the reward, to quote the brochure."

With that Mr. Song handed Lee an envelope. "In this envelope is a brochure explaining the REIT. It does actually exist, but it is a shell company created by my country. At the very worst, you will appear to be a duped investor if the IRS should investigate your investments. Also in the envelope is a computer disk. It contains several telephone numbers. All of them except one are bogus. The real telephone number comes after a telephone number ending in 10. Do you understand that?

"Yes, I understand, but what is the real number for?"

"The number is for you to call if something has gone wrong, and you wish to cancel a scheduled shipment of product."

"How do I find out when product is coming and how much is coming?"

"You will be contacted by a messenger who will give you a slip of paper with the date and the amount of product and the amount of cash to be wired. Each messenger will be different, and they will never be duplicated. Do I make myself clear, Mr. Regret?"

"Yes, you do."

"Do we have a deal, Mr. Regret?"

"I'll try it one time to see how it goes. If it works like you just described, then of course we have a deal."

"You will be pleased you agreed to this business arrangement, Mr. Regret."

"I've hard that before, Mr. Song. How do I get in touch with you if I need to?"

"You do not, Mr. Regret. You will never see or hear from me again, unless you have done something stupid to betray my country. It is better for you if you never see me again. Is this clear?"

"It is."

With that Mr. Song got to his feet, straightened his tie and walked out of the bar in to the dark, humid Charleston night.

Lee was jolted back to the present by the slamming of a patio door behind him. He turned in his chair to see the source of the unwelcome noisy intrusion into his quiet morning and was not too surprised to see his lovely sister on the warpath about something.

Lee and his sister shared the old family home on Meeting Street in Charleston. He used it when he was in town. His sister, Wendy, had taken up permanent residence in Charleston and become a well known and successful realtor. Neither real estate commissions nor the income from the sale of hay and grain was their main source of income and Wendy knew it. She and her brother were partners and that included their smuggling of North Korean counterfeit cigarettes.

Lee could see she was fuming about something and knew there was no escaping what was coming. He had learned to politely listen to his sister and hear her out. Once she was done venting, he could usually deal with her. When she was pissed, Wendy usually didn't want to be bothered with such things as facts and figures, let alone reason and logic.

"Goddamn stupid bastard," she yelled out as she slammed herself into a cushioned patio chair.

"Whoa, Wendy, slow down. What the heck are you yelling about?"

"Our stupid asshole cousin, that's who," she screamed at him so loudly it hurt his ears.

"Calm down. This is very unladylike, and we don't want the help or the neighbors to be privy to whatever this problem is."

Somewhat slightly mollified, Wendy paused in her screaming to look carefully around to see who might have heard her outburst.

Seeing no one around, she leaned toward her brother and said in a low voice, "Have you heard what that moron of a cousin of ours did? How the hell could you let him go to the DAR charity auction last night. I thought he was supposed to stay at the farm."

"He is supposed to stay at the farm, and he does. You told me to have him come to the auction so we could make a good family showing for you in front of the DAR. You also told us to spend some money and we did. What are you talking about?"

"I just got off the phone with Mandy Walker, you know, the lady I sold the house to on King Street last year. Apparently her husband was at the bar at the charity auction last night and he managed to see our stupid cousin making a public spectacle of himself."

"What did he do, pee on the floor?"

"Don't be crude. If he did do something like that, I would not be a bit surprised."

"Well, what did he do that was so bad?"

"Apparently he got into some sort of argument with the bartender. Harlo was upset about not getting the kind of drink he wanted and the poor boy tried to explain that they didn't carry the specific type of Scotch he wanted. This is, after all, a charity auction, not an alcohol convention."

"Yeah, so what happened?"

"Our dear cousin became enraged and he grabbed the little bartender by the throat and threatened him with great bodily harm unless he produced the proper kind of Scotch. And he did this in front of all the men at the bar."

"So far it's a little embarrassing, but not unforgivable. Is that all he did?"

"No. Then a gentleman intervened and tried to get Harlo to back down and let go of the bartender. Apparently Harlo tried to get nasty with the stranger and then the stranger somehow got the best of Harlo and had him face down on the bar. He forced Harlo to apologize to the bartender."

"What happened then?"

"Harlo threw down some money and disappeared into the crowd."

"Well, it could have been worse. At least Harlo knew when to get out of the line of fire."

"That's not funny. I work for years to bring the Regret name back up to the highest level of society in Charleston and our pea-brained cousin tries to pull us down into the mud in one night."

"I'll talk to him and make sure this doesn't happen again. Do you know who the bartender was?"

"I believe it was young Will Corey."

"I'll stop by the hotel and talk to young Mr. Corey. I'm pretty sure a few dollars will keep him from repeating the story and save us from any problems with the hotel. I admit I am a little surprised you seem to have forgotten it was your idea to have Harlo attend the DAR shindig. You know Harlo has a hard time covering up his true feelings in polite society."

"I remember nothing of the kind. Harlo has the feelings of an animal. Someday he is going to get us in real trouble. The last thing we need is to provide anyone with a reason to come snooping around our business."

"Has it ever occurred to you that keeping a low profile and trying to maintain a position in the high society of Charleston are not on the same page?"

"Being part of the high society of Charleston is one of the reasons we're above reproach. Nobody would suspect us of anything. I don't mind attention, I just mind bad attention."

"Very well, Wendy. I'll talk to young Mr. Corey and I'll talk to Harlo. I'm kind of curious as to how this stranger got the better of Harlo. Few men have been able to do that in my memory. Did Miss Mandy happen to mention the name of the stranger?"

"No, she didn't. Her husband said he'd never seen the man before."

"That may be in our favor. He might have been an out of town guest and will be gone from Charleston before he repeats much of the story to someone he shouldn't."

"You keep that idiot Harlo on the farm where he belongs. You hear!"

"I hear you Wendy. I'll take care of it just like I always do."

Lee picked up his cell phone from the charger on the kitchen counter on his way through the house to the garage. He hit the electric garage door opener and backed out his new black Range Rover. Once on the street, he clicked the console control to close the garage door and pushed the sound system controls. The lush interior of the luxury vehicle was immediately filled with soothing classical music. He smiled as he felt the air conditioning system automatically kick in. "Makes you wonder what the poor people are doing today," Lee thought.

He pulled the Range Rover in front of the Charleston Place Hotel and handed the keys to the valet. Lee stopped at the front desk and asked to see Skip Miller, the special services manager. After a short wait, Skip Miller stepped out of an elevator and walked quickly across the lobby to shake hands with Lee.

"Mr. Regret. It's good to see you again. How can I be of service to you?"

"Good to see you too, Skip. How are things going with the hotel?"

"Great, great, Mr. Regret. We're almost completely booked for the rest of the summer."

"Glad to hear that, Skip. I hope the big dogs here appreciate what you are doing for them."

"They have been very good to me, Mr. Regret. I have no complaints."

"I'm sure they appreciate you, Skip. I stopped by to see if you could do me a small favor."

"Of course, Mr. Regret. What can I do for you?"

"You have a young bartender named Will Corey?"

"Yes, I do. Will does a very good job for me."

"It seems he had an altercation with my cousin, Harlo Clay."

The smile disappeared from Skip's face. "Yes, Mr. Reget, Will and I were discussing last night's incident in my office just before you got here."

"Well, Skip, I'm here to apologize to you and to Will. I'm very disappointed in Harlo. You know he has a history of not handling his liquor very well, and I suspect that last night was one of those occasions. I want to make things right for you, Will, and the hotel."

"I'm sure whatever you choose to do with be satisfactory to me, Will, and the hotel, Mr. Regret. We value the business we get from you and your sister Ms. Regret."

"I'm glad we see eye to eye, Skip. I knew I could count on you to make last nights incident disappear."

"It never happened, Mr. Regrert."

"Thanks Skip. Here's a little something for your trouble."

Lee pulled out a roll of bills from his jacket pocket and peeled off ten $100 bills and handed them to Skip.

Skip pocketed the bills and shook hands with Lee.

"Thank you Mr. Regret. You are very generous."

"Thank you, Skip. I appreciate your discreet handling if this incident."

"I have no idea what you are referring to, Mr. Regret."

"Well done, Skip."

Lee strode to the front of the hotel and handed his valet chip to the attendant. Five minutes later he was heading south on King Street in his Range Rover.

CHAPTER TEN

Kit and Swifty were sitting at a sidewalk table outside a small café just across the street from the Cooper River. Between the street and the river was a large public park area with a huge fountain system. The fountain system was part of a concrete play area where children ran and played. Water spurted up from various fountain holes on a random basis so the children never knew when or where the water would suddenly erupt. Each time a new fountain of water spurted out, it was accompanied by squeals of joy from the children.

Kit was enjoying the children's antics. Swifty was scoping out their young mothers. Kit had just ordered a second round of cold beers when his cell phone rang. It was Ellie Lynn.

"Hi there, cowboy."

"Hey, Ellie Lynn. It's good to hear from you."

"Actually, I'm glad I found you. I have some news."

"Great. What did you find out/"

"I ran a computer search on Lee Regret, Wendy Regret, and Harlo Clay."

"And?"

"We hit pay dirt. Ambrose Regret was Lee and Wendy's great-great grandfather. Harlo Clay's great-great grandfather was Allison Clay."

"What else did you find?"

"Actually I found quite a bit. I printed off the results of my search and am faxing them to your hotel. I think you will find them very interesting. Call me after you've read them and let me know what you think."

"I will. I appreciate this, Ellie Lynn. I really do."

"It truly is my pleasure. Now I'd like to know what your next move will be."

"You'll be the first to know when I finally figure it out, myself. Thanks again."

"You're welcome, cowboy. Talk to you later."

Kit hung up the phone and turned to explain the call to Swifty. Swifty hadn't even turned around nor interrupted his intense scrutiny of every young female within eyesight.

"Man this place is full of gorgeous females!"

"We interrupt this program for a message of great importance."

"What the hell are you babbling about?"

"We have breaking news, Swifty."

"Dude, you've been watching way too much television."

"Swifty, we need to get back to the hotel. Ellie Lynn has found the information we were waiting for and is faxing it to us as I speak."

Swifty downed his beer and looked Kit in the eye. "Why is it that you keep interrupting my fun?"

"Because your idea of fun is rude, crude, and socially unacceptable."

"God, Andrews, sometimes you are such a pilgrim."

"Whatever. We need to head to the hotel."

"Why don't you go, and I'll stay here and observe the local wildlife."

"No deal. Let's move it.'

"All right, all right. I'm coming. God, you can be so anal."

"I'll introduce you to something anal if you don't get moving."

"The child makes threats to the master."

"Reluctantly Swifty rose from his chair and followed Kit as they headed back to the hotel.

When they arrived back at the hotel, the faxes were waiting for them at the front desk. Swifty insisted they stop in at the hotel bar and read the faxes instead of heading back to the room. They found a table at the back of the almost empty bar and Kit proceeded to read the faxes Ellie Lynn had sent.

Kit read the faxes while Swifty ordered two cold beers. By the time the beers arrived, Swifty had appropriated a sizeable bowl of peanuts and Kit had finished reading the faxes.

Swifty belched as he quickly drained his beer and asked, "Well, what's the verdict, partner?"

"Bingo," said Kit.

"Bingo?"

"Yep. Lee and Wendy Regret are brother and sister. They are the children of Thad and Lyddia Regret. They lived in Charleston and owned a rice plantation near Hanging Rock. Thad served as a state district judge in Charleston for over twenty years. Thad was the only child of George A. Regret and Andrea Regret. George had a house in Charleston and owned a rice plantation near Hanging Rock, which is now the hay and grain farm. George served two terms in the South Carolina State Senate. George Regret was one of three children of Ambrose and Cecilia Regret. They had one son and two daughters. One of the daughters married a Brock Clay, one of three sons of Allison Clay. They had six children including two sons. One of the sons, Carleton Clay married a Maxine Woodridge. They had two children, a boy and a girl. The son, Wilson Clay, married a Patience Phelps and they had four children, two of which were boys. Guess what one of them was named?"

"You lost me at Thad and Lyddia. How the hell would I know?"

"Come on, Swifty. Use that mind that's been so underutilized for so long."

"No, not Harlo Clay."

"Give the man a nickel cigar!"

"So we definitely have a direct tie-in to both Clay and the Regrets to the Civil War killers!"

"Yes, we do. The question is now what do we do with the information."

"You mean, what do they know about the gold, if anything?"

"Exactly!"

"Just how do we do we find out what they do know?"

"We need to find out if there is any connection to the gold and when the Regret family bought the former rice plantation now known as Hanging Rock Farm."

Swifty grinned. "We could do this the hard way or we could just call Miss Ellie Lynn. I'll bet she has instant access to the real estate records in this state."

"Sometimes you're smarter than you look, Mr. Olson."

"That's why I'm still alive at the ripe old age of 28, partner."

Kit picked up the phone and within twenty minutes he had a return call from Ellie Lynn.

"What do you have for me, Ellie Lynn?"

"Not what you're looking for, Kit. Ambrose Regret inherited the plantation from his father, James Regret. According to state records, the plantation was purchased by Watson Regret in 1789. That was a long time before the gold was buried in 1865."

"Well thanks for checking it out for us, Ellie Lynn. You've been a great help."

"Were you surprised by the faxes I sent you?"

"No. I sort of expected that our original premise was correct. Your records just clarified the chain and the tie-in between the Clay and Regret families."

"What do you plan to do next?"

"Well, since we now know the gold wasn't used to buy the plantation, I think Swifty and I need to head up to Hanging Rock and do some looking around. We'll check out the farm as well as the area around it to see if we can get a clue to the location of that old barn where the treasure was buried."

"What can I do from this end?"

"Well, it might help if you can do some checking into the Regret's business to see if there is any clue as to how they made their money. If the gold wasn't used to buy the plantation, maybe it was used to buy the house in Charleston or even to help them now. The gold could have been found anytime between 1865 and now. Any one of the descendents of Ambrose Regret could have been the one who was lucky enough to discover it."

"Maybe the gold is still buried and was never found."

"I would label that as possible, but not probable. If they didn't dig it up, where is it?"

"I don't know, but I would love to find out."

"So would we and with any luck we will find out what did happen. Let me know what you find out about the Regret's business."

"Will do. And Kit?"

"Yes."

"Be careful out there."

Kit laughed and hung up the phone.

After Ellie Lynn hung up the phone, she left her office and headed down the elevator to the second floor to see her friend, Samantha Butler. She was pretty sure that Sam would be very helpful in checking out the business activities of the Hanging Rock Farm.

CHAPTER ELEVEN

Dawn found Kit and Swifty headed northeast from Charleston in Swifty's big Ford pick-up truck. The sun rising in the east was visible through a hazy sky. They could already feel the heat beginning to rise.

As they drove north, the landscape became more heavily wooded and the trees seemed taller and thicker. To Kit it seemed like they were driving through a narrow band of prairie that was fenced in on both sides by the woods. Occasionally they passed through small towns. Some were prosperous looking, but most of them seemed to be engulfed with poverty. The buildings were often run-down and in need of paint. There were no signs of recent economic prosperity except for the occasional familiar fast food franchises.

They did not stop for lunch, subsisting instead on the candy bars and sodas they grabbed when they stopped to fill the truck up with gas and to hit the restroom. Kit tried the combination of an RC Cola and a Moon Pie, as part of trying to absorb some of the southern culture. One moon pie was all Kit could stand. He reverted to dark chocolate Hershey bars. Swifty did all the driving, and he controlled the radio stations. For Kit that meant a steady diet of country and western music. Kit was okay with country and western music, but by the time they finally got to the small town of Hanging Rock, he was hoping for the radio to somehow burn up and die.

Hanging Rock was a small town that had somehow built itself out of a crossroads and expanded the business district to an entire two blocks. It then had managed to shrink back to just four active buildings. Three of them stood on a corner of the cross roads that made up the center of town. There was a combination gas station and post office, a general store, and a tavern. An old church was located about two blocks away from the crossroads.

Kit studied the church. It was a small white frame building with a steeple. The back of the church and one side of it were occupied by a graveyard. A sign hanging in front of the church identified it as "Hanging Rock Church, established 1812." Kit reasoned that the church was probably there when his great-great grandfather, William Andrews came marching through Hanging Rock with the 102nd Illinois. Swifty pulled into the gas station to fill up the Ford's gas tank.

Swifty worked the gas pump while Kit went into the station to use the restroom. When he came back out, Swifty had finished filling up the truck. Kit winced when he looked at the total amount due of $55.00. Kit went inside and up to the grizzled old man who stood stooped over the battered wooden counter. The old man wore greasy cover-alls with a battered Atlanta Braves baseball cap. His hands were heavily calloused and stained with dirt and grease. His fingernails were caked with grease and what gray hair he had left on his head looked like it hadn't seen shampoo and water in over a month.

Kit handed the old man three twenties and waited for his change.

"Five bucks is yer change, sonny."

"Thank you, sir," said Kit. "Is there someplace around here we can get something to eat?"

"Yup. You'all kin git a san'wich over to the deli at Wilson's General Store or you can git a burger and fries at the King Kotton Bar across the street."

Kit thanked the old man and he and Swifty drove off the gas station lot and parked in the dirt lot next to the tavern across the street. The lot had once boasted some gravel, but now was mostly red clay. There were about half a dozen dusty pick-up trucks parked in the lot. Trash littered the perimeter of the property, and the tavern itself was a seedy looking one story wooden building that had obviously seen better days. Apparently appearances were not high on the local priority list.

Kit and Swifty walked around to the front of the tavern to the entrance. There was a roofed front porch that ran across the entire front of the tavern. On the porch were several beat-up round wooden tables with assorted types of wooden chairs. There was also a long wooden bench located next to the entrance. The wooden sign over the front porch proclaimed the location as the King Kotton Bar. Even the paint on the sign was peeling off. No one was seated on the front porch as Kit and Swifty went through the entrance. Inside the bar it was dark and cool, just like a million other such bars in small towns across America. The colored neon signs still announced Bud Light, Miller Light, and Coors were available. A smaller neon sign announced Dixie Beer was also on tap. A long bar ran across the back of the large room divided at the end of the building by a hallway that led to the back of the bar and the restrooms. There were several men setting at tables and the bar. All of them were dressed in work clothes and most were bearded. None of them were small men, but some were heavier than others. The bartender was a small older bald man wearing a loud Hawaiian shirt, cut-off jean shorts, and flip flops.

"What'll it be, gents?"

Kit and Swifty ordered two Budweisers and burgers and fries. The bartender wrote down the order and shoved it through a small opening behind the bar that Kit had not noticed at first. He then pulled two bottles out of a cooler behind the bar. After a short pause and no glasses had been produced, Kit and Swifty opened their beers and took their first swigs of the cold brew.

"It'll be a few minutes fore your burgers are done, gents. That'll be eleven seventy-five for the beers and the food."

Kit paid him and told the bartender that he and Swifty would be sitting out front on the porch. The bartender said he would send the food out to them. Kit had noticed that any conversation in the bar had ceased when they'd entered. He decided that by going outside they would allow the locals to resume their banter.

As he and Swifty went out the front door, he could hear conversation begin to start up even as the door was just closing.

They found a table and chairs that seemed to have the least amount of possible splinters or exposed nails and sat down on the shade of the porch to enjoy their beers.

They had just finished their beers, and the bartender came out with the food. He took their empties and returned shortly with two more bottles. Kit paid him, and he disappeared back inside. Across the street was a larger wooden building with a sign proclaiming it to be Wilson's General Store. Like the bar, it had a roofed front porch running across the entire length of the building. Against the entire front of the store was a series of wooden benches. All of the benches were empty, and there were no vehicles parked in front of the store.

Kit and Swifty had finished their meal and were savoring the last of their beers when the door of the general store opened and two teenage black girls came out and walked across the street to the bar. They tried not to stare at the two strangers in cowboy hats, but failed miserably. Swifty grinned at them, and they both giggled and then went through the door into the bar.

Kit drained his beer and waited for Swifty to finish his. He was trying to figure out what they should do next. Kit could see nothing in the town that looked like anything they could use as a resource in their search for the Confederate gold. He decided that he and Swifty would check out the general store and see if they could learn anything there. Kit was about to lean across the table and tell Swifty what he had in mind when the door to the bar burst open and one of the two black teen-age girls came running out without even looking at the two startled cowboys.

With the door open they heard laughter and screaming coming from inside the bar. Before Kit could even say shit, Swifty was out of his chair and heading back into the bar. Kit was quickly out of his chair and following in Swifty's wake.

Inside the bar the other young black girl was struggling in the grasp of a large man with curly red hair. Her white blouse was torn and clearly visible was the plain white bra encasing her small breasts. A half circle of men were standing around her, laughing and cheering on the red haired man holding her. By their chants, it was obvious that the man was named Red.

One of Red's hands was around the struggling girl's waist and the other was fondling her small breasts. She was screaming loudly and Red took his hand off of her breast to cover her mouth. She promptly bit him, and he let out a loud curse.

"The black bitch bit me!" he yelled incredulously as he looked at his now bleeding hand. The men surrounding him roared with laughter at his show of pain and embarrassment. Enraged, he roughly turned her in his arm and promptly backhanded her face, knocking her to the floor. He leaned forward to pick her up and pulled back his other hand to hit her again. Before he could deliver the blow, Swifty had stepped forward and grabbed his wrist and then pulled it down and backward, causing the man to go into an involuntary summersault and land in a heap on the floor. Kit was helping the black girl to her feet when things got ugly. The group of men closed in a circle around Swifty and Kit, cutting off their exit route to the front door. Red had gotten to his feet and joined the angry group of men.

"We got us a couple of nigger lovers, boys," he said.

"Nigger lovers ain't welcome here," said another.

Kit noticed that Swifty had assumed a fighter's stance, and he tried to cool things off.

"Hey, we're just here having a beer, and we're not looking for any trouble."

"Well, the nigger lovers are Yankee boys. Nothing I hate worse than Yankee nigger lovers," said a tall thin man with a terrible complexion.

Just then there was a loud bang. All of them turned to see the bartender holding a sawed off shotgun in one hand and a baseball bat in the other. He had just slammed the ball bat on the top of the bar. "There ain't gonna' be no fightin' in mah place. You boys got problems you settle them outside in the parking lot, not in mah bar." By the way he held the shotgun it was obvious he was not inexperienced and no one challenged him.

The young black girl took advantage of this sudden lull to dash out the front door of the bar.

"You heard the man," said Red. "Let's settle this outside." He then walked out the door followed by four of his friends including the tall, skinny guy.

Swifty turned to Kit and said "Let's go outside, partner."

Kit reached out and grabbed Swifty by the shoulder and brought him to a stop. "In case you didn't notice, partner, there are five of them and only two of us."

"Hell, Kit, they aint' gonna kill us. They're just gonna beat us up a little."

"Unbelievable!" thought Kit as he followed his friend out of the tavern and back to the parking lot where the five men awaited them.

Swifty walked straight up to Red, who was the biggest of the five men and said, "First thing we gotta settle is the rules."

"Rules? There aint' no rules in a bar fight," said an incredulous Red as he threw up his hands in disbelief.

Before he got the entire sentence out of his mouth, Swifty had kicked him expertly in the groin and Red went down like a pole-axed steer.

Swifty then pivoted on his right foot and his left cowboy boot clad foot shot out and nailed the tall skinny guy in the face, and he went down like a sack of potatoes.

Shocked by the suddenness of Swifty's attack, the other three men recovered in time to lunge forward. Two came at Swifty and one at Kit. The first man swung wildly at Swifty who ducked under the swing and grabbed the man by his groin in one hand and his shoulder with the other hand. By using the attacker's momentum, Swifty lifted him up over his head and then threw the man against a nearby pickup truck.

The second attacker managed to connect with a wild swing to the side of Swifty's head, and the force of the blow knocked him to the ground. Swifty quickly jumped up with a handful of dirt he had picked up from the parking lot and threw it in the face of his attacker, temporarily blinding him. Swifty then punched the man solidly in the stomach and knocked the wind out of him. With the man bent over in front of him, Swifty swung his elbow at the side of the man's head and knocked him to the ground.

Kit's lone attacker had failed to connect with a couple of wild punches before Kit grabbed his wrist and swung the man's arm behind him and forced him face down on the parking lot dirt. Before Kit could make another move, Swifty came up and kicked the prone man in the head with his cowboy boot.

Kit got to his feet and dusted himself off. He looked around and saw that three of their attackers were unconscious and the other two had fled.

"What the hell just happened?" asked Kit.

"We just made ourselves unpopular with the locals," replied Swifty.

They went around to the front of the bar and found the door guarded by the shotgun armed bartender.

"Where's the girl?" asked Swifty.

"Long gone," said the bartender. "You boys would be wise to do the same. Them boys has friends, but I must say I enjoyed watchin' the fight. It was better than watchin' one of them no holds barred fights on the TV."

Kit decided that going over to the general sore was probably a bad idea and getting out of town was probably a better option. Within minutes he and Swifty were looking at Hanging Rock in the rear view mirrors of the Ford.

They drove northeast out of Hanging Rock and after about twenty minutes Swifty pulled into a small gas station and convenience store.

"Why are we stopping here? We don't need gas," said Kit.

"I need some ice to put on my hand and my elbow," said Swifty. "I must be getting old."

"Because you hurt yourself?"

"No, dummy, because it took me so long to knock four of them down. Of course it's because I hurt myself. I want to make sure there's no swelling. I also want to look at the maps of the area that I got when I was in Columbia. I have some aerial maps that I marked as possible places to look for our landmarks. While we're here, we ought to take a look."

Swifty bought a small bag of ice and used some clean rags to hold the ice and tied some on his hand and some on his elbow. Then he drove until they came to a turn-out in the road and pulled the Ford under the shade of the large pine trees bordering the roadway. Swifty pulled the maps out of a compartment located behind the driver's seat and spread them out on the hood of the truck. After orienting the maps to true north, he began to study the detail on the maps.

"So what are we looking at here, partner?" said Kit.

"Give me a few minutes, Kit. This isn't something we can call up Triple A to find." After about five minutes, Swifty had eliminated all but two maps and motioned Kit over to his side.

"See this space here? I think this could be our meadow. It seems about the right size and is located about eight miles from Hanging Rock."

"Maybe, but I don't see any barn in the meadow."

"It could have burned down or been moved."

"I don't see any creek, nor do I see a stone bridge."

"The creek dried up and the bridge fell down."

"I can't seem to find any sign of a church or a graveyard next to it."

"Picky, picky, picky. The meadow is a starting place. Maybe all that other stuff is there, but we can't see it because of the trees that have grown up over the past 140 years."

"What else have you got, partner?"

"Well, I have this map that has a creek, but a much smaller meadow."

"Is there a barn, a stone bridge, or a church?"

"Nope, but there is a group of buildings and a parking lot."

"Let me see that aerial photo map."

Kit pulled the map up close to his eyes, but that was not much help. He still couldn't make out enough details to be sure what he was looking at.

"You wouldn't have a magnifying glass stowed back in that gear compartment somewhere would you?"

"Do I look like Sherlock Holmes? What the hell would I be doing with a magnifying glass?"

"Well you could always use it to start a fire if you ran out of matches."

"I use a windproof butane light, you dolt. Only big Dave Carlson still uses matches. I once saw him strike one on the whiskers of his face. Man that guy is tough."

"You are so full of crap, Swifty. Don't you ever tell the truth?"

"I'm pretty sure I have almost always told you some version of the truth."

"That is so reassuring."

"Hey, the truth is a relative thing. Sometimes I adjust it slightly to fit the audience and the moment."

"Well, I think we need to check out these two locations and see what they look like up close and personal."

"Sounds like a plan to me. Let's check out the one with the creek first. It looks like it's the closest to where we are."

"Ok, let's mount up."

"Mount up? You've seen way too many John Wayne movies."

"Just shut up and drive, Swifty."

CHAPTER TWELVE

Samantha got off the elevator on the lower level of the Bank of South Carolina building in Charleston. She strode purposely to the office of Ted Silverton, the Senior Vice President in charge of the IT department of the bank.

"Well, Samantha, what brings you down to the dungeon level of the bank," Ted said as he rose to greet her, his hand extended.

Samantha took his hand in a brief, but firm handshake. "Actually I'm here to get some information, Ted."

"Well, you came to the right place, Sam. Information is what we do. What kind of information do you need?"

"I'm looking for a historical activity report on all of the accounts under the name of Hanging Rock Farm and all of the related accounts as well."

"That's a pretty tall order. As I recall, they're a pretty large customer with some really active accounts."

"I'm sure it is, but I need it as soon as you can put it together."

"How far back do you want us to go?"

"I would like at least five years. Is that possible?"

"Yes, we can easily go back at least seven years."

"Great, make it seven years. How soon can you get me the report?"

"Since you want it as soon as possible, I think we can have it to you by about noon tomorrow. Is that soon enough?"

"Noon tomorrow would be great. Thank you, Ted. I really appreciate this."

"Can I ask what this is about?"

"Sorry, Ted. This is an internal investigation that may turn out to mean nothing, or it could mean a lot. Either way I can't say anything about it."

"I understand, Sam. I'll make sure you get it tomorrow."

Before Sam had returned to her office in the bank, Ted had turned the research job over to one of his vice-presidents, Marty Snyder.

After Ted left his office, Marty filled out the necessary research request forms and gave it to his assistant to be processed. Then he closed his office door, unlocked his desk drawer, and pulled out a small notebook. After consulting the notebook, he dialed a number on his cell phone and after giving an oral password, he proceeded to leave what he was sure was an important message about the research being done on the Hanging Rock Farm accounts.

Lee Regret hung up his cell phone. The call from his office at the warehouse was not what he was expecting. He and his sister had worked very hard to provide an excellent cover for their smuggling of counterfeit cigarettes. The past five years had made them very wealthy. Regret had used his alleged investment losses in the Cayman Islands REIT as losses against his increased income.

He had also hidden a good deal of the profits and retained them in cash that was hidden in places known only to him and to his sister. Lee knew there was always the possibility that someone might become suspicious of their wealth and success. Lee had taken steps to provide himself with a tripwire, so he would have advance notice of any such investigation. Marty Snyder at the bank was just one of several people he had on his secret payroll. Now that the tripwire had been sprung, he needed to decide what to do about it.

He knew Samantha Butler was an ex-cop from Atlanta. He wondered why she would be looking at his company's accounts. He had never actually even met her. He knew his sister knew Butler and wondered if something had happened with Wendy that had caused Butler to get suspicious of them. He found his sister on speed dial and hit the number on his cell phone. "Sis, this is Lee."

"Lee, what's up?"

"One of our tripwires went off this morning. We seem to have a problem."

"What happened?"

"Samantha Butler at the bank is doing an investigation on us and is having our accounts researched."

"Why?"

"That's what I was going to ask you, dear. You're the one who knows her. Did something happen between the two of you?"

"No. Nothing I can think of."

"What about that other gal banker, Ellie Lynn Main. Did you say something to her?"

"I did talk to her briefly at the DAR auction, but it was just social chit-chat. She was with some cowboy I've never seen before."

"Somebody said something or somebody heard something or something happened to make Butler suspicious of us."

"I have no idea what that could be."

"Neither do I."

"What are we going to do about it?"

"You are going to do nothing. I'm going to set a trap and if this investigation gets too close, then Butler is going to have an unfortunate accident and disappear."

"Nothing would make me happier. I never did care for her or the prissy Ellie Lynn. If both of them were to disappear, it would make Charleston a better place. Keep me posted, Lee."

"I will, Sis."

Lee hung up his phone and turned his Range Rover in the direction of his warehouse. He had plans to make and traps to set.

CHAPTER THIRTEEN

Sam came back to Ellie Lynn's office and closed the door behind her. She strode across the office and seated herself in one of the armchairs in front of Ellie Lynn's desk.

"Well the train is in motion and I hope we are doing the right thing, Ellie Lynn."

"I'm sure we are, Sam. We'll either find something or we'll find nothing. We have reason to believe that something unusual or illegal might be going on that is connected to the Regret's business operation at Hanging Rock Farm. By the letter of the law we are required to investigate and to report our finding to the bank board and the federal regulators if we should turn up anything suspicious. You know the drill."

"Yes, I do, Ellie Lynn. But I like my job and I'm no stranger to politics and all that they entail when you piss off a very good customer of the bank."

"No one outside the bank knows what we're doing and unless we find something sinister, this whole investigation will wind up in the dumpster and disappear into a landfill somewhere in South Carolina."

"We should have the data reports by noon tomorrow and maybe then we can put this thing to rest."

"Or maybe not."

"God, you're an eager beaver. Just remember that old saying, be careful what you wish for."

"I'm just wishing for the truth. Something about the Regrets smells bad. I never did like that woman, and I'm beginning to figure out why. Should we notify the police about this?"

"About what? We've no proof of anything they've done wrong, let alone a crime. Let's get some facts before we get ahead of ourselves. I'd like to keep my job, and creating unnecessary trouble for a good customer of the bank is politically a pretty unhealthy idea. Just cool it until we have some real facts."

Ellie Ann nodded her agreement, and Sam left for her own office and a waiting pile of work.

CHAPTER FOURTEEN

Kit and Swifty had been following a gravel road for about eight miles when they stopped to check their position against the map and aerial photos. Kit parked the truck under the shade of a large pine tree and spread the map and aerial photos on the hood of the truck. Swifty then pulled out a small GPS unit and turned on the power. He waited a few minutes while the small unit connected with three satellites and confirmed their location. Then he used the small controls to scroll down the commands shown at the bottom of the small lighted display. Finally, he obtained the exact longitude and latitude of their location and compared it to the map in front of him.

"Looks to me like we're about ten miles south of where we need to be," said Swifty.

"Why don't we go a little farther on this road and then turn north at the first good looking crossroads we come to?"

"It's worth a shot. Let's go."

They both got in the truck and Swifty fired up the engine. They continued to head west on the same road. The road was narrow and curved often, so they were unable to see very far ahead. The tall, dark pine forest came right up to the side of the road and made it almost seem like a dark tunnel. They had just rounded a curve when Swifty jammed on the brakes to bring the Ford to a sudden halt. In front of them was a small, battered sign that declared "Bridge Out!"

They both exited the truck and walked forward on the road for about forty yards. There they found the remnants of an old wooden bridge. A small, but fairly deep and swiftly flowing creek surged about eight feet below them.

"Well, we ain't going to get far going this way," said Swifty."

Kit didn't bother to respond. He spun on his heel and headed back to the truck.

After almost two hours of backtracking, they finally turned onto a blacktop road that was heading west. Swifty pulled the Ford over to the side of the road and got out to take a GPS reading. He jumped back into the cab and started the engine. "This should be about right, partner. We ought to get there in about fifteen minutes."

Kit took the GPS unit and checked the reading with the map he held and nodded in agreement. The road was fairly new and much wider than the country roads they had been traveling on. Kit noticed that even the painted stripes on the road were new and the trees had been cut back so there was about fifteen yards between the shoulder of the road and the beginning of the forest that bordered the road. After about five miles, they saw a road sign painted brown with white lettering. "Andrew Jackson State park, 10 Miles."

"Did you see anything about a state park on that map?" asked Swifty.

"Nope. The map shows no sign of a park."

"They must have been asleep when they did South Carolina, unless that sign we just saw is some kind of a joke."

"It looked like the real deal to me."

"Well, we'll find out in about ten minutes."

Before ten minutes had passed, they came to a modern steel and concrete bridge that spanned the same creek they had been stopped by about two hours before. After they crossed the bridge, Swifty pulled the truck over to the side of the road and shut off the engine. He and Kit got out and went to the back of the truck where Swifty pulled out a large black duffel bag. He zipped open the bag and withdrew two H&K 45 caliber pistols, the silencers for them, and four magazines of full metal jacket hollow point ammunition. Swifty pulled out two hard plastic paddle holsters and handed one to Kit. Kit slipped on the holster and put the silencer in his jacket pocket.

Kit then loaded the pistol with a magazine and pulled back the slide to chamber a round. He put the gun on safety and placed it in the holster on his right side. He looked up to see that Swifty had done the same.

When they climbed back into the cab of the truck, Swifty put the keys in the ignition and turned to Kit. "You ready to rock and roll?"

"I was born ready," replied Kit.

They pulled back onto the road and picked up speed. Very shortly they saw a large sign proclaiming they were entering the Andrew Jackson State Park. They came to a small booth that was occupied by a park ranger in uniform. She was a middle aged black woman with a toothy smile.

"Welcome to Andrew Jackson State Park, gentlemen. Admission is five dollars a person or ten dollars for a car load. Which will it be?"

"Well, ma'am, it seems like heads it's ten bucks and tails it's still ten bucks so I guess it's ten bucks," said Swifty as he handed her a ten dollar bill.

The ranger handed Swifty a receipt and a brochure and map of the park.

Swifty thanked the ranger and pulled ahead to a fairly large parking lot that was almost empty. The asphalt parking lot was ringed with a split rail fence. On one side it was bordered by tall pine trees that seemed to signify the end of the continuous forest that had stretched for miles to the south. Beyond the parking lot, was a large meadow that seemed to extend for almost a mile. About fifty yards into the meadow stood what appeared to be a small village made up of old log structures.

"What the heck is his?" said Swifty.

Kit pulled out the brochure and after a couple of minutes he looked up and said, "It's a collection of historic buildings that have been moved here to the park to preserve them. They were taken down at different locations around the state and brought here and reassembled and repaired so that the citizens of the South Carolina could enjoy them for years to come."

"You sound like the Chamber of Commerce."

"Hey, I'm just quoting from the brochure, genius."

"Well, we're looking for a barn that has been here for over 140 years, not a bunch of crappy old log buildings that came here from somewhere else."

"Well, we have another site to take a look at."

"Was that the place that didn't have a creek?"

"That's the one. For all we know the creek could have dried up or been re-directed somewhere else. I think it's still worth a look."

"The list of suspects is getting pretty shallow. We have to check it out, partner."

"Let's check the maps and see where we have to go to get there."

They returned to the truck and again spread out the map and the aerial maps on the hood. A quick check confirmed that they were about twenty-five miles from the site.

"The quickest route seems to have a lot of twists and turns. Doesn't this state believe in any straight roads?" asked Swifty.

"You're right. I think this is going to take longer than twenty-five minutes. It looks a lot like driving in the mountains."

"We ain't going to get there while we stand here jawing. Let's go while we still have some daylight left."

They climbed in the Ford and headed back out to the entrance and the ranger booth. As they passed on the other side of the booth, Kit noticed a box set up to collect brochures from visitors leaving the park so they could recycle the brochures to future visitors. For some reason that he could not identify at the time, Kit elected to keep the brochure and map in his coat pocket.

With Swifty driving and Kit serving as navigator, they began the arduous task of tracing their designated route through the country roads of South Carolina.

Kit noticed the tall pine forest that bordered the roads did a good job of keeping the late afternoon sun hidden and made it seem even darker on the road than it actually was. Swifty had been right. They needed to hurry or they would lose the daylight they needed to check out the next meadow site.

The big Ford truck seemed to handle like a sports car with Swifty at the wheel. They roared around tight blind corners and Kit could feel the tires digging into the dirt and gravel for traction as the truck slid through some tight turns before the tires grabbed sufficient traction to propel them forward once again. Kit found himself gripping the armrest so hard he was sure he would leave his fingerprints imbedded in the plastic.

With each turn he was bracing his body with his handhold and his feet. Even then he felt his body slipping from its position in his seat. Finally they hit a semblance of a straight stretch of road and Swifty promptly floored the accelerator. The big Ford engine roared, and the truck surged ahead with a sudden increase in speed. In no time they were at the end of the straight road, and Swifty was downshifting as the truck's engine whined in protest while they hurtled through yet another tight turn. The light continued to fade on the road as the sun became hidden behind the pine tree wall they raced along side.

"We sure as hell aren't going to sneak up on anyone," said Kit.

"What do you mean?"

"We've got a rooster tail trail of dust behind us that must be about thirty feet high. An eighty year old man could see us coming."

"Who cares. We're making great time."

"Define making great time."

"We're almost there. Give me another five minutes, and we'll have arrived."

Swifty was better than his word. In less than three minutes the truck slammed to a stop at the edge of an asphalt road. It took another three minutes for the dust trail to completely pass them by and settle down so they could see what was in front of them. Less than fifty yards to their left, the road entered a large clearing.

"That's got to be it." said Swifty.

"Not much light left. Let's see what we can see before we lose the sun."

Swifty pulled the Ford into the clearing and they found themselves in the middle of a large meadow. The meadow covered about eighty acres and was entirely devoid of any trees or brush. They drove the length of the road through the meadow and saw nothing except for some dried up cow pies.

"If this is a historical site, somebody should put up some kind of a sign."

"Our location could be an undiscovered historical site, Swifty. Those types of sites don't have any signs."

"Well, they should."

Kit pointed at the east end of the meadow. "That part looks a little higher. If there had been a barn there like the one my great-great grandfather described, it would have been higher than the rest of the meadow."

Swifty drove the truck to the middle of the beginning of the higher ground and parked it. They both got out and decided to walk the area in grids. They walked side by side from the front to the back of the meadow. Then they each turned to the outside of the high ground and walked back toward the Ford.

They walked slowly back to the truck scanning the ground as they continued to cross the area on foot. After about twenty minutes of walking in grids they met back at the truck. They had found nothing to indicate that there had ever been anything there but the meadow.

"Rats."

"Rats? Where?"

"I don't mean rat rats. I mean rats as in crap."

"You city boys are so complicated."

"Better to be complicated than simple."

"Who are you calling simple?"

"The same honyock who damn near got us killed driving here like he was doing the Indy 500 on a dirt road in the woods."

"I'll have you know that was all skill."

"Seemed a lot more like luck than skill to me."

"Well, partner, I've always been lucky. It's my nature."

"If you're so lucky why haven't we found anything here?"

"Well, I actually have found something here. Look alive, cowboy."

Swifty came to a half stance and backhanded a flat round object, sending it sailing towards Kit. The object suddenly came apart right in front of Kit and half of it went to the right of him and half of it went to the left.

Kit leaned over to see a piece of dried up cow pie slightly hidden in the tall grass.

"Very funny."

"You have to admit it is something."

"So, how about this." Kit rose up from the grass with a newly found pie in his hand and he sent it sailing towards Swifty.

"You realize this means war, cowboy!"

"Hah. Defend yourself, cowgirl."

"Cowgirl?"

"You throw like one."

"Oh, yeah. Try dodging this, girlyboy."

For the next five minutes the air was full of dried up cow pies and two scrambling cowboys who were laughing hysterically while they tried to nail each other with their flat natural saucer shaped missiles. Each of them kept on the run, changing directions as they tried to launch their own missiles while attempting to duck from the airborne missiles of the other. Each of them would eventually score a hit on the other which would be accompanied by a great deal of whooping and laughter. Finally they ended up lying flat on their backs in the tall grass, both of them totally exhausted.

"Was it good for you, cowboy?"

"I've had better, but I think I needed that."

"We both did."

"I don't understand it. According to the aerial photos we looked at one of these two sites almost has to be what we're looking for."

"Well there's nothing here, and it doesn't look like there ever has been anything here."

"We must be missing something. Can there be another site, and we didn't see it on the aerial photos?"

"I think not. It's getting dark, and we should find a place to put up for the night. We can try looking at those photos again in the morning."

They piled into the Ford and Swifty headed back over the road they had come, but at a much slower speed.

CHAPTER FIFTEEN

Sam returned from the employee break room with a fresh cup of coffee. As she set the cup on her desk and sat down in her chair, she noticed a large pile of paper filling her in-box. She took a sip of the coffee and then lifted the pile of papers onto the top of her desk. On top of the pile was a handwritten note from Ted Silverton.

"I hope this is what you wanted. Good luck. Ted"

Sam went through the pile of printouts and began sorting them into piles she felt would represent a good search base. Then she pulled out a yellow legal pad and a mechanical pencil and began reading and taking notes.

After about three hours, numerous cups of coffee, and most of the yellow legal pad, Sam put down the mechanical pencil and rubbed her eyes. On the right side of her desk was a large pile of computer printouts and on the left side was a smaller pile of printouts that were neatly stacked.

Sam picked up her phone and called Ellie Lynn's extension and got her voice mail. Sam left her a message to come down to her office and then she headed to the ladies room. When she returned to her office, Ellie Lynn was sitting at her desk going over the neatly stacked pile of printouts.

"How did you know that was the right pile, Miss Smarty Pants?"

"Duh. Let's see. A messy pile of paper and a neat pile of paper. Which one is important?"

"O.K. So I'm a little bit of a neatnik."

"A little bit! That's like calling Madonna a little bit sexy."

"So sue me. Everyone else has."

"I'll skip the lawsuit. What did you find in all this computer crap?"

"You want the Cliff Notes or the long version?"

"Cliff Notes, please."

Sam picked up her yellow legal pad and began to read.

"These are the records of the depository and loan accounts of Hanging Rock Farm and also of Lee Regret, Wendy Regret, and Harlo Clay."

What did you learn?"

"Well, apparently Lee and Wendy inherited their great-great grandfather's old rice plantation and turned it into a hay and grain farm. They had loans with the bank and struggled to make it until about five years ago."

"What happened then?"

"I'm not sure, but some sort of pixie dust seems to have been spread on all of them."

"Pixie dust?"

"They call it cash in some countries, but I prefer pixie dust."

"Where did they get cash?"

"I don't think they got it the old fashioned way."

"The old fashioned way?"

"You know, hard work."

"So where did the cash come from?"

"I can't tell yet, but I plan to find out. I'd bet you a month's pay it's not legal."

"How much cash are we talking about?"

"Somehow, in the past five years they have managed to double their cash deposits each year. And they also managed to keep their expenses the same for the entire five years."

"So how do we find out how they did it?"

"We find out how they are doing it now. My guess is that nothing has changed. I think I know a way we can find out just how they are doing it." With that Samantha reached for her cell phone and searched for a name and a phone number. When she was satisfied, she picked up the phone and dialed.

CHAPTER SIXTEEN

Swifty had finally found a paved road and using the GPS, Kit had guided him back to Hanging Rock.

"So explain to me why we are returning to the scene of the crime?" asked Swifty.

"There was no crime. I doubt if five good old southern boys want to admit they got their asses kicked by two Yankees. My guess is nobody saw anything. Nobody heard anything and nobody said anything."

"God, I hate optimists."

"Either way, we need to make sure we have no problems with the law. We've done nothing wrong and all we did was step in to protect an innocent girl and then defend ourselves."

"Man, this is the South. She was a black girl and we're two Yankee cowboys from Wyoming. They'd lock us up and throw away the key."

"You have been watching too many old movies again. I suppose you think some overweight deputy with big sunglasses is going to pull us over and say something like "You boys in a heap of trouble.""

"Something like that. You know, like the cop car behind us with the flashing lights."

Kit turned in his seat to look behind them while Swifty slowed down the truck and pulled off to the side of the road. Sure enough, there was a marked police car with its lights flashing right behind them. Kit swallowed hard and said, "Oh shit."

Swifty turned off the motor and pulled down the sunshade where he kept his registration and insurance card for the truck. By the time he was done, the deputy sheriff had emerged from the parked police car. He was about six feet tall and he was about fifty pounds overweight. He wore a light tan uniform with a brown straw cowboy hat. The shirt of his uniform was soaked with sweat and he had small mean looking eyes. The deputy had apparently forgotten to shave that morning, which gave him a slightly intimidating look. An odor from the deputy permeated the truck as soon as he stuck his head in the open truck window giving rise to the speculation that the deputy might have an aversion to deodorant. He also wore leather driving gloves and large reflective sun glasses.

"Put your hands in your lap where he can see them," whispered Swifty.

"Morning boys," said the deputy as he leaned into the open window on the driver's side of the truck. "Kin I see your license and registration?"

Swifty produced the registration and insurance cards and then went to pull his wallet from his right hind pocket.

The deputy stepped back from the window with a fearful look on his face and said, "What the sam hill are you doin'?"

Swifty replied that he was reaching for his wallet to produce his driver's license.

"O.K., but do it very slowly and both of you keep your hands where I kin see them."

"Certainly officer," replied Swifty. He slowly pulled out his wallet and removed his driver's license, handing all three items to the deputy.

"You boys stay right here till I git back."

"Certainly officer," replied Swifty.

The deputy then retreated back to his patrol car and picked up his radio microphone.

"What's he doing?" asked Kit.

"He's checking me and the truck for any wants or warrants."

"Do we have a problem?"

"Not with me or the truck. But I'll bet you five bucks he comes back and says, you in a heap of trouble, boys."

Kit had to stifle a laugh.

"Just let me handle this," said Swifty.

After about five minutes the deputy returned to the driver's side of the truck and handed the documents back to Swifty.

"Just what are a couple of cowboys from Wyoming doin' in this part of South Carolina?" he asked.

"We're just doing a little sight seeing, officer."

"You boys on vacation?"

"Why yes, officer. We're doing some visiting of historical sites while we're here," answered Swifty.

"Is this your first time in South Carolina."

"Yes, sir, it is."

"Well, let me give you a little advice, son. This here is the South and we like things nice and peaceful. This morning I got a call from Mabel Lovejoy in Hanging Rock. Seems like there was this fist fight in the parking lot of the King Cotton Bar about eleven this morning. Miss Lovejoy claims two guys in cowboy hats beat the crap out of five local boys and then left in a black Ford pickup truck with Wyoming license plates. A truck kind of like this one you got."

"What's that got to do with us, officer?" said Swifty.

"Well, none of them alleged five victims filed any claims, so officially nothin'. I just don't like getting' calls from citizens like Miss Lovejoy about no disturbin' of the peace on my shift. You boys get my drift?"

"I believe we do, sir," replied Swifty.

"If I was you boys, I'd do my sightseeing in some other state. I hear tell Georgia is nice this time of year. I don't want to see you boys around here again. We clear on that?"

"Yes, sir," responded both Swifty and Kit at the same time.

"Well good. You'all have a nice day."

With that the deputy spun on his heel and went back to his patrol car. A few minutes later the patrol car pulled out and sped past their parked truck.

"What the hell was that?" asked Kit.

"That was a warning, my friend. Mr. Deputy was letting us know he considers us unwelcome in his county and was trying to scare us into getting the hell out of here."

"So are we sufficiently scared?"

"No, but he is."

"He sure didn't look scared to me."

"You can bet he knows who the five jaspers are who we beat up in the parking lot. He might not be real bright, but he knows that if two guys he doesn't know beat the crap out of five he does know then he wants no part of us and hopes we'll just leave."

"So what do we do?"

"We do what we intended to do. We go to Hanging Rock and get some lunch. Then we go back to Charleston and see what the ladies have found out about the Regrets. I get a feeling we might have more to worry about with them than some overweight deputy sheriff. By the way, you owe me five bucks."

"I owe you five bucks for what?"

"The deputy forgot to say you boys are in a heap of trouble. Pay me."

*   *   *

Harlo Clay was on the phone to his cousin Lee trying to explain why two deliveries had been delayed. "Look, Lee, I can't help it if five of my drivers decided to get into a bar room fight with a room full of cowboy types. Two of them are at the doc's and the other three are barely fit to drive."

Harlo listened to the loud and angry response from his cousin by holding the phone away from his ear. Finally he said, "Yes sir," and hung up. He was disgusted. He hated to get yelled at by his cousin and especially when he had no defense. He had just been yelled at by his cousins for creating a scene at the DAR charity auction. Harlo hadn't wanted to go in the first place, and he was still pissed because some cowboy he had never seen had sucker punched him.

Harlo was also smart enough to know when to shut up. He could afford to be patient. He often disliked his cousin Lee and his sister for their highbrow ways, but he always reminded himself of how good he had it and that usually calmed him down. He knew that Lee and his sister were the brains in the outfit and he was the muscle. That was his job and he really liked his job. Harlo was one of those individuals who enjoyed inflicting pain on others. He took pleasure in the punishment he could inflict. In the past five years Harlo had been in charge of the farm, he had become even more and more vicious. Harlo hated that he was the poor cousin and he took his anger out on others.

Harlo was an impressive physical specimen. He lifted weights every day in the small gym he had built in the old stable he had converted into his personal quarters. The main floor contained his one bedroom living space and the basement contained his gym, his shop, and his special hobby room. His hobby room was built to entertain "guests." Occasionally Harlo would hire some derelict to work at the farm and after they had done something to displease him, he took them to the hobby room. The room was windowless except for one entire wall that was a mirror. Actually it was a one way mirror window with a viewing room on the other side. The walls were poured concrete and the only way in and out of the room was through two heavy steel doors.

The room was equipped with state of the art digital video recording equipment and what could only be described as primitive torture devices. In addition to the occasional derelict, the room had hosted some small town prostitutes Harlo had picked up and the occasional runway teenage girl. All of them had ended up in the hog pen located at the backside of the farm. Harlo knew that legend had it that the pen had been there since before the Civil War and that his ancestors had also used it to dispose of a body or two. There was never any proof of the claim, so it was just a legend. For Harlo it was a good working arrangement. The hogs got additional meals and Harlo got rid of any evidence of his activities.

Harlo was soon back on the phone trying to find some backup drivers to take the deliveries out. He still couldn't figure out what really happened to his five drivers in Hanging Rock. He'd called the bartender at the King Cotton Bar and gotten no information. Willy Baugh, the bartender, had told him that the five drivers had gotten into an argument with some cowboy types and he ordered all of them out to the parking lot to finish their argument. Baugh didn't follow them out and said he didn't bother to watch out the window of the bar to see the fight so he didn't know any details.

Harlo didn't believe Willy. He knew Willy wouldn't have missed a chance to see a fight like that. Still this was probably Willy's way of staying neutral. Harlo didn't push Willy because he knew Willy would go running to Sheriff Horton and the last thing Harlo wanted was any confrontation with the law. Horton was an older guy and pretty smart. Harlo and his cousins didn't need him snooping around their affairs or the Hanging Rock Farm.

After getting two hands to agree to be drivers for a day, Harlo got in his pickup truck and headed to Hanging Rock. He had a shipment of porno DVD's due and would stop in at the post office before stopping in at the King Cotton Bar for a beer and a chance to see if Willy might add any further details to his story.

CHAPTER
SEVENTEEN

Chester Luck had spent about three hours setting up his equipment, and now he stepped back to admire his work and make sure that he had not forgotten anything. He had obtained a small space in an old warehouse on the second floor. Most of the warehouse was empty and run-down, a victim of the closing of the naval base in Charleston. The market had recently improved and the warehouse was scheduled to be refurbished by a new buyer. In the interim, Chester had gotten the watchman to let him use the space for thirty days for a cash payment the owner of the building would never know about.

His video equipment was powered by electricity in the warehouse, but backed up by a battery system. The equipment was state of the art and was motion activated. A time clock in the lower right hand corner of the picture showed the date and time. The digital image was immediately stored on a DVD.

After checking everything again with a final test, Chester closed and locked the door to the space with his own personal padlock. He also powdered the door knob and the surrounding frame with a dust that was invisible to the naked eye so he would be able to check to see if anyone had tried to enter or tamper with the room. In his business, a man couldn't be too careful.

Luck emerged into the warm damp air of the harbor and stopped at the base of the warehouse, right below where he knew his equipment waited for motion to activate it. The equipment would record any and all activity at the warehouse across the street at 313 Concord Street in Charleston. He knew the owners of the warehouse were the Regrets, but that meant nothing to him. He was being well paid for his work and would return every third night to check his equipment and switch DVD's. Luck whistled as he walked to his car. He checked his watch. He could get home in time to watch the last few innings of the Braves game in Denver.

*   *   *

Kit waited in the lobby of the hotel for Swifty. When they were doing most things, Swifty was as alert as Kit had ever seen anyone, but when it came to getting up in the morning, Swifty was slower than molasses in January. While Kit waited, he took a seat near the entrance to the hotel where he could see the bank of elevators clearly. Kit studied the rest of the hotel main lobby. To his left was the bar which ran along the side wall of the hotel before ending next to the reception desk. Beyond the reception desk was the bank of elevators. To his right was the dining area, a restaurant called "225". There were numerous tables occupied by people enjoying their breakfast on a bright sunny morning in Charleston. Kit's people watching session was ended abruptly by a voice from his past.

"What the hell is Carson Andrews doing in that ridiculous cowboy getup?"

Startled, Kit looked up at the entrance of the hotel to see a tall thin handsome man with jet black hair and tanned skin. He was dressed expensively in a linen suit with Gucci loafers and a belt to match. He had a brilliant smile filled with perfect white teeth. His dark brown eyes sparkled with mischief.

"Good god! Is that you Billy?" said Kit.

"Who the hell else would it be, you idiot."

Kit rose and the two men hugged as only two old friends can. Billy broke the hug, stepped back and said "Is the circus in town? Does your mama know how you're dressed?"

Kit grinned and said, "Carson Andrews, Kemmerer, Wyoming, at your service, sir."

"Wyoming! How the hell did you wind up in Wyoming?"

"It's a long story, but since you asked, what's a smooth operator like you doing in Charleston?"

"Well Carson, I'm taking a little vacation from the arduous work of my profession."

"Arduous work! That'll be the day. The Billy K I know always did the supervising, while he had the others doing the manual work."

Billy joined Kit at his table and ordered a cup of coffee. While they waited, Kit brought Billy up to date on how he wound up in Wyoming and what he was doing in Charleston. Carson and Billy had gone to high school together in Kankakee, and also to college at Eastern Illinois University where they had been roommates and fraternity brothers. They had not seen each other since graduation from college.

Billy smiled at Kit when he had finished with his account of how he had ended up in South Carolina. "And I thought I led an interesting life. That's awful close to a tall tale if I ever heard one, Carson."

"Every word is the truth, Billy."

"Coming from you, I know that's true. But it's hard to believe. You need any help with this deal?"

"It's starting to look like I could use all the help I can get."

"Well, my social calendar is sort of blank at the present and helping you just might help me."

"What do you mean by that?"

Billy then brought Kit up to date on what had happened to him since college. After Billy graduated, he enlisted in the Army, winding up in military intelligence. He worked on a loaned basis to the CIA and NSA. Needless to day he did a lot of traveling and much of what he did exists only in sealed records marked "Top Secret" filed away somewhere in the depths of the Pentagon.

"So about all you can tell me is that you worked for the government?"

"Actually I can tell you anything you'd care to hear about. I'm sort of out of favor with the government at this time."

"Why is that?"

"I was sent on a mission and I was misled as to what I as supposed to do and lied to about the identity of the target."

"Target?"

"Yeah, target. I spent three years being a government assassin. Finally I got sick of the lies, the misleading crap, and the politics. I was very good at my work, so I had a little trouble "resigning" from my job. I finally settled things so that all I have to do is report my whereabouts and activities to the FBI on an annual basis."

"The FBI?"

"They take a dim view of a professional assassin running around without some sort of supervision."

"So they assign you a supervisor?"

"No, Carson. They put a tail on me twenty-four hours a day. They change them regularly, but I always spot them. I left my last tail stuck in an elevator in Atlanta."

"So they don't know you're here in Charleston?"

"They have no idea where I am and that's fine with me. I got sick of looking over my shoulder and a few bus trips later, here I am. I must say that seeing you sitting here was a shock."

"No more than seeing you walk in the hotel door!"

"Do you need any help in this missing treasure mystery?"

"I just might. As soon as he rolls out of bed, I'll introduce you to my partner, Swifty Olson."

"With a name like Swifty he sounds like my kind of guy."

"He is our kind of guy. Very much the cowboy, but he is ex-Delta Force and absolutely the guy you want with you when serious trouble breaks out."

"I can't wait to meet him."

"So what line of work are you in now?"

"I'm more or less a professional gambler."

"Gambler?"

"Yep. I specialize in card games. You know like poker and blackjack."

"You can make a living at that?"

"Absolutely. You'd be surprised at how well one can do. I know the FBI is surprised. The bastards have had the IRS audit me for the last three straight years. They found nothing."

"So where do you hang your hat now?"

"I have a condo in Hawaii, and I still have my parent's house in Kankakee."

"Your parent's house?"

"They were both killed in a hotel fire in California about five years ago."

"I'm sorry to hear that."

"Thank you. It was quick and they didn't suffer. At least that's something. I just couldn't bring myself to sell the house and I have a management company look after it. I don't think I've been in it for at least two years."

At that moment they were interrupted by the entrance of Swifty Olson. He was dressed in his standard uniform of blue jeans, denim shirt, polished cowboy boots and a cream colored Stetson cowboy hat. He looked like he had spent the past hour getting ready when in fact Kit knew he hadn't been out of bed for more than fifteen minutes. Swifty's brown curly hair just peeked out from under his Stetson.

Kit made the introductions and watched as his two friends sized each other up like a couple of male jungle cats.

Finally Billy K. broke the silence. "Anybody stupid enough to be a friend of Andrews is O.K. in my book."

"I couldn't agree more. How did you stand it growing up with this moron?"

"It was a chore, but I struggled through it and did the best I could with what I had to work with, which wasn't much."

Both Swifty and Billy K broke into laughter.

"Just out of curiosity, why do they call you Billy K?"

"I'm Polish. My last name is rather hard to pronounce or spell. I've been Billy K since I was in first grade with Carson."

The three of them walked down East Bay Street to a small café and sat down to a mixed breakfast. Kit had orange juice and Eggs Benedict, Billy K had coffee and an English muffin, and Swifty had coffee, eggs, sausage, potatoes, and a cinnamon roll.

Kit caught Billy staring at the enormous collection of food on Swifty's plate. "I know, you can almost hear his arteries filling in."

Billy grinned and Swifty paid no attention to either of his companions and continued his attack on the mound of food in front of him.

After answering more of Billy's questions, Kit told him that basically they were stumped on how to find the site of the barn and the buried treasure.

"What have you used so far?" asked Billy.

"We've used satellite photos, maps, tax records and have come up empty."

"Usually something like this is right in front of you, but you can't see it because it looks like something else."

"Even if this thing were disguised to look like a whorehouse, I could still find a damn barn that was like the one described in he journal," said Swifty.

"What if the barn burned down? What if it was moved? What if it was built on to and looked totally different today?" said Billy.

"Anything is possible," said Kit.

"Do you have a list of the names of the five Confederates who stole the gold and killed their friends?" asked Billy.

"Of course we do. Why do you ask?" responded Kit.

"It just occurred to me that if I were burying stolen gold in a barn, I just might bury it in a barn I owned," replied Billy.

"This guy is smarter than he looks," said Swifty.

"We should have thought of that," admitted Kit.

"I suggest that you boys go to the county seat where this Hanging Rock is located and do a little search on the names of the five rebel soldiers," said Billy.

"How do we do a title search?" asked Kit.

"Let's go up to your hotel room, and I'll show you how to do a title search by name and maybe even find out what happened to each of the five survivors. Could be the land is in the name of one or some of their heirs."

Kit tossed down some money to cover the check for their breakfasts and followed Swifty and Billy out the door and back to the hotel.

CHAPTER EIGHTEEN

Ellie Lynn saw she had an e-mail from Sam and quickly pulled it up to read. She grinned as she read the message. Sam had some news and wanted to have lunch at 11:30. Ellie Lynn looked at her watch. It was already 11:00. She finished up a report she was working on for the bank's board of directors and then headed out the door to meet Sam at Anson's Restaurant.

Sam was already there, sitting at a table in the corner of the back of the dining room. Ellie Lynn was pretty sure she had picked it for a little privacy. She seated herself opposite Sam and said, "What's the news?"

"I hear the sea bass is just excellent" said Sam.

"What the hell does sea bass have to do with lunch? You know what I meant."

Sam laughed. It was a deep heart-felt kind of laugh that meant she was thoroughly enjoying herself.

"You'll have to forgive me. This is a lot like my days as a cop in Atlanta. I tend to enjoy myself too much when I feel like I'm doing something really meaningful."

"And just what is it that you find so meaningful?"

"I hired a local private detective to do a little electronic snooping for us."

"You mean the bank is paying for him?"

"No, I'm having him bill me direct. I don't want to have any paper trail connecting him to the bank unless this turns out to be what I think it is."

"And just what is that?"

"I think your good friends, the Regrets and their cousin Mr. Clay are involved in some illegal activity that has nothing to do with hay, horse feed, or straw."

"How do you know that?"

"One of the first things I learned in police work is that a picture is worth a thousand words. Look at these."

Sam then slid several 8x10 glossy black and white photos across the table to Ellie Lynn.

"Where did you get these?"

"I took them off a video I had the PI take from some remote video equipment he installed in an old building across from the Regret's warehouse at 313 Concord Street."

"So what am I looking for or is this going to be twenty questions?"

"Those are shots of activity at the warehouse over the past two weeks. I took out photos of each activity I saw on the video. Please note that while 80% of the warehouse is used for the Regret's supply business, the other 20% is leased out to a shell corporation that was set up in Delaware. The shell corporation is called Signet LTD. What I see here is very limited activity at Signet. Once a week they receive a shipment. They never appear to send any shipments out from the warehouse. Unless they have a huge hole dug under their part of the warehouse, they should be running out of room to store all the things that have been delivered to them."

"How about the idea that Signet is using the Regret's part of the building?"

"It seems that the Regret's use almost all of the space in their part of the warehouse and there is no room for anyone else's stuff."

"So, a shell corporation named Signet takes in stuff, but doesn't seem to ship anything out. It does seem a little strange, but you only have a few days of video."

"Bear with me. In addition to the Signet mystery, the pictures you see of activity on the Regret portion of the warehouse also seem a little strange. They use small delivery trucks to service the various stables in Charleston where they deliver hay, grain, etc. and bring back metal sealed containers of horse manure. They use big trucks to bring in the hay, grain and straw. Those trucks go back to the Regret Farm empty, except for one that arrives and leaves twice a week. Guess what it carries?"

"I have no idea."

"It brings in hay, feed, and straw and it returns to the farm carrying all the horse manure that they've been collecting from all of the Charleston stables."

"What's odd about that? They have to take it somewhere to get rid of it, and they probably take it back to the farm and use it as fertilizer."

"I think you're right about that part. What's strange is the method they use to take the horse manure back to the farm."

"What do you mean by method?"

"The horse manure comes into the warehouse in sealed metal containers. It leaves the warehouse in a large open bed trailer behind a truck. Why would you take the trouble to hide the sight and smell of horse manure when you collect it and store it and then allow it to be transported out in the open when they ship it back to the farm?"

"That does seem odd. You would think there are laws on the books to prevent someone from shipping horse manure in an open bed trailer. The smell has to be pretty bad. I wouldn't want to be the poor guy driving behind that trailer as it heads up the interstate to the Regret farm."

"Look at this picture of the manure trailer coming back to Charleston with a load of hay. See how high the box of the trailer sets and how high the bed of the trailer is. Look carefully at the base of the trailer bed. It appears to be a series of parallel metal drawers. Notice that the manure trailer only returns to the farm during the night. It never leaves in the daytime."

"So what does that mean?"

"I think it means that there are some secret compartments under that trailer bed and the Regrets are smuggling something into and out of Charleston."

"What would they be smuggling?"

"I have no idea, but it has to be something pretty compact or they couldn't hide it under the bed of the trailer."

"So they are using the horse manure to hide a secret shipment of something they are smuggling?"

"Bingo. Who is going to look under a load of smelly horse manure?"

"What on earth are they smuggling?"

"I have no idea, but I intend to find out."

CHAPTER NINETEEN

Marty Snyder came back to his office at the bank with a fresh cup of coffee in one hand and a large sheaf of computer print-outs in the other. He set the cup and print-outs on his desk and carefully closed the door to his office. He wanted to get this job over quickly, and he did not want to be interrupted or to have anyone discover what he was doing. Marty seated himself behind his desk and sipped his coffee as he began to read the print-outs.

What he was reviewing was a list of all of the outgoing calls on Samantha's Butler's phone at the bank. He had a master list of numbers and who they were assigned to that he had compiled from earlier reports he had created. Whenever he found a number that he had not previously identified, he highlighted it with a yellow high-lighter.

After about fifteen minutes he was finished and he began to do a computer search on the new numbers he had gleaned from the print-outs. He found one new number that appeared no less than four times. He ran the number on his computer program and almost spilled his coffee when the listing name associated with the number came up on his computer screen.

"Oh shit," he said. He quickly reached for the notebook in his desk drawer and began to dial the special number he had. He then gave a password and after a short wait, he left a detailed message and hung up. Marty paused and took a sip of his now lukewarm coffee. He was pretty sure he had just earned himself a $500 bonus, maybe more.

Lee Regret entered his sister's office at her realty firm without knocking. Startled, Wendy looked up and was not pleased to see the grim look on her brother's face.

"What's wrong?"

"It's that nosy Samantha Butler. She's trying to create trouble for us."

"What's she done?"

She's hired that private dick, Chester Luck. He specializes in electronic surveillance, and I'll bet money she's having him spy on us."

"Spy on us? Where?"

"My money is on the warehouse."

"What are you doing to do?"

"I'm going to have my boys search the area around the warehouse and see if we can find anything."

"What if you do find something. What do you do then?"

"Then I'm going to make sure the Mr. Luck has an unfortunate accident."

"What about Butler?"

"I'll find out if she has anything from Luck before I kill him. If she does, then I'll need to get rid of her as well."

"That'll be no loss to Charleston. What if she's talked to others?"

"That I'll find out before I kill her. My guess is if she's told anybody anything, then she probably has talked to her friend Ellie Lynn Main."

"Then you better make sure you get rid of her as well. I don't want anyone screwing up our deal. How will you get rid of them?"

"I'll use the pig pen just like a great grandpa did. It worked for him and it's worked for us before. Those pigs don't leave much and I doubt any forensic experts will be spending any time in a pig pen."

Wendy smiled at the thought.

"I'd like you to turn them over to Harlo before you kill them and let him and his boys have a little fun with them before they become hog slop. Have Harlo take some videos. I'd enjoy seeing those two stuck-up women getting taken down a few pegs."

"If that's what you want, sis, you got it. Harlo will certainly like the idea. I swear that boy has sex on the brain. I think those two ladies will welcome the hog pen after having Harlo and his boys work them over."

"Don't get ahead of yourself, Lee. Let's make sure they actually have some evidence. If they don't have anything we just get rid of Mr. Luck and wait."

"I don't agree, sis. If that Butler broad is suspicious and we get rid of Luck, she'll just find someone else. People like her tend to be relentless. Besides, I don't like the idea of sitting around waiting for something bad to happen. When we have a problem, we get rid of it."

"All right, Lee. Just make sure you're careful and you cover your tracks."

"Don't worry, sis. I'll take care of this deal just like I've taken care of all the others. Luck and those two women will be no problem."

Wendy smiled as she watched her brother leave the room, closing the door behind him. She would look forward to seeing the videos. She had seen videos that Harlo had taken before and she had thoroughly enjoyed them. Watching the helpless women suffer in Harlo's previous videos had been strangely arousing to her.

CHAPTER TWENTY

Kit called Ellie Lynn, but all he got was her voice mail. He left her a message letting her know that he and Swifty were headed to Kershaw to check out the title records in the county to try and find a link between one of the killer Confederates and the site of the mysterious barn. He also let her know about Billy K and left Billy's cell phone number with her so she could contact him if she needed any help.

Kit then called Big Dave in Wyoming and brought him up to date on what had happened and what they were currently doing. Big Dave told Kit that he had heard from Connor and that he had decided that his contact in Sicily was just trying to con him out of money and had no real information on what had happened to Kit's father. Connor had also told Big Dave that he was going to return to Wyoming unless he turned up something else.

Kit called Billy K and told him he and Swifty were headed to Kershaw to do a title search in the county records. He told Billy that he had given Billy's name and cell number to Ellie Lynn in case she needed some help.

"Who you gonna call if you need help, Kit?"

"I assume I can count on you, Billy K."

"Anytime, any place, against anyone. Just make sure you call me when you get done at the courthouse in Kershaw, Kit."

"Okay. I'll call you when we leave the courthouse."

"If I don't hear from you by the time the courthouse closes, I'll come looking for you, Mr. Andrews."

"I look forward to that, Billy K," laughed Kit as he shut off his cell phone.

After making sure he had the notes on how to do a title search, Kit joined Swifty in the hotel lobby. They waited for the staff to bring up Swifty's Ford from the hotel's valet parking facility.

Half an hour later they were headed north toward Columbia on the interstate in Swifty's big Ford pickup truck. Two hours later they pulled into Kershaw, the county seat of Lancaster County. The town was small and seedy-looking. There was not much of a business district, and they had no trouble finding the courthouse. It was one of the few buildings of real substance in the entire town.

After checking with a clerk in the entryway, they were directed to the office of recorder of deeds which was located on the second floor. After Kit explained to the clerk he wanted to do a title search, she directed him to a library like section of the office where large leather bound volumes filled the shelves around several old, long wooden tables with even older wooden chairs. With the clerk's assistance, Kit began reading through the grantee's books beginning with the year 1820.

Kit felt that if he could find one of the four names of the surviving Confederates, then he could follow it forward to 1865 and find out what property they owned. The books were large and the entries were hand-written and sometimes hard to read. After two hours Kit was up to 1849 when he finally found not one, but two of the names. In 1849, Ambrose Regret had purchased 200 acres of land in Lancaster County. In the same year a Wilson Clay had purchased forty acres. Kit wrote down the legal descriptions of the land and kept searching.

In 1858, he found where a Samuel Walsh had purchased a two hundred forty acre parcel of land. When he reached 1865 and found nothing more, he went back to 1820 in the Grantor's book. He found that Wilson Clay had sold his forty acres in 1852 to a William Seacrist. He also found that Samuel Walsh had sold his two hundred forty acres to a Walter Jackson in 1860. None of the other names of the four Confederates appeared in the grantor or grantee books.

Kit had assigned Swfity to check the real estate tax records, and he had come up bleary eyed and empty.

Kit compared the three legal descriptions to a map of the county and copied them into his notebook. He compared the locations on the map to the satellite maps they already had and checked to see if any of them matched up with the two locations that they had already found. Maybe they would point to a new location.

Kit grabbed Swifty and after thanking the clerk and giving her a ten dollar tip that she tried to refuse, the two men made their way back to Swifty's truck in the courthouse parking lot. Kit and Swifty came to a sudden stop as they noticed an older gentleman dressed in a sheriff's uniform leaning against Swifty's Ford as though he were waiting for the owner of the truck to show up. He was tall and lean, his skin tanned by the sun. He had white hair under a sheriff's cowboy hat and his tanned face was decorated with a bushy white mustache. As they drew closer Kit could see that the man had bright blue eyes that seemed to twinkle. He was smiling, not frowning as they approached.

"Good afternoon, officer," said Kit.

"Good day to you, sir," replied the gentleman.

"Can we help you with something?" asked Kit.

"I assume you two boys are the owners of this here truck with Wyoming plates?"

"Well, actually the truck belongs to my partner, here."

The gentleman held out his hand and said, "I'm Peck Horton, sheriff of Lancaster County."

Kit and Swifty identified themselves and shook hands with Sheriff Horton.

"It's almost noon, boys. How about we walk over to Alma's café and grab a spot of lunch and have a little chat?"

Kit and Swifty nodded their agreement and followed the sheriff across the street to a small café.

Alma's café was not large and probably seated about thirty people, counting the eight who sat on stools at the counter. The sheriff led them to a table near the back of the café and motioned to the waitress, a heavy-set older woman wearing a well-worn uniform that seemed a little small for her ample frame. Stitched across the pocket on the right front of her uniform was the name "Peggy".

Peggy passed out menus and promptly began pouring coffee into three large mugs that magically appeared in her large hands. As soon as the last cup was filled, she hurried onto the next table. The café was starting to fill up with patrons.

Kit looked up from his menu to see the sheriff was studying him intently. Peggy was back in a flash and took their orders then disappeared as quickly as she had come.

"What can we do for you, Sheriff?" asked Kit.

"Well, boys, it seems as though I got this report from one of my deputies that he ran into two cowboys from Wyoming and he felt they were somehow involved with a fight that occurred in a parking lot in Hanging Rock a couple of days ago. He told me he advised them that they might find sightseeing a bit better in some other state and thought that was the end of it. I found it quite fascinating that two cowboys beat the crap out of five locals that work for the Hanging Rock Farm. I decided that if I had the opportunity, I would make their acquaintance."

"It was a fair fight, Sheriff," said Swifty.

"I'm sure it was, son. To my way of thinkin' them five boys are pretty bad actors and no one I know would be at all upset to hear that they got their comeuppance, even if it was from two Yankees. Course we tend to look down on incidents that are considered disturbing the peace."

"Did someone file a complaint, Sheriff?" asked Kit.

"We did get a call from an old widow lady in Hanging Rock, but I would hardly call that a complaint."

"What did she say?" asked Swifty.

"She said two guys dressed like cowboys beat the crap out of a bunch of ruffians who worked for Harlo Clay, and she said it was better than watchin' a movie."

The sheriff paused as Peggy appeared out of nowhere to refill his coffee mug.

"I figured that you two were the culprits. Normally we don't put up with fighting in public, and we throw both parties in the cooler."

"And this time?"

"Well, son, my only regret was that I wasn't there to see it. I've been sheriff here in Lancaster County for sixteen years and them five jaspers have been nothing but trouble for me since they were young boys. Having someone come along and punch their lights out makes me feel like there really is a little justice in this world. On the other hand, I don't want no more fistfights breaking out in public places in my county, so I wanna make sure you ain't planning on having no more fights around here."

"We didn't have much choice, Sheriff. They were the ones who started it."

"I'm sure that's true, son. Just promise me you'll stay out of trouble during the rest of your visit."

"That's the plan, Sheriff. We're just here doing a little sight seeing and research, that's all," responded Kit.

"Where're you boys from?"

Kit explained he and Swifty were from Kemmerer, Wyoming, and they had been down in Charleston. Kit told him they also had been doing a little research in the Lancaster County Recorder of Deeds office.

"You said your name was Peck Horton?"

"Yep."

"How did you get a first name like Peck?"

"Well, son, Peck is actually a nickname I got as a young boy."

"What does it mean?"

"As a youngster I was always in a peck of trouble, and it sort of stuck."

Both Kit and Swifty laughed, and Peck joined in.

"Since you asked, Mr. Andrews, I must say that there is something very familiar about you."

"I've never been in South Carolina before, Sheriff."

"You look like someone else I knew who also had the last name of Andrews. You wouldn't happen to be from Illinois originally, would you son?"

"Yes, sir, I was born in Illinois. In Kankakee, Illinois, to be exact."

"What was your daddy's name?"

"My father's name was Wayne, Sheriff."

"I'll be damned."

"What do you mean?"

"I was in the service after I got out of high school and I served under a real tough hombre named Wayne Andrews. And he looked a hell of a lot like you, especially the eyes. Was your daddy in the service?"

"Yes, sir, he was."

"So you're Wayne Andrew's boy. I can hardly believe it. How in tarnation did you wind up in Wyoming? And how is your daddy?"

"It's a long story, Sheriff, but my dad has been missing for a couple of years."

"Knowing your daddy I ain't surprised. He was always being sent out on some mission that he could never talk about. I hope he turns up O.K., son."

"I hope so too, Sheriff. I thank you for your kind words."

"Nothing kind about them, Kit. Your daddy helped make a man out of me and got me out of trouble more than once. I was a slow learner when I was younger. Thankfully I got smarter when I got older. I'll take care of the lunch bill, boys. You let me know if I can be of any help to you."

"Thank you, Sheriff. I appreciate the offer," answered Kit.

"You don't need to thank me, Kit. I owe your daddy."

With that Peck Horton tipped his hat, stopped to pay Peggy, and slipped out the front door.

"You're the luckiest son of a bitch I ever met, Andrews."

"Hey, can I help it if we keep running into people who knew my dad?"

"I'm glad this one was a sheriff. Knowing him might come in real handy before we are done down here. Speaking of being done, what did you find out on those legal descriptions and maps?"

"I haven't had time to look. Let's head back to your truck and look them over."

Back at Swifty's truck, Kit dropped the tailgate and used it for a temporary desktop. The legal description for Regret's deed matched the land around the present day Hanging Rock Farm. The other two legal descriptions were nowhere near the two areas that they had previously identified with the help of the satellite maps.

"This looks like we made this trip for exactly nothing," said Swifty.

"It just could be the barn we're looking for is on one of two sites we already had."

"I'll bet a cold beer our missing barn is not on either one of those sites."

"You're on, Swifrty. Make mine a Bud Light."

"I don't think so. Get ready to buy old Swifty a cold Coors."

After checking the maps, they set out for the Walsh property, which was located about three miles from the courthouse.

CHAPTER

TWENTY-ONE

Harlo had a big smile on his face when he hung up the phone after talking to his cousin Lee. The thought of having that big blonde Butler under his absolute control began stirring feelings of arousal in him. The idea that he would get to do the same to the little Main broad was twice as good. It was a mood that did not last long.

Harlo's fantasy was rudely interrupted by Red pushing his way into Harlo's office without stopping to knock on the door.

"God damn you, Red. How many times have I told you to knock before coming into my office."

"I'm sorry, Boss, but I just got a call from Wendell Cooper. He saw them two cowboys who we had that fight with. They was in Alma's café in Kershaw having lunch with Sheriff Horton."

"What do you mean two cowboys? You told me there was at least a half a dozen of them."

"Well, actually there was only two of them, but they fought real dirty."

"So these were the same two cowboys who beat the shit out of you, Skinny, and the boys?"

"The very same two cowboys."

"What the hell were they doing talking to the sheriff?"

"I don't know, Boss."

"Shit. That can't be good. All I need is to have the damn nosy Sheriff Horton snooping around the farm. I thought you told me them cowboys were just passing through and were already gone out of the state?"

"I thought so, Boss, but they is still here."

"Take some of the boys and find them cowboys and make sure they get the hell out of South Carolina by tonight. Do whatever you have to do, but make sure they are convinced that staying around here is unhealthy for them. Understand?"

"Yes, Boss. I'll take care of them."

"Red."

"Yes, Boss."

"Don't screw this up, or I'll put you on the hog pen menu."

"Yes, Boss. I understand."

With that, Red was out the door as fast as he could move. Red was a lot more afraid of Harlo than he was of the two cowboys. After all, he told himself, the reason they got beat was them cowboys tricked him, and he wasn't about to let that happen again. He stopped by the main barn and picked up three of the toughest guys he had.

The four of them grabbed weapons from the main barn locker and piled into a crew cab pickup. Red drove and headed for Kershaw to try and pick up the trail of the two mysterious cowboys.

Meanwhile, Kit and Swifty had stopped for gas in Kershaw and asked for directions. They got directions based on a map they got from the station attendant, a high school drop-out named Leon who had a bad case of acne. Leon was able to read the map and show them the quickest way to the former Walsh property. They each bought a can of pop and set out following Leon's directions. Soon they were driving down a dusty dirt road with a rooster plume of dust rising behind the Ford.

*   *   *

Walt Jagger was a former special forces soldier who had received a dishonorable discharge from the Army for selling Army supplies on the black market for his personal gain, something the Army frowns on. Walt wound up in Lee Regret's employ because of his training and the same instincts that made him a good soldier, albeit a dishonest one. Walt liked to work alone, and he never carried a gun. He always carried at least three knives concealed about his body. His theory was that guns always got you in trouble and if caught with one, the sentence was always more severe. Knives were hard to trace and easy to dispose of. Walt was very good with a knife and he prided himself on his skill. He was tall and lanky and had dark hair and dark skin. His eyes were dark brown, almost black. When people looked into his eyes, what they saw looked almost lifeless and certainly without any pity.

Walt had drifted from job to job until he found employment with Lee Regret. Regret quickly determined that Jagger's criminal mind combined with his special forces training and natural instincts were ideal for managing the Regret warehouse in Charleston. Walt had turned out to be the perfect employee, and he ran the warehouse with an iron fist. He tolerated no mistakes and did his job with skill and enthusiasm. Occasionally Walt began to feel closed in by the walls of the warehouse so he would go for walks. His walks were more like patrols. He carefully memorized every detail of the area around the warehouse. If something had been changed, he seemed to know it instantly.

Today Walt was on a mission. He went out on his morning walk and did a careful patrol of the perimeter of the warehouse. He was looking for video surveillance equipment being used to take pictures of his warehouse. He knew that today's video equipment could be made extremely small and difficult to detect. He also knew that most such equipment was sensitive to the environment and often was hidden in a building or a structure. His second stop on his patrol took him to an old warehouse that was being renovated, located directly between his warehouse and the harbor.

With his worn work clothes and boots he blended in with the work crews working on the building, and he was able to wander around the building unchallenged. After about fifteen minutes, he hit paydirt. He found a small closet on a wall that faced the Regret warehouse that had the door locked with a new padlock. Taking out one of his heavier knives, he worked the screws on the hasp out of the rotting old wood and opened the closet door.

Inside he found a very sophisticated state of the art digital video system set up. A small hole had been drilled in the outside wall, allowing the camera to view the entire front of the Regret warehouse with a zoom lens. As Walt studied the equipment, he saw it was motion activated and was operated by a portable battery pack. He checked the voltage meter on the pack and saw it was down to less than a third of battery power.

Walt knew someone would have to come by that night and change the batteries and retrieve the digital video disk. Walt pushed the screws on the hasp back into the soft wood so nothing looked disturbed to the naked eye. Then he casually walked out of the building and headed back to his office in the Regret warehouse with a grim smile on his face.

CHAPTER
TWENTY-TWO

Leon had never liked Red or Skinny or any of the rest of the Hanging Rock Farm guys. They were a mean bunch and treated people like Leon as if he was dirt under their boots.

Leon saw them ride into town acting like they owned the place. Pretty soon they were in and out of several of the stores across the street from the gas station and finally Red and one of his unfriendly buddies came into the station.

Red did not waste time on any pleasantries. "Leon, you little turd. Have you seen two guys dressed up like cowboys in your place today?"

Leon swallowed hard and shook his head to signify that he had not seen any such people. He did not like Red and was not inclined to tell him or any of his cronies what he may or may not have seen that day.

"Leon, you little turd, I think you're lyin' to me."

Leon tried to keep a poker face and not make any kind of expression, but before he knew what was happening Red had hit Leon along the side of his head and sent him flying into the painted concrete block wall of the station.

Before he could recover from the suddenness of the blow, Leon felt himself being pulled up by the front of his shirt by Red.

"Answer me, you miserable dipwad. Did you see these two cowboys in here today?"

Leon was so frightened that he found himself needing to take a piss immediately, if not sooner. As Red drew back his fist, Leon managed to choke out the words he did not want to say. "I saw 'em, I saw 'em. They was here and left a couple of hours ago."

"Where were they headed, you worthless piece of shit?"

"They was headed to the old Walsh place out on Country Road 21."

"Why the hell would they be goin' there?"

"I got no idea. They had some kind of satellite map and wanted to know how to get to the old Walsh place. You gotta believe me, that's all I knows."

Red's response was to backhand Leon across the face and break his nose. Blood soon began to run down over Leon's mouth and chin.

"You broke my nose, you broke my nose," wailed Leon.

"You're lucky that's all I broke, you piece of shit."

Red kicked the prone Leon in the ribs and stomped out of the gas station.

Leon got up off the floor and grabbed a paper towel to try to stop the bleeding, while Red and his crew all jumped in the crew cab pickup and roared out of town.

* * *

Chester Luck finished off his third beer while watching the end of a movie on cable television. He noted that it was almost dark, so he headed out to the garage to get his car. After making sure he had freshly charged batteries and a new blank digital disk, he backed the car into the street and headed for downtown Charleston and the empty warehouse where he had placed his hidden camera and equipment.

By the time he reached downtown Charleston and parked his car about two blocks away from the old warehouse, it was finally dark. Chester put the batteries and cartridges in a small knapsack and slung it over one shoulder. He made sure he walked slowly and casually and acted as normally as he could, while still keeping his eyes moving and checking out everything he saw around him. It was completely quiet with no traffic on the street, and he saw no one on the sidewalk during the two block walk. Chester let himself in the unlocked door to the warehouse and stopped in the darkness to listen. All of the workmen had gone home and he heard nothing. He pressed the button on a tiny flashlight on his key chain and used the miniature light to find his way to the second floor and the small closet that held his camera equipment.

With the limited illumination of his small flashlight, Chester failed to notice the two screws that he had used to keep the hasp on the closet door were not in the same position he had left them. He unlocked the padlock with his key and opened the closet door. He quickly threw down his small knapsack to the floor and after opening it, he replaced the batteries in the battery pack and then removed the digital disk and replaced it with a new one. Chester placed the old batteries and the current cartridge in his knapsack and stepped back out of the closet. Chester stopped and froze as he sensed something behind him. Everything seemed to go black, then there was nothing.

When Chester awoke, he was securely tied to a heavy wooden chair with what seemed to be climbing rope. He tried to speak, but found he was gagged as well as tied up. As his eyes adjusted to the dimness of his surroundings, he could see he was in a small room with no other furniture or anything else he could see. The only opening was a heavy wooden door that was closed and probably locked as well.

After about half an hour had passed, the heavy wooden door opened and tall lanky man dressed in black and wearing a black ski mask came into the room. He brought a four legged stool with him, and he sat down on it and stared at his captive.

"I see you're finally awake. Welcome back to the land of the living."

Chester tried to answer, but the gag made his response sound unintelligible.

"Having a little trouble expressing ourselves, are we? Let me fix that."

The man stood up and with a flick of his wrist he held a short sharp knife in his hand. With one swift motion, he cut the gag and it fell away from Chester's mouth and dropped on the dirty wooden floor.

Chester greedily gulped in fresh air through his mouth.

"A mouth-breather, huh! I shoulda known."

Chester did not respond. He just kept his eyes on the man in black.

"I've a few questions for you, mouth-breather. You give me truthful answers, and you'll get out of here with your hide intact. You lie to me, and I'll kill you and dump you in the Cooper River. You understand me, mouth-breather?"

Chester nodded his head up and down signifying that he did understand.

"That's not good enough, mouth-breather. When I ask a question, I want an answer I can hear. You understand that?"

Chester was filled with fear. He knew he could not take a chance on telling this man any lies, and he decided to tell him all he knew and hope he would let Chester go in exchange for the information.

"Yes, sir."

"That's more like it. All I need is the truth, mouth-breather. But I warn you. You lie to me and you won't be breathing no more. You savvy?"

"Yes, sir."

"That camera equipment that was hidden in the closet in the old warehouse belongs to you?"

"Yes, sir."

"Why did you put it there?"

"So I could photograph the activity on the warehouse at 1313 Concord."

"Who hired you to do this?"

"I was hired by Samantha Butler. She's in charge of security for the Bank of South Carolina."

"Was this a job for the bank?"

"No. She had me bill her directly, not the bank, so I'm pretty sure it was just for her."

"Why would she want to have surveillance done on the warehouse?"

"I don't know, sir."

"Do you know who owns the warehouse you were filming?"

"Yes sir. It belongs to Hanging Rock Farm. I think Lee and Wendy Regret own the farm."

"Why would this Butler woman want to have surveillance done on the Regrets?"

"I don't know. She didn't tell me."

"What did she tell you?"

"She told me she wanted surveillance of the warehouse, so she could see what kind of activity was going on there."

"Was there anyone with Butler when she talked to you about this job?"

"Not as far as I know, sir. She did everything on the phone."

"Did you deliver her any pictures so far?"

"Yes, sir. I delivered a packet of pictures to her three days ago."

"I thought you said you didn't talk to her in person?"

"I didn't. I left the packet with the receptionist in the front of the lobby of the bank. The packet had Ms. Butler's name on it."

The man in black shifted his weight on his stool and stared intently at Chester. Seconds seemed to tick away. Finally the man spoke.

"I'm going to talk to my boss and see what he wants me to do with you. In the meantime, you'll stay tied up in this room. I'll leave the gag off, but if you so much as utter a sound, the guard will come in here and slit your throat. Is that clear?"

"Yes, sir."

The man in black stood up, picked up his stool and left the room. The heavy wooden door closed behind him. Chester could hear a metallic click as the lock was turned.

Outside the room, in the open warehouse, Walt took off the black ski mask and motioned to Frenchy to come to him. Frenchy was a short, stocky man with a swarthy complexion and dyed blond hair. He had the powerful build of a weight lifter. He was supposedly a former veteran of the French Foreign Legion. Thus he came by his nickname of Frenchy. His real name was Hans Von Listek. He was born in Germany and was an illegal alien living in the United States.

"Wait about fifteen minutes, and then go in and kill the bastard. Wrap him up in one of these old drop cloths and make sure you clean everything up and leave no evidence. Then take him out and wrap some chains around him and dump him in the Cooper River tonight while it's still plenty dark. You clear on all that, Frenchy?"

"I got it, Boss. No problem."

"There better not be any problems. For your trouble, you can have all the camera equipment I left in the cardboard box by the back exit and anything you can find in his wallet. Leave the watch, any jewelry, and his credit cards on him."

"Why can't I have the credit cards?"

"Because I want nothing that can link him to us. Sell the camera equipment to the Mexican in Savannah. Take whatever he gives you with no arguments. You understand?"

"Yes, Boss."

CHAPTER
TWENTY-THREE

Lee Regret listened carefully to every word Walt told him. Walt had come in person to Lee's home office to tell Lee what he had learned. Walt had a complete distrust of phones of any kind, especially cell phones.

"So that Butler woman is after us, and she already has some evidence of what we're doing. Is that what I'm hearing?"

"Yes, Mr. Regret, it is."

"We don't have to worry about Mr. Luck?"

"We have nothing to fear from the late Mr. Luck."

Regret chuckled.

"I'd like to put Ms. Butler in the same category. How do you suggest we do that, Walt?"

"Sounded to me like she was due to get more photos from Luck. When she doesn't get them and she can't get him on the phone, she'll more than likely go to his office to try to find him."

"What does that mean to us?"

"We can break into Luck's office and home and make sure there is no other evidence or photos that can be used against us. But we need to do it quietly and cleanly so no one will know we were ever there. Then we can have the office watched with one of our people and nab Butler when she comes in."

"What if she's not alone?"

"We can handle two just as easy as one. Surprise is on our side."

"Once you have her, I want her taken to the farm. I promised Harlo he could deal with her. He'll be very happy to see her."

"I'll see that it gets done."

"How can we get her out of town without anyone seeing her?"

"We drug her, then put her in the back of a van and take her over to the warehouse. Then we put her in one of the cigarette compartments under the shit truck and send her up to Harlo at the farm when the truck makes its return run."

"We need to find out if she's talked to anyone else about what she was up to, Walt."

"We can do that at the warehouse before we send her to the farm."

"I like the plan. Make it happen, Walt."

"Okay boss, I'll make it happen."

Lee hit the remote to turn on the huge plasma television on the wall of his home office as Walt slipped out the side door of the house and into the warm Charleston night.

*   *   *

Swifty pulled his Ford truck over to the side of the road and shut off the engine.

"Okay, genius. According to your directions we should be right next to the old Walsh place. Does this look anything like a farm meadow to you?"

Kit didn't bother to answer. He'd seen the endless wall of tall pine trees that edged the road like some giant tree fence, and he was busily studying the map he had spread out on his lap.

'Earth to Kit. Earth to Kit. Where the hell are we?"

"Quit your whining. God! You act like you've never missed a turn in your life. We can't be that far off."

"I'd settle for just knowing where the hell we are. Not how far off we are."

"I think we turn around and back track about one and a half miles and then we take the turn to the north."

"Okay, okay. I get the drift. I see an old driveway about half a block ahead. I can pull in there and get us turned around."

"What driveway?"

"It's not really a driveway, just a small dirt track over there to the left. You can just see the old tire marks going between the trees."

Swifty pulled slowly ahead, and soon they could clearly see the old roadway that cut through the protective wall of trees that surrounded the road. He pulled into the roadway and the trees immediately blocked out any view of the road they had just been on.

"Hold it here a second, Swifty. I want to double check our position on my map."

The words were hardly out of Kit's mouth when they heard the sound of a truck engine being pushed hard and a large dust-covered crew cab pickup truck roared past their hidden roadway. The truck was going so fast, they only got a glimpse of it and then their viewing space was filled with an impenetrable curtain of dust.

"Holy shit! That looked like some of the yahoos we tangled with back in Hanging Rock."

"Brilliant deduction, Swifty. This time I think there were four of them packed into that truck and I saw at least one shotgun."

"You don't suppose they're on this road looking for a couple of cowboys from Wyoming, do you?"

"I don't think they were coming out to sell us tickets to the local pancake breakfast."

"Damn. You know how I like pancakes."

"I suggest we shitcan the pancakes and get the hell out of here as fast as we can."

"Which way?"

"We go back the way they came from. I sure as hell don't want to be following them."

Swifty pulled the truck out of the narrow roadway and turned right onto the road and headed back the way they had come.

After they had gone a little over a mile down the road, Kit tapped Swifty on the arm and said, "Stop."

Swifty brought the truck to a screeching halt and waited until the clouds of dust had drifted past the truck before asking, "Now what, genius?"

"This is the turn I thought we should make. Since we're here, I vote we take the road and see what we can see."

"I suppose this can't be any dumber than what we've already done." With that said, Swifty turned left onto the new road and soon they were roaring down a dirt road that was throwing up huge rooster tails of dust behind them.

After about three miles, they came to a dead end.

"Shit. What a waste this trip turned out to be," said Swfity.

"Maybe so and maybe not. Look over to the right," said Kit pointing his finger out the passenger side window.

Swifty followed Kit's pointed finger and there between the trees he could see an opening. Through the opening in the trees he could see a large fenced-in meadow and what looked to be a horse farm with barns, out-buildings, and a sizeable corral. He could see some horses in the corral, but no sign of any people. Not even a pick-up truck or a car could be seen.

"Oh shit," said Kit. "Look behind us."

Swifty turned in his seat and could clearly see the big crew-cab pickup truck that had passed them earlier coming down the road at a high rate of speed. A huge dust plume trailed the fast moving truck.

"How do we get out of this one, partner?" asked Swifty.

"Maybe we can reason with them," replied Kit.

Just then a bullet smashed into the back of Swifty's pickup truck.

"So much for reasoning with them. Let's get the hell out of here. We're sitting ducks in this truck."

Swifty grabbed his H&K 45 caliber pistol from the glove box, and Kit pulled his Kimber 45 out from under his seat.

"Let's make for the farm," yelled Swifty and he led the way out of the truck and through the opening in the tall pine trees.

Swifty was in front as they ran up to the fence surrounding the meadow. "Well move around the meadow and stick to the edge of the trees and get to that farm. We might find some help there. We have to stay out of that meadow. There's no cover, and we'll get our asses shot off."

Kit did not stop to agree or to argue. He just kept running and trying to keep up with Swifty. They dodged in and out of the edge of the tree line that was about five yards outside of the fence. Twice bullets thudded into trees that were just behind them and once leaves shredded by bullets fell in front of them.

They had run about two hundred yards when Kit paused to look behind him. He could see what looked like three or four men chasing them and all of them appeared to be carrying some kind of firearm.

It was soon apparent that while the gunmen were not gaining on Swifty and Kit, they were not losing much ground, either.

Kit and Swifty reached a point in the woods about fifty-five yards from the corral. To reach the corral and the nearest barn, they would have to run across about fifty yards of open meadow. Swifty suddenly stopped and shouted to Kit to keep running to the barn.

Kit complied and Swifty dropped behind a pine tree and pulled out his H&K pistol and steadied his aim by learning against the side of the tree trunk.

Swifty's gun boomed twice, and Kit heard a distant scream. He looked over his shoulder, and he could see Swifty was running about thirty yards behind him. Back toward the trees, he could see three men milling around one man lying on the ground.

Swifty had slowed down the gunmen long enough to allow he and Kit to safely make it across the open ground and get to the relative safety of the nearest barn. They skidded to a stop behind the small barn and Kit dropped to the ground and crawled to the edge of the barn. There he carefully looked around the side of the barn to see what was happening with their pursuers. He could see that while Swifty's shots had knocked down one man and temporarily scattered the rest, the gunmen had regained their courage and were again headed toward them, dodging from tree to tree just outside the fence line.

Swifty stuck his head around the side of the barn for a look and then said, "Okay, genius. Now what do we do? We can hold them off for a while, but we only have about a dozen rounds between us. Seventy five yards is a long way off for a good pistol shot, even for me."

Kit looked back at the corral and saw about half a dozen horses nervously milling around the corral. The gunshots had obviously upset them. Kit immediately noticed that all of them had halters on. He smiled to himself and he reached down and grabbed a large handful of tall, fresh green grass and handed it to Swifty.

"What the hell is this, camouflage?"

"Nope. This is our way out," replied Kit.

"We're going to beat them to death with grass?"

Kit ignored Swifty and with a large handful of grass in each hand, he slipped through the gate in the corral. The barn they had been hiding behind was between them and the pursuing gunmen.

Kit slowly walked to the center of the corral and stood there motionless, holding the grass out in his outstretched hands. Pretty soon two of the horses overcame their nervousness with curiosity and came up to sniff the handfuls of fresh green grass. As they began to eat the grass offered to them, Kit slipped his hands under their halters and led them over to Swifty.

Kit whispered softly to the two mares and handed the halter of one to Swifty. They led the horses through the gate and closed it shut behind them. Each of them mounted their horse and using the halter as a clumsy bridle, they urged the mares to a trot heading across the meadow away from the oncoming gunmen. Kit was careful to keep his horse on a line that kept the barn between him and Swifty and the gunmen, preventing them from seeing what was going on.

By the time the gunmen had cautiously crossed over the meadow to the barn and moved around it to the corral, all they could see was the outline of a pair of horses and riders galloping across the far side of the meadow and away from their position.

Red couldn't believe his eyes. Goddamn cowboys on horses. This was like a bad movie. He yelled at his men, and they started running back across the meadow to where their truck was parked. Red's jaw was set in a grim line as he sprinted back towards the truck. No damn horse could outrun a truck, and he was ready to shoot both the cowboys and their horses for good measure.

CHAPTER TWENTY-FOUR

Billy K found himself nervously pacing the lobby of the Market Pavilion Hotel. He knew the desk clerk was getting tired of him asking if Carson Andrews had checked in or left any message. He pulled his cell phone out of his pocket for about the twentieth time to check for any messages from Kit. There were no messages, just as there had been none each time he'd previously checked.

Billy looked at his watch. It was almost five thirty. The courthouse closed at five. He called information and got the number for the courthouse in Kershaw. His call to the courthouse got a recording saying they had closed at five P.M.

Billy called the number Kit had given him for the lady banker, Ellie Lynn Main. After two rings she answered. Billy identified himself and said he had heard nothing from Kit and was getting worried. Ellie Lynn told him that she had not heard from Kit either. Billy hung up after agreeing with Ellie Lynn that each would let the other know if they heard anything. Billy gave her his cell phone number and asked Ellie Lynn to call him within an hour and they would trade updates, if any, on what was going on.

Billy headed for the front door. He needed to stop by his hotel room and pick up some "tools". Then he needed to rent a car. He was so preoccupied with what he needed to do that he failed to look up and plowed right into a huge giant of a man wearing a cowboy hat, who had just entered the lobby of the hotel. The impact knocked Billy flat on his back on the hotel lobby floor.

He found himself looking up into the giant's bright blue eyes.

Then he heard a deep voice. "You ain't hurt none, are you, partner?"

CHAPTER TWENTY-FIVE

Walt and Kenny drove up in front of the small old office building located just off Calhoun Street in Charleston. They left their van in a tiered parking lot a block away and casually walked up to the front of the building. The office building was old and had been restored more than once. The three story structure had a small elevator and a tiny lobby. Walt and Kenny entered the lobby and checked out the office directory, a small dusty glass covered panel on the wall next to the elevator. Their job was to search Luck's office while another team led by Frenchy would be searching Luck's apartment. Everything depended on speed and stealth. Neither team could afford to be discovered.

"Luck Investigations Ltd." was located on the second floor in suite 201 according to the building directory. Walt noted that the other office on the second floor was currently vacant. He scanned the small lobby and saw no surveillance cameras. He also walked around to the side of the elevator shaft searching until he found the service entrance in the back of the building. The entrance opened up to an alley behind the structure. Walt made a mental note of what he had seen and then he and Kenny took the stairs to the second floor rather than the elevator. Walt did not want to step out in front of surveillance cameras on the second floor. After all, Luck was supposedly a private investigator who specialized in electronic surveillance.

Walt cautiously opened the second floor stairwell door and swept the hallway with his eyes. He could see no cameras. Even better, the light above the elevator was out and the hallway was darker than it normally would have been.

Walt knocked on the vacant office first, just to be certain it was truly empty. There was no response to his knock. He checked the door. It was locked. Then he knocked on the office door for Luck Investigations Ltd. Again there was no response. He stood still for a few seconds just to listen for any sound and let his eyes adjust to the gloom. He held up his hand to keep Kenny silent and motionless, and fortunately Kenney obliged. Kenny was a young up and comer. He had the skill to be a good soldier, but he was emotionally not real stable. Between his substance abuse problems and his financial problems, Kenny was not one to disobey someone as important to his world as Walt.

Walt took a small leather packet out of his coat pocket and extracted a set of lock picks, which he immediately used to pick the lock of the office. In about thirty seconds the lock was open and a smiling Walt opened the door and motioned for Kenny to enter Luck's office ahead of Walt.

The office was dark and since he had no fear of discovery, Walt flipped the light switch on the wall, which turned on the ceiling light for Luck's office.

It wasn't much of an office. The desk, chairs, filing cabinets, and a few other pieces of wooden furniture were all old and pretty beat up. Some mail lay on the floor under the mail slot in the office door. Walt and Kenny took off their coats and put on some plastic gloves. Kenny picked up the mail on the floor and put it on the desk. They both proceeded to search the office from top to bottom. They were careful to drop nothing and to replace things as closely as possible to the way they originally found them.

After about two hours, they had finished and Walt sat down at the desk and began to sort through the office mail. He found nothing of interest there. He had found the file Luck had opened for the Butler investigation and he put the whole file and contents into a backpack he had brought with him. Satisfied that nothing existed in the office that could provide anyone with a link to his boss, Walt led Kenny out of the office.

Then he turned and carefully scanned the office, looking for any sign that they had been there. Nothing seemed disturbed or out of place. Walt carefully closed the now unlocked front door to the office. Then he walked over to the adjacent empty office and quickly picked the lock on the door. He and Kenny entered the dark office. It was empty except for a few cardboard boxes full of junk.

Walt then explained his plan to Kenny. Kenny would stay out in front of the building, sitting on a bench located in front of a small office building that housed several attorneys. Kenny would be reading a newspaper and keeping his eye on the front of Luck's building. When he saw anyone enter the building and use the elevator, he would call Walt on the small two-way radio he carried on his belt. Walt would hide in the vacant office and wait for Kenny's call.

After Kenny left to find his perch across the street, Walt checked the contents of his backpack.

Walt had packed plastic ties to bind his victim's hands and legs, a plastic bottle of chloroform, some clean rags, and two plastic body bags, just in case there was more than one victim. He also had a thermos of coffee and a tattered paperback book he had been reading. Walt sat on the floor with his back against the wall, propped up his two way radio next to him and poured himself a cup of steaming hot coffee. After a sip of the hot coffee, Walt allowed himself to relax. He was sure he had thought of everything.

As long as Kenny did what he was told there should be no problem. By the next morning his part in the job should be over and the Butler woman would be Harlo's problem. An involuntary shiver went through his body as he thought of what Harlo might have in store for Ms. Butler. Walt knew he would be better off if he had no knowledge of what Harlo would do to her. He just needed to complete his part of the job.

*   *   *

Ellie Lynn returned to her office and found a phone blinking with voice mail messages and her computer announcing the presence of innumerable e-mails. She checked her watch and saw she had about fifteen minutes until she needed to call

Kit's friend, Billy K. She wondered why he had an initial for a last name. She was pretty sure she would find out before long. Kit had some very interesting friends. Swifty struck her as a guy who was funny, interesting, and dangerous. That was an unusual combination. She could not seem to make up her mind about Kit. He just seemed too good to be true. He somehow seemed a little too innocent and that made her nervous. She was wary of any man, but the more she saw of Kit, the more she liked what she saw in Kit, the person.

She was almost done with her e-mails when her door flew open and in stormed Sam Butler.

"There you are. How come you haven't answered my voice mails?"

"I just got through my e-mails and voice mails were next on the list. What's up?"

"Something's wrong. I haven't heard from Chester Luck and he didn't drop off the pictures yesterday as scheduled. I called his cell phone, his home phone, and his office phone and got nothing."

"How long have you been calling?"

"Since about seven o'clock last night. I called all three phones every half hour until midnight. I started calling again about six-thirty this morning. I have a bad feeling about this, Ellie Lynn."

"Do you think he's sick or hurt? Maybe he took a trip out of town on another job."

"No matter what he was doing he would have the photos delivered on time. He only gets paid when he makes a delivery. No pictures, no dough. If he was sick or hurt, he would've had someone else make the delivery. This isn't like him. Not like him at all."

"What should we do?"

"I'm planning on driving over to his office and see what I can find out. If he's not there, I can check with the neighboring offices. Sometimes they look out for other offices when one of them is sick or gone."

"What if he's not there and no one knows anything?"

"Then I try his house and if he's not there, I check with his neighbors."

"Should we call the police?"

"At this point we don't know anything for sure. Calling the police won't help because they would deal with it as a missing persons report and do nothing about it for at least forty-eight hours. I don't want any unnecessary publicity. Remember I'm doing this deal on my own nickel and the bank is not officially involved. I'd like to keep my job, so I don't want the bank involved."

"Okay, so the two of us get to play junior G-Men?"

"You got it, sister. If we do find out something, then we bring in the police."

"You want to go now?"

"It's after working hours and starting to get dark. Now works for me. I'll go get my car and met you in front of the building in ten minutes."

"I'll log off my computer, answer a couple of voice messages, and be out there in ten."

"Thanks," said Sam, and she swept out of Ellie Lynn's office as quickly as she had appeared.

Ellie Lynn had finished logging off her computer and then quickly worked her way through her voice messages, making notes to return calls and look up answers for callers. She was getting up to put on her jacket when she remembered she had promised to call Billy K. She decided to try Kit's cell phone one more time. She got the "Not now in service" message and waited to leave her own voice mail.

"Kit, this is Ellie Lynn. The detective Sam hired to do surveillance on the Regret's warehouse has disappeared, and he didn't deliver the second set of photos as promised. We're going to his office and then his home to see if we can find him. Sam thinks we're on to some criminal activity with the Regrets and their farm operation in Hanging Rock. Probably includes that creep Harlo Clay as well. Call me when you can."

She hung up and then dialed the cell number for Billy K. Billy answered on the second ring.

"Did you hear from Kit?"

"No, I didn't. Our security officer Samantha Butler and I are headed over to try to find the private detective she hired to snoop on Regret's warehouse. He's late with a delivery of surveillance videos, and he seems to have disappeared."

Ellie Lynn then proceeded to give Billy the background of Chester Luck's work and their subsequent suspicions about the Regrets and their cousin Harlo Clay. She gave him the address of Luck's office and his home so Billy would know where they were headed. She promised to call him back within half an hour.

Billy checked his watch so he would know when to expect Ellie Lynn's call. Things were starting to get complicated. He was uneasy about not hearing from Kit and now this new development.

Sam and Ellie Lynn pulled into a vacant parking space about a block from Luck's office. As they exited the car, Sam opened her purse and checked the contents. She pulled out her cell phone and checked that it was on and had a good battery charge. Then she pulled out a snub-nosed Smith and Wesson 38 caliber chrome plated revolver and checked to see it was fully loaded.

"You have a gun in your purse?"

"Never leave home without it. It's more reliable than a man and easier to take care of than a dog."

"Very funny. You think this trip could be dangerous?"

"You never know. It's always wise to make sure you're prepared for the worst."

"How about me?"

"You're too little and too skinny to have any concealed weapons. Do you have your cell phone?"

Ellie Lynn slyly reached into the inside of her suit jacket and pulled out the smallest cell phone that Sam had ever seen. It was about four inches long and very thin. Ellie Lynn showed Sam how easy it was to operate and how the pocket that contained it was kept shut with a tiny patch of Velcro.

"Very cool," said Sam.

"I got tired of having them on my belt or digging in my purse for a phone so I got one I could always get at in a hurry."

"I think I need one of those."

They began walking down the sidewalk toward Luck's office building.

Kenny waited until they got to the front of the office building and went in the front door. When he could see them step into the elevator he switched the 2-way radio on and Walt answered immediately.

"Two broads, one tall and blond and one short and thin with brown hair just went in the building and into the elevator."

"Come on up and use the stairs and don't come out in the hall until you can see me in the hall. I'll wait until they go into Luck's office. Pull on your ski mask before you come out into the hall. Got it?"

"I got it, Walt."

Walt turned off his radio and frowned. He would have preferred that the Butler woman had come alone. Two of them made things more complicated. His guess was that the second woman was the Ellie Lynn woman that Lee had mentioned. Who knew? Maybe getting both of them out of the way could turn out well for him. A little more bonus wouldn't hurt.

CHAPTER TWENTY-SIX

Once they were out of range of any gunfire from their pursuers, Kit and Swifty let their horses run at an easy lope. The sun was setting behind the trees and it was rapidly getting dark. Swifty pulled his mare to a stop and Kit quickly followed suit. They both sat on horseback and listened. They heard nothing to indicate that there were any gunmen chasing them or that anyone was in the area.

"I think we lost them."

"I sure as hell hope so, Kit. I ain't real fond of riding bareback."

"It sure beats getting shot."

"No argument there. It was the same bunch we had the run-in with in the parking lot in Hanging Rock. Guess they wanted to even up the score."

"Even up the score! They were shooting at us! They were trying to kill us! What kind of score is that?"

"I got a feeling that we stuck our fingers in something pretty sensitive and we stirred up a real hornet's nest."

"What could be so bad you would try to kill somebody?"

"I think them boys work for Regret and we must have stumbled close to something Regret don't want nobody to know about."

"So he wants us killed?"

"It would appear so, partner."

"Well screw him and the rest of his family. I take this real personal. We need to notify the sheriff."

"Just how do we do that? Do we use our horse phones?"

"As a matter of fact, yes."

Kit pulled out his cell phone from his pants pocket. He hit the power button and waited for the phone to come to life.

"Shit. I've got power, but no service."

"Hell, Kit. We don't even know where we are."

Kit continued to play with his phone and suddenly announced, "I've got voice messages, but I can't raise them." He continued to work the phone and then said, "I've got a text message."

"What is it?

"It's from Billy K."

"What does it say?"

"Where R U?"

"Now that's a question we'd all like to know the answer to."

"I have no idea where we left the truck, let alone where we're standing right now."

"Then I think the smart thing to do is find a place to spend the night and find out where we are at first light."

"That does make more sense then stumbling around in the dark. Hopefully we can find someplace where my phone gets service in the daytime."

Swifty grunted his agreement and began walking through the woods, leading his mare behind him. Kit followed with his mare.

They had walked for about an hour when the ground beneath them began to angle downward. They slowed their walk and hung onto their horses for support as the downhill angle got more and more steep. Finally it began to level out again and Swifty put up his hand to signal a stop. Kit came up next to him and Swifty whispered "See the road just slightly below and ahead of us? You can just make it out in the moonlight."

Kit looked and sure enough there was a gravel road that looked like a stream of water in the dark night. It was about fifty yards ahead of them. The tree line had already thinned out so that more moonlight flowed down from the tree tops as the forest canopy began to dissipate. They stood there in silence, carefully watching their surroundings and listening for any sign of other people, creatures, or an ambush. They heard nothing but the sound of the crickets. Other than a few tree branches which moved with the occasional gust of wind, they could see no movement of any kind.

Swifty motioned to his left and they began to walk slowly and as quietly as possible on a path that was parallel to the road below them. After about twenty minutes they stopped and Swifty motioned for Kit to take hold of the halter of his horse. Swifty then went behind a large bush to relieve himself. He returned quickly and took his horse back from Kit.

"The pause that refreshes!"

"You are such a moron, Swifty."

"You're just jealous."

"I'm aware of nothing to be jealous of."

"You city boys are all alike."

Both men looked at each other and burst out laughing. The laughs seemed to break the tension that they had been toiling under for the past several hours. It felt good to laugh instead of worry. Suddenly Kit held up his hand and they both fell silent.

"What is it?" Swifty whispered.

"I hear something. It sounds like an engine. Get down in the grass!"

Both men dropped down and lay flat in the tall grass, still grasping the halters of their mounts.

Their horses looked down at them as if they had no idea what these stupid humans were up to now.

Soon both men heard the whine of an engine. It sounded like a truck or a car with a V-8. Within a couple of minutes, they could see headlights on the road coming from the direction they had been heading. Soon the vehicle drew closer and they could see it was a pickup truck painted a light green color.

"Damned if that don't look like a forest ranger truck," whispered Swifty.

"It is a forest ranger truck!" said Kit.

As the truck passed below them, they could see the familiar lettering of "U.S. Forest Service" with the emblem on the side of the door.

"What the hell is a forest ranger doing driving around in this neck of the woods in the middle of the night?"

"Maybe he had a sudden urge for a doughnut," replied Kit.

"I ain't seen no doughnut shop, no coffee shop, or a shop of any kind nor even a damn house in the last several hours," said Swifty.

"Well, he had to come from someplace up ahead of us."

"We'll check it out in the morning. Let's find a place to sleep."

They proceeded next to the road for about another ten minutes and then found a slight depression on the hillside that was hidden from the road. Right behind the depression was a stand of stunted pine trees.

"We'll tie up the horses behind these little pine trees and that way nobody coming down the road can see us or them."

"Sounds good to me," said Kit.

Swifty tied off the horses and made some makeshift hobbles for the horses' forelegs using some vines he pulled off a larger pine tree.

"Are you sure those vines will hold them horses?" asked Kit.

"They're pretty tough. They should work fine."

Kit broke off the ends of the lower branches of some of the pine trees around them, and soon they had a temporary pine needle mattress.

"All the comforts of home," said Swifty.

"Smells a lot better than your home," replied Kit.

"I'm so tired I don't care what smartass remarks you make. I just want to sleep."

Within minutes all that could be heard was the chirping of the crickets and the snoring of two very tired cowboys.

CHAPTER
TWENTY-SEVEN

Sam and Ellie Lynn stood in front of the door to Luck's darkened office like they were trying to decide what to do. Sam broke the impasse by putting her hand on the door knob and opening the door.

"It's unlocked!"

"Maybe we shouldn't go in."

Sam's response was to push open the door and step inside the office. She quickly found the light switch and motioned for Ellie Lynn to join her.

"Isn't this illegal?" asked Ellie Lynn.

"Of course it's illegal, but only if we get caught."

"Oh, boy that's sure a relief to know."

"Relax. We're just going to check out the office and see if we can find any clues as to where Mr. Luck has disappeared."

Suddenly the door to the office slammed shut and both women whirled around to find themselves facing two men wearing black ski masks and pointing pistols at them.

"Oh shit," said Sam.

Ellie Lynn found herself unable to even scream. Her throat felt like it was tied up in a knot. Both women almost involuntarily put up their hands.

The taller of the two men whispered something to the shorter man, and he responded by stepping forward and relieving each of the women of their purses.

"Help yourself," said Sam. "All my money and my credit cards are in my purse."

"Me too," Ellie Lynn managed to get out in a high squeaky voice. She just wanted this to be over and for the men to leave.

"Turn around and put your hands flat on the desk," commanded the tall man.

Both women turned around so their backs were to the two gunmen, and they placed their hands flat on the desk. The next thing Ellie Lynn knew someone had grabbed her by the hair and jerked her head backwards and then a strange smelling cloth of some kind was placed over her mouth and nose. Everything went black.

Walt nudged each of the two women lying on the floor with his toe. Neither woman moved. He took off his ski mask and motioned to Kenny to take his off as well.

"Well, we got two for the price of one, Kenny. It must be our lucky day. It certainly ain't their lucky day."

"What do we do with them, Boss?"

"You go get the van and drive it around to the alley and pull up in back of this building to the service door we saw. Inside the van is a janitor's cart. Bring it up the elevator to this floor and leave the van parked in the alley. Got that?"

"Yes, Boss. I'll be right back."

As soon as Kenny was gone, Walt tied each woman's hands behind them using the plastic restraints he had brought with him in his backpack. He tied each woman's ankles together as well using more of the plastic restraints. He opened up the two body bags he had brought with him and gently rolled Sam into a bag and zipped it up, leaving the bag open at the end so her face was still uncovered. Then he did the same with Ellie Lynn.

He picked up the cloths soaked in chloroform and placed them in a small plastic bag and placed the bag in his backpack. Then Walt stood up and carefully surveyed the room. Walt was looking for anything that might indicate that either of the women had been in Luck's office. Satisfied that nothing seemed disturbed or out of place, he sat down in an office chair and waited for Kenny.

When Ellie Lynn regained consciousness, she found herself lying on a cold and rough concrete floor in a small dimly lit room. She could see Sam lying next to her and at first she feared that Sam was dead. She found that her hands were tied behind her, and her ankles were also tied. She managed to wiggle her way across the three feet that separated her from Sam. Ellie Lynn managed to get Sam's wrist in her hand and she could feel a pulse and could hear Sam's shallow breathing.

She lay there quietly listening for some clue as to where she was being held. At first she could hear noises, but she could not make out what they were. After about an hour had passed, the large steel door to the room began to open with the noise of metal being scraped against concrete. Ellie Lynn immediately pretended to be as unconscious as Sam. She could hear two men enter the room, and she steeled herself to remain motionless no matter what happened.

"Well, they're still out cold, Boss."

"They should be with all the chloroform we gave them. Still we better check them in an hour to make sure they will be nice and quiet for their ride to the farm."

"The big blonde one has nice looking tits."

"She certainly does," laughed Walt.

Kenny bent down next to Sam. Before Walt could stop him, he had ripped open her blouse and was fondling her bra-encased breasts.

In an instant Kenny was rolling across the hard concrete floor as a result of Walt having belted him in the side of the head.

"What the hell was that for?" yelled a bruised Kenny.

"We get the merchandise, we deliver he merchandise, but we don't use the merchandise. These two broads are going to be Harlo's private plaything before he gets tired of them and puts them out of their misery. I've known Harlo to let the rest of the hired help bang the women he has used when he was tired of them, but never before he was done with them. You want some of the blonde, you go to the farm with these two and when Harlo gets done with them, you'll get your chance along with the rest of his guys."

"Sorry, Boss, I just got carried away."

"I understand, just don't let it happen again. She does have a nice body. The little one isn't too bad either, but she doesn't have much in the chest department."

"She does have a nice ass though, Boss."

"That she does, Kenny. That she does. Nevertheless, our job is to keep these two on ice until the shit truck gets here in about an hour. Then we load them in the cigarette compartment and send them off to Harlo at the farm. In the meantime, nothing happens to them, understand?"

"I understand, Boss. Nothing will happen to them.'

"It'd better not or you'll be deader than a doorknob. You understand, Kenny?"

"Absolutely, Boss."

The two men left the room, closing and locking the metal door behind them.

Ellie Lynn slowly opened her eyes to make sure they were gone. Then she rolled over on her side. She couldn't believe what she'd just heard. This was a nightmare. It just couldn't be really happening. She glanced over at Sam and gasped as she saw that neither man had bothered to rearrange Sam's clothing and she lay on the floor with her bra exposed, her breasts rising and falling with her breathing.

Ellie Lynn was shocked by what she saw. She was in shock from what she had just heard from the two men. She and Sam were both going to be raped and abused by that sick and depraved Harlo Clay. Then he was going to turn them over to his men to be gang raped. Then he was going to kill both of them. She could see how his ancestor was capable of stealing from the Confederacy and killing his fellow soldiers. His family was just evil and so was Harlo.

Ellie Lynn knew she must get her emotions under control. She had to be calm. She had to think. She had to find a way out of this situation. She had to help herself and Sam. She felt her panic beginning to overwhelm her and then remembered that taking deep breaths had often helped her gain control over her emotions before.

Ellie Lynn remembered how out of control she had been when Carl had left her. She had been emotionally devastated to learn that the man she loved and believed loved her had lied to her, cheated on her, and stolen from her. She had taken a great deal of therapy back then and the deep breathing exercise was one of the things her therapist had taught her.

She began to take slow deep breaths, holding them for an instant and then slowly letting them out. After about five minutes her heart rate had slowed and she felt the rising panic subside and slowly begin to flow out of her.

When her breathing returned to normal, she began to think. What did she have at her disposal? Did she have any weapons? Did she have any tools?

Then she remembered the cell phone in her jacket pocket. She shifted her body around so she could rub her upper arm against the pocket area of the jacket. Yes! The cell phone was still here. She had been afraid that they had been searched and the cell phone confiscated. Now, how was she gong to be able to use it?

Ellie Lynn tried to estimate the distance between her wrists that the plastic ties allowed when she pulled her hands as far apart behind her as she could. She was surprised to find that there was almost ten inches of slack between her wrists. Then she tried to remember the details of an exercise she had done as a gymnast in high school. She was not a great deal larger than she had been back then, but she was not nearly as limber.

She now fervently wished she had continued with her Yoga and stretching exercises she used to do to improve her flexibility. Coming home tired from too much work at the bank had ended that schedule over a year ago. Still, it was worth a try. She flexed her knees several times, pressing her legs tightly against the bottom of her thighs. Then she found herself focusing almost Zen-like on the task before her.

When she felt she was ready, she rolled over onto her knees and then paused to rest before her next move. Her desire to turn the tables on her captors seemed to provide the extra motivation that she needed to complete the exercise. When she felt she was sufficiently relaxed, she began her move. With her hands behind her and held as low below her buttocks as she could manage, she tilted backward onto her back while she kept her legs tightly against her thighs.

With agonizing slowness she worked her hands down and over her feet until they were finally clear. Now her manacled wrists and hands were in front of her, not behind her back.

Ellie Lynn went down to her knees and carefully brought her hands up and pulled the cell phone out of her jacket pocket. With the slack in her plastic ties, she easily pushed the power button and waited for the phone to warm up and find local service. After what seemed like an entirely too long of a wait, the phone come to full service mode.

Ellie Lynn moved the phone to text messaging and tapped out the following message:

"Sam n I bn takn to farm w Harlo. Use GPS my fone to find us."

Then she scrolled to Kit's cell number in her directory and pushed send. She then scrolled to Billy K's cell number and sent the message again.

Ellie Lynn then shut off the phone and replaced it back in her jacket pocket. She was afraid to try to make a phone call fearing that if they heard her talking on the phone, they would rush in and kill both her and Sam. She worked on the plastic cuffs and managed to lengthen the distance between her wrists. She paused to make herself as relaxed as possible. When she felt fully relaxed, she did a reverse of her previous exercise so that once again her bound hands were behind her. Then she scooted sideways on the cold concrete floor until her body was resting against Sam. Ellie Lynn lay there in silence, and she prayed for their rescue.

CHAPTER
TWENTY-EIGHT

Kit awoke to the sounds of Swifty snoring and the cold, soft light of dawn. He slowly scanned his surroundings and saw nothing other than the pine trees, brush, rocks, grass, and the gravel road about forty yards below him. After a quick poke from Kit's elbow, Swifty was awake. Both men kept silent and listened carefully for any sound that could indicate trouble. Other than the wind in the tall pine trees and a few birds, they heard nothing.

After motioning for silence to Swifty, Kit led the way as they moved back up the slope to the grove of stunted pine trees where they had left the horses tied. As he rounded the group of small trees, Kit was greeted with the sight of nothing. The horses were gone. All that was left was the remnants of the vines they had used to tie them up and hobble them.

"Shit, Swifty. Using vines was a great idea. We provided them horses with a good meal and a quick way out of here," said Kit in disgust as he threw down the small piles of vine he had found on the ground.

"It don't matter, Kit. I think we're close to wherever that truck came from. The horses are probably back at the corral by now, and we're no longer officially horse thieves."

"That's a comfort, Swifty. A real comfort."

They began walking parallel to the road about twenty yards up on the slope. After a walk of about four miles, they could see the pine trees began to thin out and about a quarter of a mile ahead of them was the beginning of a sizeable meadow.

"I hear water running," said Swifty.

Kit paused and then he too could hear what sounded like a stream between them and the distant meadow. He motioned forward with his hand and they again began walking through the grassy hillside. Now the grass was almost waist high and the land was flattening out. They were getting lower and closer to the same level as the road.

Suddenly Kit went flying and he rolled about ten yards down the hill toward the road before he stopped.

"What happened? Are you all right?" yelled a concerned Swifty.

"I'm fine" said a surprised Kit. "I just tripped over something I didn't see in that tall grass. Kit got to his feet and walked back to where he had tripped. He knelt down and pushed back the grass and said, "I'll be damned."

"What is it?"

"It's a gravestone. I tripped over a gravestone."

"Gravestone? This don't look like no cemetery!"

"Maybe it's just one marker. Let's check it out."

They started to carefully walk through the area near where the gravestone was located and sure enough they were on the edge of a small graveyard.

"This must be pretty old to be deserted. Who would abandon a graveyard?"

"I think I see the answer to that," said Kit.

"This is a small group of maybe twenty-five to thirty graves. The headstones are simple rocks, not formal monuments. I can make out a few dates and words, but most of what was on the stones has worn off with time. It looks like most of these folks died prior to the Civil War. Some of them only have one name. My guess is this is a slaves' cemetery. After the war they probably left the plantation where they were slaves and went elsewhere, and this graveyard was abandoned."

"That makes pretty good sense, Kit, but why was it here?"

"I suppose the plantation was nearby, and it probably got burned down by the Union troops when they came through in 1865."

"You mean your great-great grandpa was a house burner?"

"He was one of Sherman's men and Sherman made sure that whoever his army ran into got a taste of how bad war can be. Sherman's march was easy to follow. Just go from one burned building to another."

Swifty had wandered past the small graveyard and looked down to see something unusual.

"Hey Kit, come take a look at this!"

Kit walked over to where his partner stood and Swifty pointed to a small line of rocks hidden in the tall grass.

"What do you make of this?"

Kit followed the line of rocks and after a few turns he looked up at Swifty and said, "This is an old stone foundation for a building."

They walked along the foundation, beating down the grass and soon they could see the outline of the foundation quite clearly.

"It wasn't a very big place," said Swifty.

"Nope it wasn't. By the looks of it, I'd say it was an old schoolhouse or a church."

Kit paused, realizing what he had just said. Both he and Swifty looked at each other and then back at the foundation and the graveyard beyond it.

"Partner, I think this is it!"

"You mean the graveyard and the church that you great-great grandpa saw on his way to where the gold was buried?"

"Exactly. I'll bet that stream we can hear is at the edge of that meadow and there is, or was, a stone bridge going over it. Let's head down the road and find out."

They scrambled down to the road and jogged toward the sound of the stream.

The road began a slight decline and as they rounded a small turn that was partially hidden from view by a stand of small pine trees, they came to a stop. There below them was the stream they had heard from their overnight camp. Spanning the creek was a fairly modern concrete bridge that could easily handle two lanes of traffic. Beyond the bridge lay the open expanse of a large meadow. To their right they could see a cluster of buildings that seemed to hug the far right side of the meadow.

Kit took a look at the sign just beyond the bridge and groaned.

"What's wrong, Kit?"

"Check out the sign on the other side of the bridge."

Swifty looked past the bridge to the large sign on the right side of the road.

"Andrew Jackson State Park? Hell, we were here a few days ago. This ain't the place!"

"Maybe it is, and maybe it isn't. Maybe we didn't look hard enough. Let's hoof it up to the park and get a land line phone we can use. My cell phone is still not getting enough of a signal to use it."

Minutes later they were in the small visitor's center. Kit used the pay phone while Swifty got coffee and rolls from the snack bar.

Swifty was hard at work consuming his third roll when Kit sat down.

"Have a roll. They're pretty good. What did you find out?"

"Thanks," said Kit as he sat down at the table and took a bite out of the cinnamon roll in front of him. "I couldn't raise Ellie Lynn at all. I left her a message. I couldn't raise Billy K either, but I left him a message to let him know where we were and I left him the pay phone number."

"Why the pay phone number?"

"Because my cell is still not showing we have any real service here."

"What do we do now?"

"We finish breakfast and try to find some transportation. Maybe we can hitch a ride with one of the visitors."

"Look around, partner. It must be too early for visitors. We appear to be the only guests in the park."

Kit looked up from his coffee and surveyed the room. Swifty was right. Except for the two ladies working at the snack bar and the ranger at the information desk, the two of them were the sole occupants.

Just as Kit was putting the last of the cinnamon roll in his mouth and reaching for his cup of coffee, the pay phone rang loudly.

Kit spilled his coffee as he leaped up from the table and tried to swallow the remnants of the roll left in his mouth.

He dashed to the phone and answered with a muffled, "Hello."

"Is this Kit?"

"Yes!"

"You sound like you got a mouth full of cotton, boy."

Kit swallowed the last of the roll and managed to retort, "Screw you."

"How unpleasant of you, Kit. Where are your manners?"

"You're a fine one to talk about manners, Billy K. Where the hell are you?"

"Actually I'm not far from you. I'm much closer than you might think, and I have a little surprise for you. Stop stuffing your face and look out into the parking lot."

Kit turned from facing the pay phone and looked out through the glass door of the welcome center to the parking lot. When he and Swifty had arrived, the lot was almost empty. Now smack dab in the middle of the previously empty parking lot there was an all too familiar sight that was not quite the same.

Looking like it had just rolled off the General Motors assembly line was his 1949 GMC three quarter ton pickup truck. The truck's new green paint job gleamed in the morning sun. Both doors of the truck opened and out of the passenger side stepped Billy K. Out of the driver's side stepped a giant of a man wearing a familiar cowboy hat and dressed in worn denims. Big Dave Carlson stood there with his hands on his hips looking a whole lot like John Wayne arriving with the cavalry.

CHAPTER
TWENTY-NINE

Ellie Lynn heard them coming. She pretended to be asleep when they opened the steel door and came into the room. Sam was still lying on the concrete floor unconscious.

Out of the corner of her eye, Ellie Lynn watched as the taller man knelt next to Sam and checked her pulse. Then he rearranged her clothing so that her bra was covered. She was surprised to see that small act of kindness from one of her captors. Then she saw him place an chloroform bottle against a clean cloth and press the cloth against Sam's mouth and nose. Sam's slow breathing continued uninterrupted.

Then Ellie Lynn felt the man take her pulse and when he applied the chloroform soaked cloth to her face, she managed to hold her breath and continued to pretend to be unconscious.

The two men left the room and returned with what looked like a gurney. They both lifted Sam up and placed her carefully on the gurney. Within a minute the men, Sam, and the gurney were gone.

As soon as they were gone, Ellie Lynn quit holding her breath and sucked in the cold clean air as though it were a delicious wine. Her lungs went from aching to feeling sated. She reveled in knowing that she had outwitted her captors. She reminded herself she needed to keep the celebration short. She had to keep her wits about her and use her victory to her advantage as soon as she could.

They two men returned, and they placed her gently on the gurney and pushed it with Ellie Lynn as the cargo through the large warehouse.

Soon she felt the light of the sun and the fresh air of the outside as she was pushed past an open warehouse door.

Then she was almost overcome by the putrid smell of horse manure. She was suddenly reminded of the time she and Kit were walking by the stable in Charleston after they had dined at Anson's. That seemed so long ago. She wondered where Kit was now and if he had received her text message. She knew she and Sam were in serious trouble and would need Kit's help if they were to get out of this mess alive.

Ellie Lynn carefully looked out of the corner of her eye and saw she was next to a large truck. She could see and smell the bed of the truck was full of horse manure and it was uncovered. That seemed odd to her considering how careful the people from Hanging Rock Farm had been in removing the horse manure from the small stable in downtown Charleston.

She recalled they had used a sealed stainless steel container to contain the smell. So why would they transport the manure in a big open truck? Then she heard a scraping noise and could see there were several compartments hidden beneath the truck bed of manure. They were like drawers that ran out from under the truck bed on stainless steel rollers. They were shutting one of the drawers, and she could see Sam's still body lying in the drawer.

Ellie Lynn fought back tears. She couldn't let them know she was conscious. She had to keep control of herself. She willed herself to appear unconscious.

She heard the stainless steel drawer being opened and felt the men's hands as they grabbed her body and lifted her off the gurney and into the steel drawer. No sooner was she placed on her side in the drawer than she felt a hand squeeze one of her buttocks. She fought back a gasp.

"What the hell are you doing, Kenny?"

"Hey, she has a nice lookin' ass. I just wanted to feel it. Where she's going it ain't gonna matter to her."

"You're sick, Kenny. If you worked in a morgue, you'd be screwing the cadavers."

"Well, I wouldn't get no complaints," laughed Kenny.

Then the drawer was pushed shut, and the compartment was dark.

Ellie Lynn's first fear was that she was going to suffocate from lack of air. Then she felt the flow of air over her face.

Where was it coming from? She could not see any air holes nor any light coming from the outside. Then she realized that there was some sort of system above her head that was moving air through the drawer compartments and that was what she felt on her face. She could also pick up the scent of something familiar and it was sort of pleasant, not like horse manure.

She took another whiff and then realized what she was smelling was tobacco. It smelled like cigarette tobacco, not pipe tobacco and then it dawned on her. These hidden compartments were being used to smuggle counterfeit cigarettes. That was why they were carrying horse manure in an open truck bed. The smell and the nature of the cargo kept anyone from checking the truck very closely, and it was the perfect cover for moving smuggled cigarettes. She had a feeling there was a lot more money in illegal untaxed cigarettes than there was in hay and grain. So much for the Hanging Rock Farm being the sole source of Wendy and Lee Regret's wealth.

Then Ellie Lynn felt the truck move, and she could feel the bumps in the parking lot as the truck moved out of the warehouse area and onto the street to begin its journey to Hanging Rock Farm.

Ellie Lynn remembered what the man called Kenny had said about what was coming next. She knew she and Sam were being sent to Hanging Rock Farm and were to be turned over to Harlo. She knew what a sick psychopath he was, and she feared for both Sam and herself. Although she tried to fight against it, Ellie Lynn found herself softly sobbing in the darkness.

CHAPTER THIRTY

Wendy Regret sat impatiently on the sofa of her office while she waited for her brother to finish his conversation and get off the phone. Finally he said something she assumed to be adios and shut off his cell phone.

Lee Regret turned to face his sister. He had a hard look to his eyes, but she as used to that. In the past twenty years they had both done hard things to get what they wanted and then to hang on to it.

His stern face broke into a smile.

"Wendy, darlin'. I think you're gonna like this."

"What? What is it? What's happened?"

"I told you that the former cop Samantha Butler was getting too close to our business. Remember?"

"I remember. What's she got to do with us now?"

"She used a private eye and had figured out our cigarette smuggling deal."

"Why that nosy bitch. How much does she know?"

"I'm not sure how much she knows. The important thing is that it soon won't matter what she does or doesn't know."

"How's that?"

"That was Walt on the phone. I had him get rid of the private eye, a guy named Luck."

"So Mr. Luck has cashed out. What about Butler?"

"I had Walt search Luck's home and office. We found nothing that could incriminate either of us in any way. Walt destroyed the evidence that Luck had on him and his equipment."

"Good for Walt. It sounds like he has a bonus coming."

"That he does. Especially since he caught Ms. snoopy Butler in Luck's office and knocked her out. Seems she had Ms. Ellie Lynn Main with her, and Walt nailed her as well."

"That's great news. I never liked Butler, and I couldn't stand that prissy Ellie Lynn. What's the plan?"

"Walt took them back to the warehouse after he cleaned up the scene at Luck's office. He'll hold them there until the shit truck arrives. Then he'll load them in a cigarette compartment and send both of them back with the next shit load to the farm and Harlo."

"Harlo! How fitting! He may be our cousin and most of the time he's a pain in the ass, but he is just the right man for taking care of those two troublemakers. I want to be there to see him work them over. Then I want to watch when he kills them."

"You're getting meaner every day, sister. I think we can manage to get away from our daily work here long enough to see Harlo carry out his assignment. That way we're sure there are no loose ends."

"And make sure that any threat to our business is wiped out."

"Always a good idea, sis. I'll get the car and bring it around to the front door."

"Thank you, Lee."

CHAPTER THIRTY-ONE

Kit rushed out to shake hands with Big Dave only to find his hand engulfed in Dave's giant fist and then feel himself lifted up in the air in a great bear hug. When he finally hit the ground, he felt like he had the air crushed out of him.

"What the hell are you doing here, Big Dave?"

"Well, I got tired of you boys having all the fun down here and when old Elmer called me to tell me your truck was done, I knew it was a sign."

"A sign?"

"Yep. It was a sign that I was supposed to deliver the truck to you in person. That way I could also see what the hell was going on down here. You mention gold to an old feller like me, and I just naturally got to come and take a look see."

"How did you hook up with Billy K?"

"Well, I sort of ran into him in the lobby of your hotel."

"Ran into me is putting it mildly. I'm lucky I didn't get a concussion," said Billy.

"What the hell are you talking about?" said Kit.

"I was about to turn and head out of the hotel lobby, and I ran smack dab in to the gentle giant here and got knocked on my ass. He apologized and helped me up. Once I got my eyes to focus and could see the cowboy outfit, I had a sneaking suspicion he had to be another wild man from Wyoming. So I asked and sure enough he was. God, you hang around with some rough characters, Andrews!"

Kit smiled. So did Swifty. Big Dave was already smiling.

"Before we get carried away with the hellos and the howdy-dos, we have a problem, Kit," said Billy.

"I got this test message on my cell phone. I've been talking with Ms. Main, just like you told me to, and she let me know she was going to check out some private eye's office with the lady bank cop."

"Samantha Buter?"

"Yeah. That's the one. Anyway she said she would call me by a set time and she never did. I kept calling her and got no answer. Then I got a text message from her."

"What did it say?"

"Here, let me show you."

Billy K then pushed some buttons on his cell phone and then when he found what he was looking for, he handed the phone to Kit.

"Sam n I bn takn to farm w Harlo. Use GPS my fone to find us."

"Jesus Christ! Ellie Lynn and Sam have been kidnapped and are being taken to Harlo at the farm!"

"What in the wild blue blazes are you talking about, son?" asked Big Dave.

Kit took a few minutes to give Big Dave the basic story and filled in a few blanks for Billy K as well.

"So what do we do now?" asked Swifty.

Before Kit could speak, he heard the strong voice of Big Dave.

"Before we go off half-cocked and get our asses blown off, maybe we should make us a plan."

Big Dave's words seemed to have a calming effect on everyone, especially Kit.

"Where's your truck, Swifty?" asked Big Dave.

"To tell you the truth I ain't real sure. It's about a two hour horseback ride from here, somewhere."

"I know exactly where it is," said Kit.

"How in the hell could you know that?" asked Swifty.

Kit pulled out his small GPS and after he got it warmed up, he pointed to a wayside mark on the small screen. "The truck is right near this mark. I marked the last turn we took before we got to the horse ranch on my GPS."

"Well, how far is it from here to that there mark?" asked Big Dave.

Kit took a reading of their present location and then checked the scale. 'We're about sixteen miles northeast of the truck."

"Let's go," said Big Dave. "I'll drive with Kit in the front. You two grab some space in the back."

Half an hour later they were parked next to Swifty's truck. The truck was none the worse for wear except for a bullet hole in the back of the tailgate.

Big Dave put his finger into the bullet hole. "You boys been ridin' around in Indian Country?" he asked.

"You might say that," replied a grinning Swifty.

They broke some soft drinks and bottled water out of the cooler and then spread out the maps Swifty had in the truck as they began to plan their strategy.

After a few arguments, they agreed that Big Dave's plan was probably the best. They decided that since none of them had ever been on the farm they needed some on site information about the layout of the farm before they just walked in and got shot to pieces. Big Dave referred to it as "on site intelligence."

Big Dave's plan was for him to drive the old truck into the farm to buy some hay. To make sure no one got suspicious, they removed the Wyoming license plates. Big Dave figured an old truck with no plates would seem pretty normal at a hay farm. To complete the deception, Big Dave rolled around on the ground in the dust to make his clothes good and dirty. He ran over his beloved Stetson cowboy hat six times with the old truck. Then he had everyone pick up handfuls of dust and throw it on the truck. In no time the beautiful new paint job Elmer had done was dulled so that it just looked like a dusty old pickup truck.

*   *   *

Harvey and Jim were loading a small delivery truck with bales of hay and six eighty pound bags of grain when they heard an engine approaching the entrance to Hanging Rock Farm.

"Take a gander at that old rig, Jim!"

"Shit, that truck must be older than the two of us put together."

"Hell, the driver looks even older. I ain't never seen him around here before."

"Me neither. Let's see what he wants."

Big Dave pulled the GMC slowly up next to the delivery truck and stepped out of the old pickup. He was careful to move, very slowly.

"Hey there old timer. How's it shakin?" said Harvey

"Sonny, I'd be happy if I had somethin' to shake."

Both Harvey and Jim roared with laughter.

"What's the matter, old timer, havin' trouble getting' it up?"

"Funny you should mention that, sonny. I was just over to the Doc's yesterday and told him I was havin' a problem. He asked me what the problem was and I told him that my sex drive was too high. He said having a sex drive too high shouldn't be a problem, especially for an old coot like me. I told him my problem was that my sex drive was all up in my mind and I wanted to see if he could help me to move it down lower."

Big Dave was gesturing with his hands to illustrate his story and again both farm hands almost bent over double with laughter.

"What kin we help you with, old timer?" said Harvey

"Well, I heard tell this was a good place to get some quality hay and since I just moved to these parts, I drove over here to see if it was so."

"We got the best hay and grain in South Carolina," said Jim.

"That's right," said Harvey, "the best."

"I'm powerful glad to hear that, boys. Powerful glad. This is some spread you got here. Just how big is it?"

"The farm is about 2,000 acres, but all the buildings and shops and such are right here," said Jim. "We got us livin' quarters that are better than any motel you could find in Columbia. We got a mess hall with three meals a day, and we get paid damn well."

"Man alive, that's amazin'. Are they hiring?"

"They don't need no help and we don't hire old coots like you. We sell and deliver hay and grain all over South Carolina. Even in Charleston where we got a warehouse full of stuff."

"Man, that's a lot of land. How many boys like you they got workin' here?"

"Normally there's about twenty-two. Usually half of us are out on deliveries and the rest are working the fields or setting up loads."

"I suppose some rich guy owns the place. Let me guess. The owner is some rich Yankee from New York?"

"Not a chance in hell, old timer. This here place is part of an old Confederate's plantation and his family still owns it. Lee and Wendy Regret own Hanging Rock Farm and their cousin Harlo Clay runs it for them. The Regrets live in Charleston, and they deal in real estate. They's real successful folks."

"So they live in the big plantation house over yonder?"

"Nope, you old fool. Like I told you they live in Charleston. They stay in the big house when they come to visit the farm."

"So this here Harlo fella, he don't live in the big house?"

"Hell no. Harlo lives in the old stable over there. He got it fixed up real nice. Got a weight room, satellite TV, and everything."

"This here Harlo must be some fella."

"Old Harlo is a real mean son-of-a-bitch and hard to work for, but he pays well."

"So this is one of them real southern plantations?"

"That's right, old timer. Just run your truck over to that barn across the road and we'll fix you up with some of the best hay in South Carolina."

For the next fifteen minutes the two men loaded up Big Dave's pickup with bales of hay. They didn't notice that Big Dave was carefully looking over the layout of the farm instead of watching them load the hay on his truck. When they finished loading, Big Dave paid them in cash, got a receipt and drove slowly back the way he had come, carefully observing everything he saw along the way. When he was out of sight of the farm, he stopped the truck. He pulled a pad of paper and a pen out of the glove box and began making a crude sketch of the layout of the farm and what buildings he had identified from his conversation with the two farm hands.

*   *   *

An hour later, Big Dave, Kit, Swifty, and Billy K were pouring over the satellite map that Swifty had spread out on the tailgate of his truck.

Big Dave laid out the crude map of the layout of the farm he had made. He also had some mental notes and he added them to the crude map.

Now Swifty made a new paper map of the grounds. It included all the outbuildings and roads as well as the site of the water well and the area where all the vehicles were serviced. In front of the truck shop were two large suspended tanks that provided gasoline to the trucks and tractors on the farm. A separate suspended tank appeared to hold diesel fuel. A smaller tank had been marked "kerosene."

After taking them on a virtual tour of the farm grounds, Big Dave spoke out.

"We have to assume that there will be at least fifteen able bodied men at the farm. How many of them are willing to fight might be less, but you have to assume that all of them will fight. In talking with the two farm hands, I'm pretty sure that I've labeled all the buildings correctly. I'm guessing at a few, but I'm pretty sure that the women are being held in this old stable. The workers mentioned that this guy Harlo is a guy who is obsessed with power and sex. It seems this Harlo fella lives on the main floor of the stable and he has some kind of kinky rooms in a basement under the stable. It sounded like anyone on the farm who was getting punished ended up down there and was never seen again. Not a real popular place with those guys, anyway."

"So how do we get Sam and Ellie Lynn out?" asked Kit.

"We use our best weapon."

"Which is what?"

"Surprise. We scare the hell out of these hillbillies."

"Just how do we do that?"

"We pick the best time to surprise them and we create a diversion to keep them busy while we sneak in and get the women out. We wait until about midnight tonight. By then things should be real quiet. These boys may be bad guys, but they are also doin' hard physical labor workin' on a farm and they don't tend to stay up late."

You three drive Swifty's truck to a point just out of sight of the farm without using any lights. Then you wait for my signal."

"What's the signal?"

"I'll drive quietly into the farm in the GMC with no lights on and get to the far side of the main buildings. When you see me drive into the farm, Kit and Swifty will sneak in on foot and take a position next to the stable building. After I'm in the middle of the farm buildings, I'll turn the truck around. I'll drive up close to those gas tanks in front of the shop. Then I'll light and throw some Molotov cocktails we can make with the old beer bottles in the back of Swifty's truck. This should cause a diversion and draw anyone there out towards me. Kit and Swifty will be hidden next to the stable. When they see the light from the first Molotov cocktail, they break into the stable and get to the lower level. The women should be there. If they are incapacitated or hurt, use a fireman's carry and get them out to the front of the stable."

"As soon as you have the women, call Billy K on the cell phone and then Billy is to come roarin' in the front gate in the Ford and go straight to the stable and get Kit, Swifty, and the women. Keep your truck lights off, Billy. Load everyone up and then get the hell out of there."

"What about you, Big Dave?" asked Kit.

"I'm going to use one or two of these cocktails to blow up the gas tanks and the vehicle shop. That way they got nothing to chase us with. Then I'll come blowing out the front gate right behind Swifty's truck."

"Seems to me you're the one they're gonna be shootin' at, Big Dave."

"I'm sure you're right. But that old truck has more steel in its carcass than any five of those Ford trucks like Swifty's. Them boys are likely mostly armed with 9 millimeters and 40 caliber pistols and those guns won't penetrate the doors of the GMC. Besides, I plan to use some of these hay bales I just bought to make the truck more bullet proof."

"What do we do then?" asked Kit.

"We hightail it to Kershaw and the sheriff. We may need to get them girls to a doctor and a hospital."

"There should be a hospital in Kershaw," said Kit.

Billy K then interrupted, "That's your plan?"

"Sonny, I was makin' plans to blow things up when you was still in diapers. Surprise is on our side and it should be enough unless one of us does something to screw it up."

"Well, I see a little problem," said Billy K.

"What's the problem, Billy?"

"What if the women are being held in a room or a cell that's locked?"

"We blow it open. Oh shit! We don't have any explosives!"

"Exactly."

"What's your solution, Billy?"

"I can open any lock. Can Swifty?"

Big Dave looked at Swifty who shook his head in an emphatic no.

"Okay. Change of plans. Billy and Kit go in and Swifty drives the truck."

The other three nodded their agreement.

"O.K. how are we fixed for weapons?"

Swifty started pulling guns from various hiding places in the truck. He checked each one to make sure they were in working order and then let each of the men take their pick. After each had chosen a gun they were comfortable with, Swifty gave each of them a couple of pockets full of ammunition. Soon the only noise to be heard was the sound of bullets being fed into magazines and the actions of weapons being tested.

Big Dave used a small length of rubber tubing to siphon some gas out of the Ford and filled six empty beer bottles. He then stuffed small rags into the bottles tops and placed all six bottles in a cardboard six-pack holder he found in the bed of Swifty's truck. He filled the holder with the modified beer bottles and placed the package on the floor of the GMC where it was within easy reach of the driver.

Big Dave looked up to see Kit rubbing his hand over the smooth fender of the restored old GMC.

"Is something wrong, Kit?"

"I'm just saying good-bye to a great restoration job, Big Dave. I got this feeling that it's not gonna last."

All four men broke out laughing.

CHAPTER
THIRTY-TWO

Lee's Land Rover pulled up next to the stable and he and Wendy got out. It was already dark outside, but at Wendy's insistence they had not stopped for supper. Wendy knew that Harlo would begin working on the two women as soon as he could, and she did not want to miss any of the action. Lee was a man who enjoyed making a lot of money and did not care what he had to do to accomplish his goal.

Lee didn't care what happened to his victims, but he did not enjoy it, and he was revolted by Harlo's love of violence and inflicting pain on others. Wendy liked money, but she liked power even more. She also enjoyed having pain inflicted on those whom she did not like or those who opposed her. She didn't like either Samantha or Ellie Lynn and was looking forward to seeing them humiliated and abused by Harlo.

They entered the front door of the empty and dimly lit stable building and immediately took a left turn to the far side of the building. Guarding a doorway was a tall skinny man with red hair. He was armed with a pistol in his belt.

"Hello Red," said Lee.

"Evenin' Mr. Regret, Ms. Regret."

"How are things going, Red?"

"Pretty good, sir. Harlo was real glad to see them two gals show up in the shit wagon. He took them downstairs, and he's bin workin' on the blonde for over two hours."

"So we're a little late for the show," said Lee.

"Damn," said Wendy as the expression on her face reflected her disappointment.

"I'm sure there is plenty of show time left if I know my cousin Harlo. You'll get to see what you want, Wendy. I'm sure

Harlo video taped the entire deal so you can see it after the fact."

"I'm real sorry we let them cowboys get away from us, Mr. Regret."

"I wouldn't worry much about them, Red. They're probably headed back to wherever they came from by now."

"Yes sir. I sure hope so."

Red hastened to open the door and Lee and Wendy went through the doorway to a set of stairs leading down to the basement of the stable building. At the bottom of the stairs was a landing with a steel door leading into the basement. Lee opened the door and ushered his sister into the basement. There they were met by their cousin Harlo.

Harlo was shirtless and wearing a pair of athletic shorts and stout leather boots. His muscular body seemed to throw off a light sheen in the well lit basement room. It almost looked like he was covered in baby oil when in fact he was covered with sweat. He shook hands with his guests and led them into a long narrow room that he had built as a "viewing room" for guests such as his cousins. It had also been used as an observation room when he wanted someone to watch or perhaps record on tape the activities of his prisoners without their knowledge.

One entire wall of the room was one way glass. There were several easy chairs as well as a counter with electronic recording equipment and video equipment. Harlo opened a refrigerator and provided cold beers for Lee and Wendy.

"You're just in time," said Harlo

"What did we miss?" asked Wendy.

"You missed all my action with Butler, but I recorded it and you can watch it later. I'm just taking a break before getting ready to take on little Miss Main and you can see all of that live and in person. Tomorrow I'll let several of my men in here and let them have their fun with both of the women.

"Tell me what you did to dear Samantha. I want all the details," said Wendy.

Harlo went to a set of control switches on the wall. He flicked one and the lights in the next room went on. There were a large number of lights recessed in the ceiling and the room was exceptionally well lit.

"Wow, that's awfully bright in there," said Lee.

"I need it to make sure the recordings are good. I've got six digital cameras mounted in the walls and ceiling and they get all the angles, but I need good light to make sure the final recording gets all the details perfectly."

"I call this room my workshop for obvious reasons. Once a woman enters this room she's mine. When I'm done with her, she's a broken woman. No matter how tough they seem when they walk in, when I'm done with them they're broken. I can then give them to my men without taking any precautions because by then they are as passive as an old whore. I love breaking their spirit almost as much as I enjoy inflicting pain on them."

"So, what happened with Butler?" Wendy had heard Harlo's rants before, and she wanted him to get back to the juicy details of what he did to hurt Samantha.

Harlo sat on a stool next to the counter with the recording equipment. He turned until he was facing Wendy, and then he smiled. It was not a pleasant smile.

"She was everything I had hoped for and more. She is this tall, well built blonde with long legs and big boobs. She is also an ex-cop and trained in all kinds of self-defense. When she finally woke up and Andy brought her into the workshop, she was full of attitude."

"Attitude?" asked Wendy.

"Yeah, attitude. You know the kind of broad who thinks she's still in control, but she's not and she's about to find that out the hard way."

Wendy was tempted to ask a question, but then decided to keep quiet and let Harlo tell his entire story uninterrupted.

Before Harlo could continue, Lee interrupted him. "I assume the rest of the story is a rerun of all the others I've heard. I have financials to check up on at the big house. You stay here and let Harlo entertain you, sis. Come on up for supper when you've had enough of Harlo and his theatrics."

Lee turned and then disappeared back up the staircase.

Harlo stared after him with an annoyed look on his face.

"Please continue Harlo. Don't pay any mind to my brother." Wendy had no intention of letting supper with her brother interfere with the Harlo's detailed story of inflicting pain on Samantha Butler.

Harlo contined on with his story to his entranced audience of one.

When Harlo finished his story, it was obvious that Wendy wanted more.

"Where is she now?"

"She's over in one of the rooms. Unless I miss my guess, Andy and Red are flipping a coin to see who gets to take her on first."

"Where is little Miss Ellie?"

"She's waiting in another locked room and after I've had another beer, I'll have Andy bring her in and give you a real show."

"Will this be just like the one with Butler?"

"No. This time I'll show you how I can get the uppity Main broad to do anything I want without having to hurt her in the least."

"So you're not going to hurt her?" Wendy sounded disappointed.

"I didn't say that. I said I would get her to do what I wanted without hurting her. I plan to hurt her a lot."

Wendy smiled.

$$* \quad * \quad *$$

Ellie Lynn was worried. She was in a small dimly lit room that was made out of concrete block. There were no windows. Just a peep-hole in the steel door. She was sure she could make out a small video camera about nine feet up against the concrete ceiling. After the truck had arrived at the farm with its hidden cargo, she and Sam and been pulled out of the drawers under the manure load and been carried over the shoulders of two very large men like sacks of potatoes.

She was carried into a brightly lit room and stripped of her clothes, leaving her clad only in her underwear. Then she was lifted up again and placed on the cold and dirty floor of this room. She was pretty sure they had not found her hidden cell phone, but that didn't mater now as she could no longer get to it. A thorough search of her room had revealed that it contained nothing but her. When they had removed her clothes, they had cut her restraints. When they were finished undressing her, they had placed new plastic restraints that tied her hands in front of her.

She had heard them take Sam down the hall located in front of her cell. Sam was yelling and swearing at her captors. She could hear some muffled screams over the next two hours, and then it was quiet. It was too quiet. Ellie Lynn desperately tried to think of a plan but could come up with nothing. She was sure her message had gotten through and Kit or Billy or both were on their way to rescue her and Sam. All she could do was try to find a way to stall for time so they could get to the farm before it was too late. She knew that Harlo was a psychopath who liked to hurt people, and she was sure he would abuse both her and Sam before he decided to kill them.

Ellie Lynn did not want to die and if help didn't arrive, she would find some way to fight back, even against a huge monster like Harlo.

CHAPTER
THIRTY-THREE

As the two truck column pulled out onto a country blacktop road that led to the Hanging Rock Farm, a county sheriff's patrol car coming from the direction of the farm stopped in front of them. Both trucks came to a stop.

"What's this?" said Kit.

"Hope it's not that dopey deputy," said Swifty.

The patrol car door opened and out stepped Sheriff Horton. Both trucks emptied with the exception of Big Dave. Soon Kit was introducing the Sheriff to Billy K. While they were talking, Big Dave remained in the GMC talking on Kit's cell phone.

"Am I interruptin' something, Kit?"

"Well, Sheriff, we're actually kind of glad to see you."

"How's that?"

Kit went on to explain to the sheriff about the kidnapping of the two women and the text message that showed they were being held at the Hanging Rock Farm.

"Why the hell would the Regrets do something stupid like that?"

"We think they have some kind of illegal activity going on and the two women found out about it. Regret kidnapped them and brought them to the farm to get rid of them and eliminate what they know," replied Kit.

"You mean he plans to kill them!"

"We think he plans to let Harlo use them first, and then have him kill them and dispose of the bodies."

"I wouldn't put anything past Harlo. He's a real mean one. But I still can't see the Regrets involved in this. You're sure this ain't just Harlo?"

"Sheriff, do you really think Harlo could be pulling off something like this and the Regrets not know anything about it. I doubt he's that smart."

"Harlo may not be real smart, but he's shrewd. You can't underestimate him and I think he'd be like a cornered animal if you try to take him down. He's plenty dangerous."

"We've had a little experience in taking down wild animals," interrupted Swifty.

The sheriff looked around at the small group. "You're gonna need some help. I'll call my office and get some deputies out here, and we can surround the place and make sure nobody gets away. I'll also call the State Police and the FBI since this sounds like a kidnapping to me."

"You do that, Sheriff," said Swifty. "But meantime we got to get them girls out of there before Harlo kills them."

The sheriff nodded his agreement and went back to his car where they could see him talking on his police radio.

"Saddle up boys," said Big Dave as he emerged from the GMC and tossed the cell phone back to Kit. Soon the little two truck column was racing down the blacktop towards their appointment with Harlo and his men at the Hanging Rock Farm.

Minutes after they left, the sheriff turned his patrol car around and headed in the same direction as the two trucks.

CHAPER
THIRTY-FOUR

"I can't wait to see how you do this with Ellie Lynn. She's such a goody two-shoes."

"Watch and learn, Wendy."

Harlo picked up a phone and hit the intercom button.

"Andy. Are you there?"

"Yes, Boss."

"Are you and Red done with the blonde?"

"Yes, Boss."

"Good. Now bring her back up to the workshop."

"Right away, Boss."

Five minutes later Andy came into the workshop. He was short and stocky with a weightlifters build. He was half carrying and half dragging Samantha Butler. Sam was wearing a torn and dirty robe that barely covered her. Her exposed body showed numerous bruises and her face was streaked with dirt and dried blood. Her hair hung in dirty tangles.

Andy placed her in a wooden chair in the middle of the room. He didn't bother to tie her feet to the arms and legs of the chair with plastic ties as he had done previously.

Wendy could see her face and upper body were bruised. She had a black eye and her nose appeared to be broken. She was bleeding from the mouth and nose and from what looked like cut marks on her neck, arms and chest. Samantha hung her head like the beaten woman she was. She kept her eyes focused on the floor.

"Why is she here? I thought you were done with her?"

"Almost. She's about to serve one very useful last purpose for me as you are about to witness."

"Andy?"

Andy was still standing by the door to the workshop.

"Yes, Boss?"

"Go get the Main woman. Make sure you blindfold her first. Okay?"

"Right away, Boss."

Five minutes later Andy led Ellie Lynn into the workshop. She was blindfolded, and she had her hands tied in front of her. Andy led her to a second wooden chair with its back to Samantha. The chair faced the one-way glass of the viewing room.

Andy pushed Ellie Lynn into the chair and then untied her hands. He tied her ankles to the legs of the chair and her wrists to the arms of the chair with plastic ties. He left the blindfold on. Then Andy went back to the door and stood there with his eyes riveted on Ellie Lynn.

Harlo stepped through the door of the observation room and into the workshop area and walked over until he was standing right in front of where Ellie Lynn was tied to the chair.

"Good evening, Miss Main. How're you feeling?"

"You bastard! What've you done with Samantha? I demand that you let us go."

"You demand. I don't think so. Here I make the demands and you may not find them to your liking."

"What demands?"

"Whatever I tell you to do, you're gonna do."

"I'd rather die."

"I don't think so, and in a minute you'll see why."

Harlo stepped forward and pulled the blindfold off Ellie Lynn. He smiled as he could see the terror in her eyes as they adjusted to he bright lights. He could also see the hate.

"As I said, first I'm going to cut you free and then you're gonna strip for me."

"Not a chance in hell, Harlo."

"I think you'll change your mind very quickly, Miss Main."

Ellie Lynn squinted as her eyes adjusted to the bright lights overhead. She could see Harlo's face twisted in a cruel smile. She could smell the stink of his sweat. She shivered.

Harlo then reached down and turned Ellie Lynn's chair around with her still tied in it. Now Ellie Lynn was facing Samantha and she was visibly shocked by what she saw.

"What have you done to her? My God, what kind of an animal are you!"

"I'm just a very powerful man and you're next on my menu, Miss Main."

"Like hell I am. I'll never let you do that to me."

"Oh, I think you will. Watch this."

Harlo moved over to Samantha. He pulled out a long hunting knife and held it up for Ellie Lynn to see. The bright metal of the long blade flashed in the overhead lights.

"It's very sharp. Let me demonstrate."

He pressed the sharp side of the blade against Samantha's throat. She cried out in pain and blood began to drip from the cut he had inflicted.

'It's very simple. You do as I say or I'll slit her throat and kill her right in front of you. You can watch her bleed to death. And it will be because you refused to do what I want. Do you understand the rules, Miss Main?"

Ellie Lynn was rendered speechless. She was frightened out of her mind. She now knew no help was coming no matter what message she had sent on her cell phone to Billy and Kit. She also knew that Harlo would probably kill her and Samantha as soon as he was done playing with them.

"Don't think I'll do it? Watch this."

Harlo took the knife and pressed the point of the blade against Samantha's throat. Then he slowly drew the blade across her throat so that blood began oozing out. Samantha screamed in pain.

"Oh, God! Please don't do that to her! I'll do whatever you ask, but please don't kill her," sobbed Ellie Lynn.

"I thought you might reconsider, Miss Main," said Harlo as he turned toward her.

He walked over to Ellie Lynn. She visibly flinched at his touch as he bent over her and cut the ties that bound her ankles and wrists. He then stepped away from her and placed his knife back in the sheath on his belt.

"Stand up!"

Ellie Lynn got shakily to her feet, rubbing her sore wrists as she did so.

"Now strip!"

Suddenly Ellie Lynn heard what sounded like an explosion followed by another explosion and the floor of the stable building seemed to shake and the overhead lights flickered, but stayed on. Harlo stopped dead in his tracks, looked quickly around the room and then turned and ran for the door to the stairwell.

"What is it, Harlo?" screamed Wendy.

"I don't know. Andy, watch these two. Wendy, come with me."

Harlo grabbed Wendy by the hand and they flew through the door and out of the room. Andy just stood by the door to the workshop. He was not sure what to do, but he had been told to stay and stay he would.

When Harlo got to the front door of the stable building, he told Red that Andy was guarding the women and he wanted Red to take Wendy to the big house while he went to find out what was going on. Harlo could see flames coming from the direction of the truck shop and he immediately thought of the fuel tanks.

"Shit," he said and he took off for the truck shop at a dead run. As he ran toward the shop he could see his men spilling out of their living quarters, pulling on their clothes as they ran.

After watching Big Dave drive silently into the farm, Kit and Billy had carefully made their way through the shadows of the farm buildings until they had reached the side of the stable building. There they waited.

At the sound of the first explosion, they quickly made their way near the front of the building and they watched as Harlo, Red, and Wendy ran out of the building. Both men crept forward and silently opened the front door a few inches. Billy K dropped to the ground and peered inside. There was no guard. Light was coming from a stairwell located to their left.

The door to the stairwell was open and Kit and Billy K entered the building and quietly made their way down the steps with their weapons drawn. Kit slowly opened the door at the bottom of the steps a crack and peered in.

He was looking in at the deserted viewing room, and he and Billy K silently slipped inside. Using hand signals, Kit motioned to Billy K to stay put and Kit slowly pulled himself up to the bottom edge of the big window that made up a wall of the room. He could see clearly in the well lit room beyond the window. Bile rose in his throat as he could see a half naked Ellie Lynn holding the shoulders of a badly beaten and bloody, partially clothed Samantha who was seated on a wooden chair in the middle of the room. Kit could see that neither woman was tied or bound. He could see only one guard, who was standing by a door in the brightly lit room. The guard had his back to the viewing room where the two men lay.

Kit crawled back to Billy K and gave him a sign that he could only see one guard and that he was going to take him out. Kit slowly and quietly opened the door of the viewing room. The door made no sound and the guard did not turn around. Andy was too intent on watching the two helpless and partially clad females in front of him. About fifteen feet separated Kit and the guard. Kit shifted the Kimber 45 to his left hand and in four quick strides he reached the unsuspecting guard and hit him right on the left temple with the butt of his pistol. Andy flopped on the floor like a dead fish and didn't move.

Kit quickly moved to the women and put his hand over the mouth of Ellie Lynn who almost cried out at his touch. Then she saw who he was and she hugged him for all she was worth. Billy K quickly entered the room and checked out the other doors. When he returned, he brought with him a couple of blankets he had found in one of the rooms. He and Kit quickly wrapped the blankets around the two women. When they were done, Billy K called Swifty on his cell phone.

"We need to get out of here now, Ellie Lynn. Billy K will help you and I'll carry Samantha. It doesn't look like she can walk out of here on her own."

Billy had Ellie Lynn make sure the blanket was well wrapped around her and helped her out of the room and up the stairwell. Kit re-wrapped Samantha in the blanket and then took her on his back with her arms coming over his shoulders in a fireman's carry. As he pulled Samantha up on his back, his cowboy hat fell to the floor. He didn't pause to try to pick it up. Samantha was tall, but not terribly heavy. Carrying her as almost dead weight was awkward, but Kit was able to get her up the stairs without much of a problem. When they reached the front of the stable building, Billy K helped Kit get Samantha off his back. They both looked at the flames from the fires by the truck shed that were turning night into day. Almost immediately they could see the outline of Swifty's big Ford pickup roaring toward them from the front gate.

*   *   *

Big Dave had managed to quietly drive the old GMC pickup into the center of the farmyard where he was surrounded by farm buildings. He drove with the lights off and slowly in low gear to make as little noise as possible. He drove to the front of the truck shop and stopped the truck. He had both truck windows open. He had learned a long time ago that unless you were left handed, which he wasn't, it was very hard to throw anything out the driver's window with any accuracy. Throwing anything out the passenger window with the right hand was possible, but it was also easy to slightly misjudge and have it bounce off the door or the window frame and end up back in the cab of the truck where you didn't want it.

Big Dave lit the fuse to a gas filled bottle and put it in his left hand. He held it out the driver's window with his arm outstretched and lobbed it over the top of the cab of the truck to land on the passenger side of the truck. It was just like lobbing a grenade. He tossed two gas bottles into the truck shop and a storage building next to it. Both buildings burst into flames. Then he drove the GMC into a U-turn and pulled up next to the elevated gas tanks.

A half-dressed man appeared out of the darkness and asked Big Dave what he was doing. Big Dave calmly reached down on the seat beside him and came up with his beloved single action Colt 45 and shot the man between the eyes. Then he tossed the last four of his Molotov cocktails at the fuel tanks using the same lobbing method he had with the buildings.

Almost immediately the tanks were engulfed with fire. Big Dave stomped on the accelerator of the old pickup and pulled hard on the steering wheel sending the truck back toward the stable building and the entrance to the farm.

Big Dave was still driving without any lights, and he could soon see men running toward the fires he had started. Thankfully only a few of them had managed to think to bring any firearms. Some had and as they realized something was wrong, they began shooting. Big Dave could hear the dull thump as bullets hit the heavy steel side of the old GMC. Big Dave had placed hay bales strategically in the bed of the pickup and on the passenger's side so that he would be protected from bullets coming in from the passenger side and from the back of the truck. He had also lowered the window on the passenger side so he could shoot out through the window without any deflection. He could hear the impact of bullets into the hay bales, and he kept the gas pedal to the floor. The old truck lurched around a corner, and two men dove out of the way to avoid being run over.

Suddenly a huge explosion rocked the farm, and Big Dave could feel the ground move under the wheels of the truck. Then he could see the entire farm bathed in a harsh searing bright light. Immediately he could feel the wave of heat from the explosion as it engulfed the truck. He couldn't help himself as he broke into a grin. He turned his head toward the open window on the driver's side and let out a familiar yell which seemed to startle one farm hand in his long johns standing on the porch in front of his quarters unsure of exactly what sort of scene from hell lay in front of him.

The farm hand watched as an antique truck with no lights seemed to burst from a background of twenty foot high flames. Over the roar of the truck's engine and the sound of the flames he could distinctly hear some one yelling loudly, "Powder River, Let 'er buck."

Harlo had retrieved his pistol from his truck and was running toward the fires when he saw a truck with no lights coming toward him. Over the noise of the fires and small explosions, he could hear some kind of strange yell coming from the driver of the truck. Harlo stepped out in front of the truck with his hands raised in an attempt to stop the driver of the truck and find out what was going on. He stood there in the darkness, outlined by the flames of the fire, with his hands raised in a signal for the driver to stop.

Instead, the driver produced a pistol and shot Harlo twice and the truck never slowed down. The first bullet hit Harlo in the upper chest and the second bullet broke his pelvic bone and Harlo's legs felt like they had suddenly become detached from his body and wouldn't work. The rest of his body crumbled to the cold, dark ground. Harlo felt nothing as the big tires of the old pickup truck rolled over his inert body and crushed his ribcage.

*   *   *

Swifty helped Billy K bring Ellie Lynn out of the stable and put her in the front seat of the truck. Swifty and Kit then carried Samantha out and carefully lifted her into the bed of the pickup and laid her on a bed of hay between hay bales Big Dave had insisted they place there. Kit stayed in the bed of the truck with Sam while Swifty ran back to the driver's side of the Ford.

"Hold it right there. All of you put your hands in the air."

Swifty and Billy stood by the sides of the truck in amazement and slowly raised their hands.

"You too, Kit. Stand up where I can see you with your hands in the air."

Kit rose to his feet in the bed of the pickup. About fifteen yards in front of the truck, he could make out the figure of Sheriff Horton. He was holding a shotgun and aiming it at them.

"What the hell do you think you're doing, Sheriff?" yelled Kit.

"I'm stopping some criminals who trespassed onto private property and set fires to the barns of local tax payers. All of you are under arrest."

"Are you crazy! Didn't you see the condition of these two women we just rescued from that stable building?"

"All I see is three Yankees who are destroying property of a friend of mine. Throw down your weapons, or I'll kill all of you where you stand."

"So you're working for the Regrets. How could you hook up with people like them?" said Swifty.

"Watch your mouth, sonny. I'd just as soon shoot you as have to worry about turning you over to Lee and Harlo."

All three men threw their weapons down on the ground. Kit knew that Horton was too far away for Swifty to use his boot knife. He felt numb from the shock of the sheriff's betrayal, and he knew there would be no deputies or other law enforcement coming to their aid. Horton had notified no one and once he turned them over to the Regrets and Harlo, they were all as good as dead.

Kit could make out the outline of the sheriff because of the light cast from the flames of the growing fires. There was no way he could get to the sheriff before Horton's shotgun would cut him down, and it was only a matter of time before some of Harlo's men arrived to help the sheriff and take them prisoner.

Suddenly an apparition appeared out of the darkness and the smoke from the fires. An old GMC pickup truck burst out of the dark, smoky night and crashed into Horton before he could even turn toward this new threat. The impact saw the sheriff hit the hood of the truck and bounce off to the side like a bag full of dirty laundry. Horton lay twisted, bloody and motionless in the dust, still clutching the now bent and useless shotgun.

Big Dave hit the brakes and the old GMC skidded sideways, throwing up a cloud of dust before it came to rest about thirty yards past the sheriff's body. Big Dave was out of the cab of the truck before the dust had settled.

"Grab your shit and let's get the hell out of here!"

Kit, Swifty, and Billy were suddenly moving at full speed as they recovered from the shock of the events of the previous five minutes. They scooped up their weapons and ran to the truck. Kit sat down in the truck bed to protect Samantha while Billy K jumped into the passenger side of the Ford and put his arms around a terrified Ellie Lynn. Swifty leaped into the driver's seat and within seconds the Ford was roaring out of the entrance of the farm followed closely by the old GMC with Big Dave at the wheel.

Lee Regret was running down the stone pathway from the big house to the stable building when he saw the taillights of the two trucks leaving the farm. He had no idea why some of the hands would leave the farm when it was on fire. He continued running towards the flames, not seeing the two crumpled bodies on the side of the roadway hidden by the darkness. In front of Lee the fires were out of control, and he could see his men trying to move equipment out of the path of the fires.

The two pickup trucks were about two miles from the farm when they met two County Sheriff's patrol cars with their lights and sirens on heading for the farm. The trucks didn't stop, and neither did the patrol cars. On the heels of the patrol cars came the flashing lights and sirens of two rural fire trucks and an ambulance.

"Where're we going?" asked Swifty.

"I'm not sure. Let me check with Kit." Billy K opened the sliding rear window of the truck and yelled back to Kit, "Where to?"

"Go to the nearest hospital. Tell Swifty to head for Kershaw. They've got to have a hospital or at least a clinic. Samantha needs medical help now."

Billy K nodded and pulled the window shut.

"Kit says to head for Kershaw and find a hospital or clinic. Samantha needs a doctor."

"Roger that. I'm puttin' the pedal to the metal."

The big Ford fairly leaped forward and the old GMC fell slightly behind, unable to keep up to the new high rate of speed that Swifty had urged out of the Ford.

Within thirty minutes, they entered Kershaw and Billy K saw a sign directing them to the hospital. They pulled up in front of the emergency entrance, and Swifty ran inside to get help. The hospital was a small two story brick structure that had probably been built in the 1960's. Nevertheless it was a welcome sight for all of them. Very quickly two nurses with wheelchairs came out to the truck and soon had both Samantha and Ellie Lynn in the emergency treatment area with the ER doctor.

"What happened?" asked the doctor who looked at Samantha in horror.

Swifty and Kit told the doctor what they knew while Billy continued to hold a trembling Ellie Lynn in his arms.

After about fifteen minutes, the three men were ushered out of the treatment room by a nurse and herded back to the waiting room. There they found Big Dave talking on a hospital phone. He hung up the phone and smiled at the three young men.

"Are the women okay?"

"We think so. Ellie Lynn seems more terrified than injured, but Samantha looks like she was the victim of a severe beating. She lost some blood, but the doctor didn't think she's critical."

"I need to talk to the doc, boys. I'll be right back."

Big Dave was back within ten minutes.

"The doc told me what she told you about the girls. That's a big relief. You boys did real good back there. I'm proud of you."

"Just what did happen with you, Big Dave? We couldn't really see anything until you showed up in the nick of time in the old pickup," asked Swifty.

"I snuck into the farm with the lights off and when I got to the truck shop, I tossed in two Molotov cocktails. Once they got goin', I drove over to the gas tanks and tossed four cocktails on them. Then I drove the hell out of there as fast as I could. I was halfway out of the farm when the tanks blew. What a sight. You guys had to feel it if you didn't see it."

"We felt it all right, and we could see the light from the fires. We also heard shooting. How did you get out in one piece?"

"I told you boys that a good plan is based on surprise. When I was coming back from settin' the fires, most of the yahoos were running around half dressed like they was part of a Chinese fire drill. Almost none of them were armed and those that were spent time shootin' at the truck, not the driver. I was almost back to the stable building when that idiot Harlo tried to stop me. I shot the son-of-a-bitch."

"Did you kill him?" asked Kit.

"I ain't sure, but if he lives, he'll remember me ever time he tries to walk cause after I shot him I ran over him with the truck for good measure."

"Then what happened?"

"I was coming back to the stable building when I saw the shitheel sheriff throwin' down on you with a scatter gun. I thought he was dirty from the get-go."

"How'd you know that? We thought he was our friend. He even told me he knew my father and had served under him."

"He served under your daddy all right. He washed out of Ranger School. I remember him. He was a coward. He was also a thief. I was just glad he didn't recognize me when he stopped us by the farm. That's why I stayed in the truck. I also didn't believe him when he said he was calling for more law enforcement to help us."

"Why didn't you tell us?"

"I didn't need to. Besides, I didn't want him to figure out who I was, and I knew I was goin' to have to arrange for our own backup."

"Backup? What do you mean?" said Kit.

"Any time soon now we are goin' to have some pissed off Sheriff's deputies, State Police, or who knows what showin' up here and wantin' to know what we had to do with what just happened at that Hanging Rock Farm."

"Who did you call?"

"An old friend with a long reach. Someone we can count on. We just need to sit tight here. No matter what happens, we insist on staying here at the hospital. Understood? We don't go no place with nobody 'till I say so."

"What about you, Big Dave? What happens when they figure out you shot Harlo? Aren't they going to charge you for shooting him?" asked Kit.

"You let me worry about that," said Big Dave. "Like I told Kit some time ago, there are some really bad people in this world that needs killing. Harlo is no loss and when they get all the evidence together, killing Harlo was a favor to the taxpayers of South Carolina."

The three young men nodded their understanding and they sat back to wait for word from the doctor. Swifty soon appeared with four cups of lousy coffee from a vending machine.

CHAPTER THIRTY-FIVE

Big Dave turned out to be quite a prophet. Within two hours three county deputies including the heavy-set deputy who had stopped Kit and Swifty arrived at the hospital. They were soon joined by two South Carolina State troopers. The deputies had attempted to take the four men into custody when Big Dave insisted they talk to someone he had contacted on the telephone. After a short conversation on the phone the deputy turned the phone over to the ranking state trooper. The trooper was on the phone for about twenty seconds and the only thing he said was "yes sir" several times. Then the five lawmen left the hospital without so much as a word to the four men.

"Who the hell was that on the phone, Big Dave?" asked Kit.

"I believe they were chatting with the FBI special agent in charge of the Cheyenne, Wyoming, office. I'm pretty sure he told them that this was a federal case and that FBI agents out of Columbia, South Carolina, are now at the farm and doing an investigation of kidnapping, smuggling, tax evasion and doing business with a prohibited foreign country." Big Dave paused to check his coffee cup.

"Swifty. Why don't you run out and find us some decent coffee. This stuff would kill a coyote."

Swifty jumped to his feet and promptly tripped over the leg of Kit's chair. As Swifty lay sprawled on the floor, all four men broke into laughter. For the first time that night, all of them were smiling.

"I should mention that when I went to talk to the doc I told her this was gonna be a federal case and she might want to work extra hard on her medical report. I also told her it would probably be a good idea to take pictures of Samantha and Ellie Lynn before she treated them. She's a right smart doc and told me she was using a video camera 'cause she thought the injuries looked like some sort of domestic abuse. I told her she was in the right neighborhood."

Within two hours, the doctor had come out and told them that both women were going to be fine.

Right after that, three FBI agents in dark suits showed up at the hospital. They took statements from each of the men and both Ellie Lynn and Samantha. One of them left and the other two remained to provide security for the women.

After a little prodding one of the FBI agents told Kit and the rest what had happened at the farm.

About an hour after their exciting escape from the farm, the FBI had showed up in a helicopter and taken over the crime scene and the investigation. The FBI had Lee and Wendy Regret and a dead Harlo Clay in custody as well as about a dozen of the farm hands that had felony records. They found the smuggled cigarettes and records of all the transactions.

Harlo had cooked his own goose by recording all of what he had done to Samantha and other previous victims. They even had a recording of what he started to do with Ellie Lynn and her subsequent rescue. The fire had burned about four buildings, but that was all. The FBI was also raiding the Regret warehouse, Lee and Wendy's home, and Wendy's real estate office in Charleston. All of the properties were being confiscated by the Federal Government for unpaid taxes and assorted fines and penalties.

After the agent had left, Kit asked Big Dave, "What about us? Are we guilty of something?"

"I'm sure the local deputies think so, but about all we seem to be guilty of is trespassing on some kidnapper's place and setting it on fire without a proper permit. Oh, yes, and probably of having too good a time doing it. We probably should have brought some marshmallows and weenies and that would have helped explained the fires we set."

"Very funny. How did you get the FBI involved. How do they know you?"

"They don't. But they do know one Harrison Woodley, attorney at law in Kemmerer, Wyoming quite well. I called Woody and he called the special agent in charge in Cheyenne and he contacted the FBI in Columbia and that's how we got to where we are."

"Amazing. Who would have though old Woody would be our hero."

"Never underestimate the power of a good old cowboy attorney, especially if he's from Kemmerer, Wyoming."

Kit laughed.

CHAPTER
THIRTY-SIX

One month later:

Kit shifted nervously in his chair. He, Swifty, and Billy K were waiting in the lobby of the Bank of South Carolina in Charleston. They had been excluded from the meeting going on in the bank's conference room. In the meeting were representatives from the South Caroline State Parks Department, the board of directors of the Bank of South Carolina, the IRS, the FBI, the ATF, the South Carolina Bureau of Investigation, the office of the Governor of South Carolina, and a Wyoming attorney named Harrison Woodley. Also in attendance was Big Dave Carlson.

The meeting had been going on for over an hour, and Kit was anxious for it to end. This was all the result of his trying to finally solve the mystery of the missing Civil War bank safes. After the women had been well enough to leave the hospital and return to Charleston, Kit had taken Big Dave back to the Andrew Jackson State Park. There he led him through the outer buildings to where the old barn was located near the center of the group of restored structures. The barn was in the second row of buildings and out of sight of the visitor's center. The old barn was located next to two other larger old restored buildings that dwarfed it in size.

"This is the barn that my great-great grandfather saw back in the Civil War. It was always here. The rest of these buildings were brought here. Under the floor of this barn, lie the bodies of five Confederate soldiers and the gold and vaults from the bank. We need to find out how we can convince the authorities to let us dig it up."

"How come nobody dug it up before?"

"According to this plaque, right after the Civil War, the Union Army established a cavalry post in this location and used the barn and the meadow for their horses. It remained a military post for over twenty years. Then it was a supply post also owned and run by the army. There was no chance for the crooked rebels to come back and get their loot. By the time the army left and the barn and meadow were sold to a carpetbagger, all but two of the rebels were dead. There was no easy way for them to retrieve the gold. The two of them died and the secret of the gold died with them."

"This sounds like a job for Woody," said Big Dave. "I'll give him a call."

That had been almost a month ago. Woody had arranged for this meeting after an initial meeting with the Parks Department had ended up with them refusing to even consider an excavation of the barn in their park.

Kit turned to the front door of the bank as there was a slight commotion and then he saw four elderly women come into the bank. Although they were elderly, they all walked with an almost military erectness and purpose. They marched right past Kit and the others and entered the conference room without knocking. The door quickly closed and again there was silence.

"Hey there, cowboy."

Kit looked up to see the smiling face of Ellie Lynn Main.

Kit jumped to his feet as did Swifty and Billy K.

"Ellie Lynn! It's good to see you. How are you feeling?"

"It's good to see you and Swifty and Billy. I can't thank you all enough for what you did for me and Sam."

"How is Sam?"

"She's still on medical leave. She's doing so much better. The physical scars are healing, but I'm afraid the mental scars are going to last a lot longer."

"I'm glad Big Dave killed that bastard Harlo."

"I hate to say it, but so am I."

"So what are you doing down in the lobby? I thought you pretty much stayed up on the third floor."

"Actually I've been summoned to the conference room by the chairman of the board of the bank. I think they may be close to a decision."

"I hope they make a good one because I'm tired of all the waiting."

"Keep your chin up, Kit. I have a feeling your long journey is about to have a happy ending."

"I sure hope so and so does Swifty."

"I'm sure he does," laughed Ellie Lynn.

It was good to see those lovely eyes and that great smile and hear that wonderful tinkling laugh again. It made Kit feel like things were back to normal.

Ellie Lynn stopped to talk to Billy K. She placed her hand on his shoulder and leaned in to whisper something to him. Then she was gone.

Twenty minutes later the meeting was finally over and Kit, Swifty, and Billy stood while all the participants filed past them and out of the bank lobby. Finally Big Dave and Woody came out and Woody said, "Let's go get a beer."

Fifteen minutes later they were all seated around a well-worn table in a small bar on East Bay Street. Woody ordered five beers and then turned to the three impatient young men.

"Usually I can handle deals like this myself, but this time I had to bring in some help," said the attorney.

"What do you mean, help. What help?" asked Kit.

"Did you see those four old ladies?"

"Of course. Who could have missed them."

"Exactly. Those four ladies turned the tide."

"How?"

"They represent the Daughters of the Confederacy. Once they found out five sons of the Confederacy lay buried under that barn they didn't care if it was in the back yard of the White House. They wanted those boys dug up and reburied in a proper Confederate military cemetery with proper military honors. The families of those boys want them to come home, even if it is over a hundred and forty some years late. They practically accused those park department boys of being traitors to the Confederacy."

"What does this all mean?"

"It means that tomorrow the floor of that old barn is going to be dug up, and we'll be there to see what your great-great grandfather saw in February of 1865."

Kit smiled.

The next day there was a huge crowd of several hundred people at Andrew Jackson State Park. Folding chairs had been set up in the barn and outside the barn for all the guests. Under the careful supervision of the Parks Department, the wooden floor of the barn was removed. Next a crew of men began to carefully dig up the ground with shovels. Each shovelful of dirt was taken in buckets to be carefully examined in a sieve over a wooden trough to recover any artifacts. The process was slow and after two hours of digging, one of the shovels hit something hard. The shovels were dropped and the men began digging with trowels and brushes. Soon they had unearthed the skeletons of five men with remnants of uniforms, buttons, and bits of leather.

As the skeletons of the five lost soldiers were reverently removed, a lone bugler from the South Carolina National Guard played "Dixie" very slowly.

Some in the crowd actually wept. These were family members who were descendents of the five. Finally their long-lost sons had come home.

The digging resumed and quickly the diggers hit the timbers that had been placed over the vaults. Carefully each timber was removed, marked and stored outside the barn. The digging continued and suddenly came the sound of a shovel glancing off of steel. After the diggers had unearthed the two vaults, a small crane was brought in and each of the vaults was lifted out of the hole in the barn floor and set outside on ground cloths that had been laid over the grass.

It took a locksmith from Columbia almost twenty minutes to open the first vault. He did much better on the second vault, opening it in just over six minutes.

The bank officials did a detailed inventory of the contents and after each item was verified, it was photographed with a digital camera. The contents were then placed in a locked steel box in an armored car to be transported to the Bank of South Carolina on Meeting Street in Charleston.

Kit was given a copy of the inventory, which he shared with Swifty Billy K, Big Dave, Woody, and Ellie Lynn. The inventory matched exactly with the one contained in the notebook written by Kit's great-great grandfather.

"I think these belong to you, Kit," said Ellie Lynn.

"What's that?" he said as he looked at the manila envelope in her hand.

"These are the postage stamps that were in our vault, but not shown as belonging to the bank or to any of the bank's customers. The board agreed that anything found that was not on the original manifest should go to you for finding the vaults."

"Postage stamps! I go looking for gold and I find postage stamps. What a deal."

"What did you get out of this, Ellie Lynn? Did they give you anything?" asked Kit.

"I got a promotion, a raise and I got the equivalent of 5% of the gold recovered in bank stock. I thought that was a pretty fair deal."

"It's a fair deal and you deserve it. You did a great job and you showed a great deal of courage."

"I'll feel better when the trial is over and both the Regrets are buried in the bowels of a federal prison."

"From what I hear that's a foregone conclusion. I hope that makes you feel better."

"Being alive and having friends like you and Swifty makes me happy."

"Don't forget Billy K."

"I haven't forgotten him. In fact I've invited Billy to move in with me until he decides what he wants to do."

"You and Billy? I didn't see that coming."

"Neither did I, but that night when you guys rescued me and he held me something seemed to click. I can't explain it, but being with him just feels right."

"Good for both of you. You'll have your hands full with Billy K, but if anyone can handle him, it's probably you. I wish both of you the best."

"Oh, I almost forgot. The bank is giving you and Swifty checks for $20,000 each for finding the gold. They told me to tell you they are mailing the checks. I think they want to avoid the publicity of having to admit that it took two Yankees to find some lost Confederate gold."

Ellie Lynn bent down and kissed Kit full on the lips. "I'll never forget you, Kit. I will always love you for what you did for me."

Then she turned and she was gone.

CHAPTER
THIRTY-SEVEN

Kit walked out of the lobby of the hotel to the front door. The bell hop hauling his meager luggage on a cart was right behind him. Swifty had left the day before and was headed back to Kemmerer in his truck. Kit and Big Dave were going to drive the old GMC pickup truck back, and Kit planned to stop in Illinois to see his cousin Beverly so he could tell her and Sky and the rest of the Andrews family in Illinois what had happened to him on his search for the lost Confederate gold.

Waiting in front of the hotel was Big Dave and the old GMC. The old truck was in surprisingly good shape with only a few bullet holes and a slight dent on the side of the hood. Big Dave had taken the truck to a detail shop and once again the dark green paint job shone in the morning sun.

"You got everything, Kit?" asked Big Dave.

Kit patted the suitcase he held in one hand and the carry-on bag he had over his shoulder and said, "Sure thing." Inside the bag was the package of old postage stamps and the gold and silver necklace he had bought in the DAR silent auction. The necklace was to be a present from Charleston to Big Dave's wife, Connie.

Kit stopped on the sidewalk and looked across the street at the old Customs House and the Cooper River behind it. He would miss Charleston.

Kit tossed his luggage in the bed of the old pickup truck and said to Big Dave, "I'll drive."

"It's your truck," said Big Dave. "By the way, I have something for you."

Big Dave reached into the truck's cab through the open window and pulled out a brand new pearl grey Stetson cowboy hat.

"I didn't want your head gettin' cold. I hear it can get damn chilly in Illinois."

Kit grinned and carefully set the new hat on his head. Then he checked his reflection out in the side mirror of the old pickup truck. Satisfied with what he saw, Kit opened the door and swung into the driver's seat of the GMC. He put the key in the ignition and started the truck. Then he turned to his passenger.

"Ready?"

"I was born ready, and so were you. Let's ride, cowboy."

THE END

ACKNOWLEDGEMENTS

The idea for this book came while reading a history of my great grandfather's regiment when he served in the Civil War. "Our Regiment: A History of the 102nd Illinois Infantry Volunteers" was written in 1865 by Stephen F. Fleharty. My great grandfather, William Main, was a private in Company I of the 102nd Illinois Infantry. While his company was camped at a place called Hanging Rock, South Carolina in February of 1865, they did discover two wagons, protected by southern civilian guards that contained two bank vaults. One was from the Bank of South Carolina.

After I wrote, *Kemmerer*, people asked me what happened to Big Dave, what happened to Kit? *Hanging Rock* is a continuation of their adventures.

I thank my wife Nancy for all her support and also for her tireless work proof reading my stories and making suggestions that I could not ignore.

I also thank my friends and family who have been very supportive of my writing efforts.

I thank you for reading my book and I hope you enjoyed it.

I appreciate receiving comments about my books and I enjoy hearing what readers think about my stories. I can receive your comments, questions, and criticism by e-mail at *rwcallis@aol.com*.

You can also post reviews of my books at Amazon.com and BN.com.

I am currently working on a new adventure for the boys from Wyoming.